ACCLAIM FOR **Andrew**

D0779955

"Vachss is in the first rank of American crime writers."
—*Cleveland Plain Dealer*

"Burke is an unlikely combination of Sherlock Holmes, Robin Hood, and Rambo, operating outside the law as he rights wrongs. . . . Vachss has obviously seen just how unable the law is to protect children. And so, while Burke may be a vigilante, Vachss's stories don't feature pointless bloodshed. Instead, they burn with righteous rage and transfer a degree of that rage to the reader."
—*Washington Post Book World*

"Vachss seems bottomlessly knowledgeable about the depth and variety of human twistedness."
—*The New York Times*

"The best detective fiction being written. . . . Add a stinging social commentary . . . a Célinesque journey into darkness, and we have an Andrew Vachss, one of our most important writers." —Martha Grimes

"Vachss is America's dark scribe of the 1990s. . . . His protagonist Burke is our new dark knight, a cold-eyed crusader."
—James Grady, author of *Six Days of the Condor*

"Burke is the toughest talking first-person narrator since Mike Hammer. . . . Vachss *can* write!"
—*Los Angeles Times*

"Move over, Hammett and Chandler, you've got company. . . . Andrew Vachss has become a cult favorite, and for good reason."
—*Cosmopolitan*

"Burke would eat Spade and Marlowe for breakfast, not even spitting out the bones. [He] is one tough, mean, pray-god-you-don't-meet-him hombre."
—*Boston Herald*

Andrew Vachss

FALSE ALLEGATIONS

Andrew Vachss has been a federal investigator in sexually transmitted diseases, a social caseworker, and a labor organizer, and has directed a maximum-security prison for youthful offenders. Now a lawyer in private practice, he represents children and youth exclusively. He is the author of ten novels; a collection of short stories, *Born Bad*; three graphic series, *Cross, Hard Looks,* and *Underground*; and *Another Chance to Get It Right: A Children's Book for Adults*. His nonfiction work has appeared in *Parade, Antaeus, The New York Times*, and numerous other forums. He lives in New York City.

The dedicated Web site for Vachss and his work is: www.vachss.com

BOOKS BY **Andrew Vachss**

FALSE ALLEGATIONS

FALSE ALLEGATIONS

Andrew Vachss

Vintage Crime/Black Lizard

Vintage Books

A Division of Random House, Inc.

New York

VINTAGE CRIME/BLACK LIZARD EDITION, NOVEMBER 1997

Copyright © 1996 by Andrew Vachss

The Library of Congress has cataloged
the Knopf edition as follows:

Vachss, Andrew H.
False allegations / Andrew Vachss. —1st ed.
p. cm.
A Burke novel.
ISBN 0-679-45109-9
1. Burke (Fictitious character)—Fiction.
2. Private investigators—New York (State)—New York —Fiction.
3. Ex-convicts—New York (State)—New York—Fiction.
4. Child sexual abuse—Fiction. I. Title.
PS3572.A33F35 1996
813'.54—dc20   96-16296
CIP

Vintage ISBN: 0-679-77293-6

Random House Web address: http://www.randomhouse.com/

Printed in the United States of America
10 9 8 7 6 5 4 3

for Ken Saro-Wiwa

a warrior, murdered by jackals
whose voice, unstilled
scars their dishonor into our souls
marking our path

FALSE ALLEGATIONS

"I have to do it the same way every time," the woman said, her voice full and steady even though she was deep into her workout on a stationary bike. She was wearing a set of dull-gray jerseys with matching head and wrist bands of the same material, her face glistening under a healthy sheen of sweat.

"How long does it last?" I asked her.

"The whole performance is about fifteen minutes," she said. "I don't know how much of it he watches."

"And you're sure he—?"

"Yes! He's *nailed* to it. A bloody junkie he is, I tell you—he doesn't get his fix, he'll go mad." The woman stopped pedaling. She climbed off the bike, pulling the gray sweatshirt over her head in one smooth motion, leaving her torso bare. She was as relaxed about it as someone who did it for a living. "Let me take a shower," she said. "I'll only be a minute."

I leaned back in the red leather recliner, turning it slightly so I could see down the hall where she had disappeared. I slitted my eyes, breathing shallow through my nose, slowing my clock, dialing my mind to wait-state—I know what "Give me a minute" means in girl-speak.

Like most things I know about women, I was wrong again. In less than five minutes, I caught a blur out of the corner of my eye— she was padding up the beige-carpeted corridor toward the living room, not making a sound. When she spotted me in the chair, she flashed a smile.

The only thing she was wearing was lipstick. She had a fluffy pink towel in one hand, patting herself absently with it as she made a full circuit of the living room, her eyes flicking from the bookshelves to the complicated-looking stereo to a solid rectangular platform no higher than a coffee table but much bigger. The platform was covered in light-blue leather, about the size of a pool table, seamless and smooth. It stood in a niche a couple of feet back from a huge window, which was completely covered by a panel of brass mini-blinds.

"That's where I have to do it," she said, pointing to the platform.

"How could he—?"

"They're adjustable," she cut in. "With this . . . ," showing me something that looked like a TV remote.

I held out my hand for it, but she pulled it away. "I'm not allowed to open the blinds until he calls," she said. "It wouldn't do for you to push the wrong button."

I let that one pass.

"Sometimes he wants the blinds open," she said. "Sometimes he wants them all the way up. If he wants it at night, I have these. . . . Look!" She hit a button on the remote, and a trio of baby spots popped into life on the ceiling, each beam trained at a different part of the blue leather platform.

"What makes you think he—?"

A telephone trilled in another room. She held up a hand for silence, head cocked to listen.

Another ring.

Another.

Nothing more. I counted to ten in my head. She pushed both palms at me in a "Stay there!" gesture, then she turned and ran out of the room.

She was back in a flash, wearing a red camisole with matching tap pants and spike heels, a white makeup case in one hand. She quickly crossed over to the blue leather platform and sat down, facing me. She put the makeup case on the floor, popped the locks, and opened the top. A quick eye-sweep satisfied her that she had what she needed. She pressed a finger to her lips, telling me to be quiet. Then she reached for the remote control and hit one of the buttons.

The mini-blinds slowly opened, angling down—you would have had to be on a higher floor to see inside. The baby spots flashed into hot, focused light.

She did the whole performance without once leaving the blue leather platform, almost fifteen minutes to the second, just like she said. Once you got past the high-tech, it was standard-issue Tijuana Teaser, right down to the disappearing sausage act—she put it inside her, worked it back and forth, her face an ice-mask imitation of a woman scaling a steep orgasmic curve. Soon as she faked letting go, she pulled out the sausage, then licked it a few times before she bit off a piece and swallowed. The curtain closed on her lying face-down, spent and exhausted from the performance, her body zebra-striped from the mini-blinds, long chestnut hair crackling with pale sparks from the artificial light.

"I know what I have to do by the number of rings," she said later, a tall iced glass of orange juice in her hand. She'd taken another shower, wrapped herself in a white terry-cloth robe. The mini-blinds were closed.

"How can you tell if—?"

"It's his line, the phone." She'd anticipated my question. "Only his. He's the only one who ever calls on it. I'm not allowed to use it to make calls either."

"What if you . . . ?"

"There's another phone. Two lines, separate from his. If I'm talking on one of those and I hear his phone, I have to hang up right away."

"But when you go out . . ."

"I can't just *go* out, can I?" she snapped.

"I don't know how it works," I said mildly.

She ran both hands through her thick chestnut mane, combing it back off her face. "I'm sorry," she said. "I get so cooped up here sometimes I feel like biting my own head off. You can't imagine how . . . trapped it makes you feel."

"That's okay," I said softly, not telling her that I wouldn't need an imagination. I grew up trapped—and not in some luxo-pad. "Tell me how it works," I urged her, still soft.

"Seventy-two hours," she said. "Three days, that's the key. Once I . . . finish, I don't have to do it again for seventy-two hours. It could be more—he could wait a long time to call me—he was out of the country once for almost a month—but it's never less, understand?"

"Sure."

"He used me," she said, her voice flat and hard. "He lied. He's a liar. Now he has to pay for it."

"What did he lie about?" I asked, moving my right hand in a sweep gesture to cover the whole setup.

"Who needs to lie to a whore? Isn't that what you mean?" She faced me, bitter-voiced. "Sure, he pays for . . . this. But it's his, not mine. His name is on the lease. Everything's in his name, even the bloody electricity."

"He lied about that?"

"No," she said, her voice a hard sneer against my muted sarcasm. "What he lied about was love."

"Okay if I smoke?" I asked her.

She looked up in surprise. "Why would you ask? You see the damn ashtray right there, don't you?"

"You don't smoke, right?"

"No, I don't."

"So if he was over here, he could smell smoke. . . . He'd know you had company."

Her laugh was a sad, dry thing. "Fat chance. He never comes here. Never."

"So how do you . . . ?"

"It's an electronic affair, luv," she said. "Very nineties, isn't it? I've got a PC in one of the bedrooms in the back. He pays my bills over a modem—anytime I want to see my balance, I can just call it up on the screen. Anything else you want to know?"

"Yeah," I said. "What kind of name is Bondi?"

A quick smile played around her lips. "It's from Bondi Beach. Right near Sydney. In Australia, where I'm from. My mom always said I was conceived on that beach, so she gave me that name. She was a young girl then, working square, before she went on the bash. All she could tell me about my dad is that he was a soldier. On leave he was. He left my mom something, all right."

"Tell me about the lie," I said. "The lie about love."

"Oh, smoke your cigarette, then," she replied, a faint trace of the smile still playing on her lips. "I'll even get you a beer if you want, how's that?"

"I'm okay," I said, settling back in the chair again. "Tell me."

She got up, came over to where I was sitting. "That one's built for two," she said. "Move over." I slid as far as I could to the left. She plopped down next to me . . . a tight squeeze. I pulled my right arm out from between us. She nestled into my chest. I draped my arm over her shoulders. She reached across her body with her left hand, grabbed my right hand and pulled it down, the way you'd pull a blanket over your shoulders. "Give us a puff, then," she said. "I haven't smoked in years, but I remember how good it used to taste."

I held out the cigarette. She moved her mouth into it, took a quick, short hit. She exhaled powerfully, making a satisfied sound, closed her eyes, snuggled even closer.

A few minutes passed quiet like that. I was going to prod her again, when she started talking in a young girl's voice, the one they use for secret-telling.

"I was a dancer when he met me. Before that, I was a party girl. You understand what that is?"

"Yeah. You don't give your friendship to just anyone . . . but when you do, it costs a bit to maintain it."

"Un huh. That's about right. Anyway, he met me in a club. Where I was dancing. He was a real gentleman. Left me his card, asked if he could call me sometime. We had a few dates. Very, *very* nice. Fine restaurants, a limo, flowers. You know how it goes. We got . . . close. But there was never any sex. I figured maybe he was afraid of scaring me off. But one night, he told me. Told me that he loved me.

"I thought he wanted me for a beard. You know, that he was gay and he needed some cover when he went out. But that wasn't it. He's . . . impotent, I guess. But not completely. I didn't really follow it all that well, but what he's got, he can get aroused but he can't . . ." Her voice trailed off, as though she was expecting me to cut in.

I didn't. Another couple of minutes went by like that. She squirmed against me, as if she was seeking a more comfortable position. I moved as best I could in the squeezed spot, trying to help.

"He said he had a fantasy. A fantasy about me. That I would get so excited just *thinking* about him that I'd . . . well, what you just saw . . . before. Do that. He said he loved me. He knew how much I was . . . earning. At the club where I danced. He said he didn't want to insult me, but . . . he could pay me just as much. A salary, like. And if I would . . . do that, what you saw . . . for him, whenever he wanted, then he would get stronger. You know what I mean. And maybe, someday, we could be together. Like for real, together."

"I still don't see the lie," I told her.

"I haven't seen him since. Not once. It's all . . . like I said. Just that. He never even calls me on the phone. Not to speak to anyway. I was . . . sad about it, I guess, but then a girlfriend of mine . . . from the old club . . . she heard about it. And she told me."

"Told you what?"

"He lets other people see it," she said, a catch in her voice. "He lets them bloody *watch*. That's why I let you . . . before. I never would have let anybody see it. But . . . you know what he does? He invites friends over to his apartment. Like to play cards or whatever. And then he calls me. And I put on a show. Not for him. Not for love. For anyone who's in his apartment. He doesn't tell them he knows me—he just tells them there's this really randy girl who lives in the building across the way. A real bitch-in-heat slut, he tells them. Gets so flaming hot she does it to herself."

I thought she was going to cry then, but she nipped a jagged chunk of air and kept it down until she was calm.

"Tell me what you want," I said.

"I'll be right back," she said, sliding the freshly loaded condom off me in one smooth move. I heard noises from the bathroom, but I kept my eyes closed.

I felt the bed react as she climbed back on. "Want another drag?" I asked, not opening my eyes.

"No," she said. "One's my limit."

"You're sure about the money?"

"Dead sure, honey," she said. "And it's cake too, I promise you—I've got it all worked out. I don't know if he even lives there, but he has to *be* there when I . . . do it. Soon as he calls, I can call you. It'd only take a second—he'd never know. I've got the key to the apartment—you could walk right in. Right in the middle of me . . . doing it. He'd never know what hit him."

"He might not be alone, right? You said—"

"I know the doorman. Bert, his name is. He's an Aussie too. I met him when I was still doing . . . you know. Anyway, I take care of Bert. He can always count on me for something, even though I never go to that place anymore. You know, the place where I danced? I tested him. Bert, that is. Twice now. I use this," she said, crawling over my chest to reach into a nightstand next to the bed. She held up a cellular phone. "See? It's perfect. I told Bert I wanted to surprise Morton—that's his name, Morton. So I ask Bert, when Mr. Morton comes in, would he give me a call? When he comes in *alone*, I say to Bert, giving him a wink, you know? And Bert did it. Twice. I gave him a hundred the next day. Both times. A hundred dollars, a wink, a little bit of hip . . . that's all it cost."

"So you want . . . ?"

"He doesn't know I have this," she said, holding up the cellular phone again. "Bert can call me while he's still in the elevator. So we know he's alone. Then, when he calls *me*, when he wants his damn *performance* . . . that's when I call *you*. He's got a safe in there. In the living room. Behind a painting—can you imagine? He showed it to me once, early on."

"You know the combination?"

"No, of course not. He wouldn't trust me with something like that. But you can . . . *make* him tell you, can't you? It wouldn't take that long, believe me. He's such a weak man. . . ."

"Fifty-fifty split?" I asked her.

"Yes," she said. "I'm going to have to leave as soon as it's done anyway. It won't take me an hour to pack—it's not like I ever needed a lot of clothes for *him*, right? He could never *prove* it was me, but . . ."

"So how do you collect your half?"

"You can mail it to me. At my girlfriend's place in the Village. He doesn't know about her. When we get the money, Sybil and me, we're going to take off. Rent a car, load up everything we can stuff into suitcases, drive right to the airport. It's a quick flight to L.A., then a nice jump over the water to home."

"What if the safe's empty?"

"I guarantee it won't be, honey. Believe me, this is a rich flower, just *begging* to be plucked, I tell you true. What do you say, then?"

"Let's do it," I said.

She threw me a megawatt smile, turned her back, wiggled her butt gently as she rooted through the nightstand drawer for another condom.

"**S**he's got the key, huh?" Michelle's voice, her creamy-silk trademark, the voice that made her a ton of green on the phone-sex circuit. She was perched on the edge of my desk, just past where I had my feet propped up on the battered surface. I was tilted so far back that all I could see was her flashy legs if I looked straight ahead.

"Sure does," I told her.

"And she wants you to go in when the guy's *home?*"

"Yeah."

"So you can make him open the *safe?*" she asked, a barely suppressed giggle in her voice.

"Un huh."

"And she's going to split the take with you fifty-fifty—?"

"Right again," I interrupted.

"And trust you to *mail* her share to her?" she asked, losing the fight to keep the laughter down.

"Yes."

"Oh baby, I don't mean to sound nasty, but . . . could she *really* think you were all *that* stupid?"

"No, I don't scan it that way. She's had a lot of experience. With men. Listening to them, sizing them up. That's the way she made her living, not just dancing. Her story's so bogus . . . it's like an open invitation to double-cross her."

"What . . . not give her an even split?" Michelle sneered.

"The best suckers are half-smart," I said. "I think that's the way she has me played. Let's say I believe *some* of her story—what do I do then?"

"Use the key when the voyeur isn't home," Michelle replied. "Duh-uh!"

"Yeah. Go in with my own safe man, pop the thing, and walk away with the cash. Only . . ."

"Only they'll have you on tape doing it. Or they'll walk in when you're red-handed. Or there's a dead body in the bedroom. Or . . . whatever."

"Sure," I said quietly. I interlaced my fingers behind my head, closing my eyes.

I went so quiet I could hear Michelle breathing, hear the faint rasp of her nylons when she shifted her position slightly.

Time passed. "You aren't any different," I said. "Even Pansy didn't notice anything."

"That mutant mutt of yours wouldn't notice Godzilla so long as the lizard left her Alpo alone," Michelle mock-snarled. "She's not exactly Rin Tin Tin."

I flicked my eyes open, shifted them to the left where Pansy reclined on the couch. Pansy's a Neapolitan mastiff. Long past the svelte hundred and thirty pounds she was when she was young, she tips the scales nearer to one sixty now. Sure, nobody'd confuse her with a genius—but Pansy would die for me as casually as she'd scarf down a quart of honey-vanilla ice cream, her personal favorite. And whatever she bites, God forgets.

"Don't mind her," I told Pansy. "Michelle gets cranky when she hasn't been shopping for a few days . . . you know how she is."

"I'll tell you what I *won't* be shopping for anymore, baby," she said. "I'm done with all that."

"It really . . . worked?"

"Oh, don't be so squeamish!" Michelle snapped. "Yes, it 'worked,' okay? Funny, all my young life, I thought it would be Denmark for me. And it turns out to be Colorado instead."

Michelle was a transsexual—a woman trapped in a man's body, she always called it. She wasn't the freak in her family—her scumbag bio-father filled that slot. So she ran. Ran *down*. First to the streets, then lower, always dropping deeper, fire-walking until she plateaued on pain. Once she got there, she did whatever it took to stay. It was dangerous as a subway tunnel full of psychopaths down there. And Michelle was scared all the time. But she was too high-instinct to touch any of the temporary tranqs—she saw what happened to the kids who go numb to escape the pain. So she spent every night surviving and every day crying.

I'd known her forever. She was my sister and I loved her, but I'd been hearing about the sex-change operation so long I'd stopped listening. Michelle would take it just so far . . . then some excuse would come up. She had to detox from the black market estrogen she'd been using. Or the doctors had to remove the cheesy implants from her chest first. Or the electrolysis destroyed the outer epidermis of her face so they couldn't risk surgery. Always something.

But this last time, she got it done. I went down into the Zero, chasing ghosts—Michelle went over the wall. When we both got back, I was me, and she was herself. For me, it was a return. For Michelle, it was the first time.

The real difference was: Michelle liked what she was.

"I'm walking it backwards," I told her, getting down to business. "But I can't see who's calling the shots."

"I got it from Harry," Michelle said. "He's never burned us."

"Harry the painter?"

"No, Harry the accountant. You know, one of my old customers from . . . before."

"Yeah. He profiles, right?"

"Yes, he *will* front a bit, baby—lots of *men* do that, yes? So he wants to tell the girls he knows a guy who knows a guy who . . . like that. So what? Harry's a sweetheart, Burke. He goes out, buys a monster stereo, pays *retail*, okay? Then he gives it to a girl, she says 'thanks.' So Harry asks me—I mean, when it comes to *l'amour*, what poor fool would *not* ask the Queen of Hearts?—why does he get treated so mean? Well, honey, I told him the truth. You give a spoiled little bitch an expensive present, she'll just trail *that* mink on the floor, you understand? But you give her something nice and you tell her you got it *dirt* cheap, baby . . . 'cause you know guys, guys in the know, know what I mean?"

"Yeah," I told her, telling the truth. She had the voice of the wise-guy wannabe down perfect. Michelle has a four-octave range—anything you want, from sandpaper to velvet. She has the purest heart of anyone I know, but she was born to steal. That proved she was my sister better than any DNA test could.

"Oh, *believe* it, sugar," she told me. "You give a girl a diamond, she'll be nice, but she'll have to fake it. You give her the same rock, tell her it was part of a jewelry heist, she gets her panties wet before she can get her dress off. Harry, he met this Bondi in a strip bar. There's Harry, flashing his pinkie ring, playing Moe Green, you know? So she tells him she needs something done. And Harry tells her, sure, he can handle that. Let him talk to a few of the boys. . . ."

"Now, as we both know, *I'm* the only 'boys' he knows." Michelle smirked. "But that's okay—we played his tips before. And we did okay, didn't we?"

"Sure, but—"

"So you went to see her," Michelle interrupted, "and it came up zircons. But you can't be the target, honey. I mean, no *way* this Bondi bitch knows about you. Especially about you and me—how many people know that?"

"She lied, Michelle. There's a game in this somewhere, and—"

"I know," she put in. "The way I see it, maybe she *does* hate this guy—the guy in the building across from her. I mean, *I'd* hate him if he was doing that to me. Or maybe she's gonna Pearl Harbor you both. Who knows? It's a pass, period."

"Right."

"You're not even curious?" she asked, dropping her voice a notch.

"About what?"

"Who's got you on their list?"

"That list is too fucking long," I told her, closing my eyes again.

I wasn't lying to Michelle. Chasing clues is fine for books, but that doesn't work in real life. Down here, they solve the mysteries with autopsies.

I don't have a problem with curiosity. I learned everything about why people did things when I was just a little kid—they do things because they want to do them, because they *like* doing them. Some of those things hurt, a deep hurt you keep with you way after the scars fade. And the more I got hurt, the less curious I got.

I kept that hurt down, deep as I could bury it. But like the toxic waste it was, it bubbled to the surface once in a while.

People died then.

I could think of a dozen reasons why Bondi could have wanted me to go into that man's apartment, and every one gave me another reason not to do it. I could sell the job to a pro heister, but I never worked as a finger. There's too many ways to get cheated on your piece of the pie, too many ways your name comes up if the thief goes down.

"Don't take the call if you can't take the fall," the Prof always says. Prof stands for Professor and it stands for Prophet—you had to listen close each time to tell which role he was playing. I learned that a long time ago, standing on the prison yard, me listening, *using* the time instead of trying to kill it. Like the Prof said.

Could be I wasn't the target at all—accidents happen. Homicide happens too. Last time a woman thought I was the right man for the job, I almost got myself dead. Belinda. Belinda the cop. So patient, so careful, she almost got it done. Got herself done instead. That happens too—you grab the wrong end of the knife, you get cut.

I'm real careful about things like that. I walk the cautious convict's string-straight walk, trying to be a blot in the darkness. I learned it in the juvenile joints, always keep my back against something solid. It wasn't until I got to prison that I learned people could be solid too. Then I spent a lot of years learning which ones.

I always take my half out of the middle. When you look up from ground zero, the tops of the city buildings lean so close together they almost seem to touch—a nice canopy to lurk under if you stay down. But if you stick your head up, the canopy can turn into a crossfire real quick.

For the next few days, I worked at keeping my head down— minding my own business even if someone else was too. Frankie was going in a ten-rounder down at Atlantic City, but I couldn't make myself interested. We still had a piece of his action, but we didn't expect to see any coin for years, even if Ristone's plans worked out and he could finesse the kid into a title fight. Besides, it was another setup, Frankie fighting some tomato can off the canvasback circuit, padding his record, waiting his turn. Before we sold his contract, the Prof had been bringing Frankie along the right way: each fight a little harder than the last one, learning as he moved up, getting ring-wise. The Prof knew Frankie couldn't keep winning just by being tougher than the next guy—the prisons are full of tough guys.

But now Frankie was off that track, running parallel to a bunch of other young guys, all with their eyes on the same prize. They wouldn't get together until much further down the line. Frankie would make it happen then . . . if Ristone didn't decide there was more cash to be made from tossing him in the tank.

We knew what the deal was when we took it, and nobody was bitching. But Frankie wasn't proud of it anymore. The money was coming, but the jolt was gone. We promised him we'd be ringside when he got his shot—until then, we only saw him when he dropped by Mama's. Even though we didn't hold his contract anymore, he was still with us. He'd earned his way in the same way we all did. In the same places too.

So I was working at letting it go, but nobody was around to do it with. I headed over to Mama's. The white dragon tapestry was in the window—all clear. I docked my old Plymouth in the alley behind the restaurant, just underneath the pristine square of white paint that held Max's chop in black calligraphy—newly painted, the lines not as precise as usual. Flower's hand. Max's baby, a little girl now, growing up. But it said the same: Stay Away. And even the empty-eyed Chinatown gunslingers didn't cross that border.

The flat-faced steel door opened before I could rap. I didn't recognize the thickset young Chinese who let me in, but he knew me. One of Mama's new boys. I could see from the way he held the meat cleaver in his left hand that he was a real expert. And no cook.

I walked through the kitchen and took my booth in the back. Mama started toward me from her post by the cash register at the front at the same time a guy in a waiter's jacket moved out of the kitchen carrying a tureen of hot-and-sour soup. They arrived together. Mama ladled me a small bowl, prepared one for herself, and sat down across from me.

"So?"

"I'm just hanging out, Mama. Nothing going on."

"Not working?"

Not stealing, she meant. "No," I told her. "I thought maybe Max'd be around and I'd give him a chance to get some of his money back."

"Max working," she said, a faint trace of disapproval in her soft voice. "No time to play cards."

Max is a courier. Gems, microchips, a tightly rolled rice-paper message . . . anything you don't want to put in the mail. Small packages only—Max had to have his hands free. And his feet. If he took your money, your stuff was as good as delivered. His life was the bond, and he posted it every time he carried a package. Everybody down here knows his word is sacred, even though he can't speak.

And that's not why they call him Max the Silent.

"He'll be back soon?" I asked.

I got an eloquent shrug in response. That and another helping of soup.

"Any calls?" I asked her.

"No calls. Very quiet. You not going to work?"

"Not for a while." I shook my head. I was kind of between professions. When I was younger, I was a cowboy, never thinking beyond cash registers and guns. I shot a man when I was just a kid. Because he scared me. I never lost that last part, but I got smarter as I got older. Probably because I didn't get dead first.

And because I met the Prof in prison and got schooled. I'll never forget the first time I saw him, watching from a distance as he faced a black man half his age and twice his size. I don't remember what the dispute was about, but I know the big guy was holding a shank and calling the Prof's name. The Prof stood his ground, capturing the other man's eyes, cutting right to it:

"Kill me? Kill *me*? You can't kill me, boy—I've been dead forever. Get wise to the lies—I'm a ghoul, fool. A spellbound hellhound. I was here before you. I am a Black Man. I was here *first*. First on this earth. You can put me in the ground, but I'll always be around.

"You so dumb you be a slave to the grave, boy. The Man turn the key, you *still* won't be free.

"Here's a true clue, boy. Some news you can *use*. Me, *I'm* the Man. I'm the only one can shorten your sentence. How much you doing, boy? How much time you got? Oh, got it *all*, huh? Got took by the book. Doing life. Want me to shorten *that*? Come on with it, then!"

And as the Prof held the crowd at bay with the hellfire of his preaching, I saw a pair of the homicidal children he was constantly fathering behind the Walls move in from the wings, eyes on the big man, hands concealed under loose jackets. By the time the big man figured it out, he was where he said he was going to send the Prof.

Nobody saw anything.

When the investigation was done, they blamed it on the serial killer who haunts every max joint in America: Person or Persons Unknown.

I never took my eyes off the perimeter again. When I hit the bricks after that stretch, I shifted into hijacking. Stole a load of heroin from the mob and tried to sell it back to them. Got dimed instead, and ended up in a subway tunnel holding the cops at bay with a pulled-pin grenade in my hand, waiting for the Prof and Max and the Mole to make it out the other end.

Back to prison. I knew how to jail by then. I had a name. I had people on the outside. And I never called another man's name. Not out loud.

Prison wasn't so bad that time. Bad enough that I wasn't going back, though. I put away the guns then. No burglaries either. Dope's too risky. I came from the same place as the hookers did, so I didn't want to be a pimp. Never minded doing some work on one, though, and I had a little business built up doing that until I shot one of them and he lived. I wasn't trying to wound him, and I guess he knew it, so he ran straight to the Law. A mobbed-up guy got me a pass on that one, and I paid him back by looking into something for him.

Turned out I was good at it: nosing around, working the edges of the angles, finding things out, keeping my mouth shut.

Then I discovered the freaks. Not "discovered," I guess—they were the ones who raised me. Them and the fucking State. I hate them both. All of us do. Children of the Secret, that's who we are. If we ever voted as a bloc, we'd elect the whole stinking Congress.

And if you ever put our hate together, this earth would shudder and spasm until it shattered like a spun-glass teardrop under a sledgehammer.

Baby-rapers. "Pedophiles" they call themselves now. Like it was a religion. They fuck their own children and call it love. Stalk other people's children too. Fondle them, sodomize them, torture them. For fun. Freaks love their fun. Sometimes they take pictures of it. They hang around the playgrounds and the day care centers. Get jobs in schools and orphanages. Volunteer as coaches or counselors. They lurk on the Internet. Marry women with children. Trade their Polaroid trophies like they were baseball cards. Fly to Thailand and rent children. They kidnap babies and raise them to *be* them. They make snuff films to order. Send kiddie porn over modems—you download to your laser printer and there's the sample. They bribe politicians. Lobby for changes in the law. They leave broken bleeding souls everywhere they walk. And when they get caught, they say they're sick and demand treatment.

I love that last part, treatment. They take some sex-snatcher and raise his self-esteem, teach him how to talk soft and walk careful. So when he gets out, he has the social skills to slide up real close to his victims before he strikes. Like putting a silencer on a rattlesnake's tail.

But the freaks are always easy. Real easy. I sell them promises. And it's not just their money I collect.

Oh, I do other stings too. I work as a mercenary recruiter, do S&M and B&D intros, traffic in credit cards, move counterfeit—only bearer bonds and certificates, never cash. And I sell guns.

And if I get paid, I find things out. Sometimes, I find kids. Mostly, I find what's left of them.

So I guess I'm an investigator. But I don't have a license. I don't have an address. I don't even have a name. I gave all that up, whatever it was. I live in a loft building, on a small piece of the top floor that doesn't appear on the building charts. The landlord knows I'm there. I know things about him too. I don't pay rent.

I don't have a phone, just a line connected to the trust-fund hippies who don't know they have an upstairs neighbor. I can make calls—real early in the morning while they're still sleeping off last night's soft dope and stupid music—but nobody can call me there. Anyone who wants me, there's a number to call. It rings over in

Brooklyn, gets bounced a couple of times until it ends up at the last pay phone in the bank of three on the back wall next to Mama's kitchen. She takes messages.

Mama gets my mail too. Over at one of her joints in Jersey. A driver picks it up every couple of weeks, drops it at the warehouse where Max lives with his woman, Immaculata, and their little girl. He has his dojo upstairs, but he doesn't teach anymore.

Unless you're stupid enough to try him in the street. And nobody ever comes back for a second lesson.

I own a small junkyard in the Bronx, but I'm not on the papers. The guy who's listed as the owner, he pays me a salary, like I work there. Pays Juan Rodriguez, actually. That's me, the name I use. Juan pays taxes, all that stuff. Even has a social security number. IRS wants to know how I survive, I got a story for them.

I live small. I have no real expenses. I can go a long time between scores. But I never put away enough to retire.

Mama came from the same place as the Prof. Different parts of the world, maybe, but the same place. That's why she raised her eyebrows when I said I wasn't working. Arguing with her was like waiting for Congress to vote itself a pay cut, so I told her I was going to check out some stuff and took off.

I found a pay phone in the street. The air had a sharp edge of cold coming on, but the sun was strong and I didn't mind standing out there for a while. I ran through the loops, looking for the Prof. Came up empty. What the hell, I decided to roll down to Boot's, see if he had any new Judy Henske tapes.

"Boot" is short for bootlegger. That's what he does, mostly from live performances, but he also steals from archives, vacuums off the radio, whatever. I heard he found a way to slip a recorder into the Library of Congress—I don't know if that part's true.

He runs a shop in the basement of a narrow building in the West Village, a couple of blocks off Houston. Boot deals only in cassette tapes: no 45s, no CDs, no 8-tracks. Whatever you want, he'll find it and put it on tape, but that's the whole deal. You can order a mix from him too, but he won't label it or break it down. Only way to crack the code is bring it back to him and play it on one of his machines. Then he'll tell you whatever you want to know. That's how I found a sweet, controlled harp version of "Trouble in Mind" by Big Walter Horton. And a different, much rougher take on Paul Butterfield's trademark "Born in Chicago." Not a studio edition; you could tell Mike Bloomfield wasn't there that night. Boot doesn't do Top 40, and he thinks rap should be against the law. But he's got the biggest collection of blues and doo-wop on the planet, so he pulls a wide crowd—anytime you visit his joint, you can find Army Surplus side by side with Armani.

There're no headphones—everything sounds like it's coming out of a radio speaker in the fifties.

I hit the long shot. The Prof was there, standing on a milk crate, treating a half-dozen guys and one Swedish-looking girl in floor-to-ceiling black to one of his lectures, holding forth like he used to do on the prison yard. He acknowledged me with a quick, sharp movement of his head. I got the message—he was having fun, not working.

"Hey, Boot!" he yelled. "Here's Schoolboy. You know what my man wants, right?"

"I got a new one," Boot said, looking out from under the green eyeshade he always wears. "Live. From Dupree's, in San Diego. Not even a month old."

"How many cuts?" I asked him.

"A full cylinder," he said. "Six beauties. Clear like you was right there too."

"Boot," the Prof put in, a teasing tone to his rich voice, "you get many calls for that Henske broad?"

"Yeah, we get *lotsa* calls," Boot said, jumping to my defense. "She got many fans, man, all over the world. They call her Magic Judy. That's why it's only a half for the tape."

"Half" was half a yard, fifty bucks. The usual tariff for one of Boot's tapes was a hundred—you got a discount if the artist was popular enough to justify his running off a decent number of copies. I handed over the money, declining the offer to listen to it first. I knew Boot's stuff was always perfect. Besides, I only listen to Judy when I'm alone—what we've got, it's just between me and her.

"Do you have a No Smoking section?" a guy in a denim shirt asked, frowning at the Prof lighting up.

"Yeah," Boot told him. "It's right out front. Under the lamppost."

I stayed there a couple of hours, just listening. To the music and to the Prof getting it on with anyone who wanted to try him. Nice to be in a place where you could play the dozens without it ending up in blood.

A young guy with a Jewish Afro and granny glasses got into it about who was the strongest bass in all doo-wop. "Herman?" the Prof mocked. "Man, Herman didn't have no bottom. Herman's bass was Mosley's *falsetto*, chump!"

The music took over. The Mystics blending on "You're Driving Me Crazy," Son Seals wailing his pain about the loss of his spot-labor job, the Coasters with Doc Pomus' immortal "Young Blood," a crew calling themselves the Magic Touch doing all *a cappella* stuff from the fifties, a nice soft blend. Charley Musselwhite's "Early in the Morning," Ronnie Hawkins and the Nighthawks with "Mary Lou," Koko B. Taylor, Marcia Ball, Elmore James, Janis, Big Mama . . .

Boot didn't just hold yesterday's treasures, he carried tomorrow's crop too. A back-country hard-edged band with a lead singer who knew all about pain pounded over the speakers. "That's Paw," a busty young woman in a white T-shirt with DON'T! BUY! THAI! blazed across the front in red letters said to me. "Mark Hennessy's singing. Don't you think he's amazing? That's where I got this shirt—at one of his concerts."

I nodded my head in agreement with whatever the hell she was saying, watching her chest hyperpneumatize the DON'T! BUY! THAI! message every time she took a breath. Somebody called her name and she turned in that direction. On the back of her T-shirt, in the same red letters, it said ASK ME WHY! I was planning to do just that when a ska-blues singer I didn't recognize came on, singing about someone named Ghost, a Badger Game man tracking a woman he called Shella. "Who's that?" I asked Boot.

"Kid named Bazza," Boot said. "Works with a crew called the Portland Robins. I pirated it off Miss Roberta's show in Seattle. Pretty fine, huh?"

"Sure is," I said, handing over some cash—the only way you vote in Boot's country.

"If he's any good, he'll be on the charts," a black guy in a khaki jumpsuit and a blue cut-down fez said. "Sooner or later, cream comes to the top."

The guy with the Jewish Afro lunged forward, but the Prof arm-barred him, saying, "Let me have this one, brother," like they'd both been challenged to a bar fight. "Boot!" the little man commanded in a tone a maestro would use to his orchestra. "Put on Number One."

Boot was too reverent to interrupt the Fascinators' version of "Chapel Bells." He waited until the last chord vibrated, then hit some switches and threw the place into silence. He rifled through his shelves, found the tape the Prof wanted, and slammed it into a slot.

"Give me some silence now, people," the Prof commanded.

A high-tension guitar opened it—just a few perfect, fluid notes. A soft, throbbing sax line came up underneath, a tenor with a baritone counterpoint. Then Little Richard walked on. But he wasn't playing this time—no shrieking and shouting: he stood on the Vegas-gospel borderland, a deep blues taproot anchoring him to the ground. Richard used the girl singers' background vocals like a trampoline, peacocking his way through his whole catalog: a pure-sweet lusty tenor, climbing the scale at will, comfortable inside himself only because he had no limits. The recipe was a rich gumbo: chain gang chants, church hallelujah, the gunfighter bars where nothing lasts long. He capped the upper-octave waves with his stylized hiccups, surrounding a talking centerpiece of blood poetry woven around sax riffs and that masterful muted guitar, driving off the black girls' storefront-choir voices, lifted by the organ. Sad enough to make you cry. Beautiful enough to do the same thing.

Ah, maybe the lunatic was right—maybe Elvis *did* steal it all from him.

The last sounds faded to the stone silence of abject worship. Nobody in that room had ever heard better.

"Now who was that, Solly?" the Prof asked the guy with the Jewish Afro, setting up his pitch.

"Little Richard," the guy answered, like he was in school. "I Don't Know What You Got."

"He was alive in Sixty-five, Lord!" the Prof intoned. "Open the door. Tell me more. Who's that on guitar."

"Jimi Hendrix," the young guy said. "Sixteen years old. Before he—"

"It was a big hit?" the Prof asked, setting up his speech.

"No, not really. Made the Top Twenty on the Rhythm and Blues chart, but . . ."

The Prof turned to his audience. "You all just heard it. The best song ever done. And never made it to number one. Even if you escape with your life, the shark always leaves his mark. Case fucking closed."

We all bowed our heads, even the black guy in the fez.

"Where's Clarence?" I asked the Prof. We were standing on the curb outside Boot's joint—the Prof high-fiving a goodbye to Solly, me waiting patiently so I could talk to him alone.

"He'll be along," the Prof said. "What's on your mind, home?"

"Weird stuff. A girl. Client, I was told. She made a pitch, but I don't—"

"Danger stranger?" the Prof interrupted.

"That's just it," I said. "I don't know. And I don't know if it's worth a look to find out."

"Run it," the little man said, lighting a smoke.

The Prof listened close the way he always does. The way he taught me to. It only took a few minutes.

"Schoolboy, you know how some fighters, they just wave the right hand at you? Like they loading up, gonna drop the hammer? And all the time it's the left hook that's coming, okay?"

"Yeah."

"Some of them, the real good ones, it's the *right* hand that's coming. They one step ahead of where you *think* they gonna be, understand? Sugar Ray—I mean the *real* Sugar Ray now—he could do that, double-fake quicker'n a snake. Bite you twice as deep too."

"So you mean . . ."

"Yeah. Whoever's in it—and no way it's just the broad—they got to be smarter than they showing. They got to figure you gonna come looking for answers."

"Only place I can go is back to this Bondi girl."

"The ho don't know, bro. And a trick can't play it slick."

"Then who?"

"This accountant, right? Michelle's pal?"

"He doesn't know anything about me, Prof."

"You believe that, you might just be as big a chump as that broad's playing you for. You scan the plan, you know he's the man. It don't play no other way."

Michelle was a vision as she walked purposefully past the stanchion with the tasteful lettering saying: ALL VISITORS MUST BE ANNOUNCED. The uniformed guy sitting behind a counter had been watching a propped-up little TV, but he snapped to attention when he heard the click of Michelle's spike heels across the black and white tiles. And one look at Michelle was all that he needed—he was skewered. Michelle doesn't do that swing-the-whole-thing, pelvis-out model's walk—she moves like the sorceress she is, with that muted tick-tock that tells you the motor's heavy on horsepower but not every key fits the ignition. I was a step behind, standing just to her right, but far as the uniformed guy was concerned, I wasn't in the lobby at all.

"Can I help you?" he asked her hopefully, his eyes wobbling between Michelle's perfect face and her slashed-silk pink blouse with its little white Peter Pan collar.

"I know you can, honey," she purred at him, red-lacquered talons splayed on the countertop, big azure eyes holding his. Just in case he decided to look anywhere else, she took a deep breath, let it out in a faint shudder.

"Uh . . . I mean, you wanna see somebody?"

"That's right, handsome. Can you just ring twenty-one G for me?"

"Sure! I mean, who should I say—?"

"My name's Michelle, baby. What's yours?"

"Manny."

"Manny? I know *that's* not it. That's a nickname, isn't it? What's your real name?"

"Emanuel. It's a family name, like. But I don't—"

"Oh, you *should*," Michelle assured him. "It's a very strong name. Suits you much better than 'Manny,' don't you think?"

"Well . . . Yeah, I guess I do. But the tenants here, they like—"

"Emanuel is a *man's* name," Michelle cooed at him. "Maybe you should just save it for grown-ups."

"I . . ."

"Can you push that button for me, honey? Tell him I'm on my way up?"

"Sure!"

Michelle twirled slowly, then started for the elevator. Old Emanuel's jaw dropped—up to then, he thought he'd been staring at the best part.

We got on the elevator together. But if a cop came around later, Emanuel would swear that it was only Michelle. And he'd be telling the truth.

Michelle disdained the discreet little black button set into the doorjamb of 21G, rapping lightly with her knuckles instead. The guy who opened the door was in his late forties, taller than me, with a pale, jowly face and a droopy mustache. His too-black hair was done up in an elaborate comb-over. His eyes had that intense look you see in guys who should be wearing glasses.

"Michelle! I wasn't—"

"Ah, Harry, it isn't like that," Michelle said softly. "Aren't you going to invite me in?"

"Yeah. I mean, sure. Why don't you . . ."

Michelle slipped past, gently bumping him with a rounded hip, moving him just enough for me to step in. He opened his mouth to say something. I showed him the pistol, asked, "You here by yourself, Harry?"

His face froze. Michelle closed the door behind her, twisting the dead bolt home with a harsh snap.

"What is this?" he asked, face going a shade paler.

"Why don't we all sit down?" I suggested, pointing the pistol at a white leather living room set: sofa, love seat, easy chair with ottoman.

Harry backed toward the easy chair, his eyes everyplace but the pistol. I nodded. He dropped into the chair. I took the love seat. Michelle perched on the arm of the sofa, crossing her spectacular legs. "You want a drink?" she asked Harry.

"Yeah. I'll—"

"Let me do it, honey," she interrupted, getting to her feet and moving off. I didn't watch her go. Neither did Harry.

She was back in a couple of minutes, carrying a little round tray. "Scotch rocks," she announced to Harry, bending forward like a stewardess. "Your usual, right?"

"Thanks," he mumbled, reaching to take the heavy tumbler.

"Vodka and tonic," Michelle said to me. I took the glass, tipped it to my lips. My kind of drink—vodka and tonic, hold the vodka.

Michelle had mixed herself a Green Hornet—gin and crème de menthe—in a highball glass. She held it in her hands, contented herself with licking the moisture off the outside of the rim. Harry watched, forgetting the pistol.

"How well do you know this Bondi girl?" I asked him, breaking the spell.

"I don't. I mean, I just met—"

"And she told you she had a problem? Needed somebody to do something for her?"

"Yeah."

"And you thought maybe Michelle might know somebody who could get the job done . . . whatever it was, right?"

"Right."

I reached inside my jacket, took out a tube silencer, held the semi-auto in one hand while I screwed the silencer in with the other.

"Hey!" Harry yelped. "I didn't—"

"Yeah, you did," I assured him. "You're lying. I'm not mad at you, Harry, but business is business. I got no time to shove bamboo slivers under your fingernails. No taste for it either. Whoever's idea it was to come to Michelle, it wasn't yours. You can tell me, and it's over. You tell me, and I'm out of here. You don't, this thing goes *pop.* And then I go and talk to the broad. Your choice."

"That's enough!" he said.

"Whatever you say."

"No! I don't mean it that way. I'm gonna tell you. He *said* I could tell you . . . just to see what you'd do first, that's all."

"And . . . ?"

"And you fucking *did* it, okay? You don't need the piece." He took a deep hit from his Scotch rocks, leaned back. "I'm a gambler," he said. "You'd think I'd know better, what with what I do for a living and all, right? I mean, I know numbers. If there's one thing I know, it's numbers. But you keep feeding the kitty, she gets used to a steady diet. You stop feeding her, she growls—you understand what I'm saying?"

"Yeah. You're a hard-core gambler, and—"

"Hard-core? Man, I'm a *degenerate* gambler, a sucker's sucker. I win, I tell myself I'm playing with the track's money. You think I don't *know* that's bullshit? I mean, you win the money, it's *your* money. But it ain't your money unless you go home with it. And me, I never go home with it. I got in deep. And then I went deeper."

"Okay, what then? The sharks?"

"Of *course* the sharks." He sneered. Not at me, at himself. "What else? And with the vig, I was getting buried alive. So I did some other stuff . . . helped a couple of clients work bust-out, ran a little laundry, did some structuring—you know what that is?"

"Yeah." Structuring: breaking big cash transactions into bite-size chunks of less than ten grand to slip past the IRS currency reporting laws. Michelle had him pegged—wannabes always love the language.

"I was chasing," Harry said. "You know what that means—no way I was gonna get out of it. I was going on the arm from one shy to pay another. Then I got this foolproof scheme." He laughed acidly. "A fucking horse, what else? An undefeated monster, going into the Meadowlands Pace. Million-dollar purse—no way anyone's gonna tank that one. So I decide, I'm gonna bridge-jump, all right? I empty the tax escrow account. All my clients' money on this horse. Not to win; to show. It'll pay two twenty minimum on a deuce, maybe even two forty, two fifty. Ten, twenty, even twenty-five percent return in less than two minutes—how could you beat that? I figure I'm golden."

He took another deep drink. "That's why they call it bridge-jumping, I guess. The fucking nag breaks stride. They pull him to the outside, get him under control. And then he *flies*, but he doesn't make it. Misses third by a goddamned neck. And then it's *my* neck. I'm done.

"I'm afraid to go out. Just sit here, waiting for them to come. But I get a phone call instead. From the guy who holds my markers. He tells me, maybe I can square it. I ask him, who does he want me to kill? He just tells me, go to this place, see this guy. Me, I figure I'm dead anyway, so I go.

"And I meet this guy. He tells me, all I gotta do is call Michelle, tell her that there's a good score, give her this Bondi's number. "'That's all?' I ask him. He says, one more thing. A man's gonna come around, sooner or later. He's gonna ask some questions. I figure you're that guy. Anyway, he says, this guy comes around asking questions, you just give him this. . . ."

He reached into his shirt pocket, came out with what looked like a business card. I walked over to him, still holding the pistol, took the card from his hand. It was slightly oversized, with deep-chiseled copperplate engraving on blue-gray vellum. Just the word

KITE

and a phone number. No area code.

"That's all I know," Harry said. "And it's the truth. Look, I just did what I had to do. You didn't get hurt, right? No hard feelings?"

I looked over at Michelle. She nodded agreement.

I sat there without moving until Harry's eyes finally came around to me. I pointed the pistol at the bridge of his nose. "You don't get a next time," I told him, holding the pose for a silent count of three before I slipped the pistol back into my jacket.

"**W**hoever he is, he went to a lot of trouble. Spent a lot of cash too," I said. Sitting in my booth at Mama's with my family, looking for a battle plan.

"Harry was telling the truth," Michelle said. "I know him a long time. He doesn't have what it takes to look at a gun and lie. Especially when a man who looks like you is holding it."

"That Bondi broad is strictly gash-for-cash," the Prof put in. "And there's the apartment, that whole setup. Plus he bought up all that fool's markers. And it wasn't to middle you either—he *knew* you was gonna go see this Harry boy."

"And even before that," I said, "he knew where I was going to be, right? Once I got inside that Bondi's apartment, there was a hundred ways for her to get a signal out. I had no cover—nothing close. He wanted to take me out, nothing to it."

Max nodded, reading my lips and following my hand signals as good as listening. He wouldn't have said anything if he could. Figuring stuff out wasn't his thing—he needed a target to do his work.

"We got three pieces," I went on. "We got Harry, we got Bondi, and we got this guy's card."

"Harry's dry," Michelle said. "He's Tap City. You could make him talk some more, but he's got nothing more to say. I'm sure of it."

"Nobody die on telephone," Mama said. Meaning why not just call this Kite, whoever he is, see what he wants?

"Bondi's probably in the wind already," I said. "Harry must've called the man, told him he gave me the word."

"Whatever the man wants, it ain't about no chump-change score. Before you book, let's all take a look," the Prof answered, putting it on hold.

Four days later, the cellular phone in my jacket purred. I flipped it open, said "What?" and waited.

"It's all like it was," the Prof's voice came. "The spot's still hot . . . and the geek's still on the peek." The connection went dead.

So Bondi was still living in that high-rise with the blue leather performance platform. And the watcher was still across the street, a few floors up, ready to look down on what he paid for.

So far, we'd already been through her apartment. Clarence kept watch until she went out, stayed with her until she got a good distance away, and used the cell to signal the team. Michelle drew the doorman outside to look at her pretty little blue BMW coupe— and her prettier little white dress. Maybe the nice man knew who owned the fat Mercedes that had put all those scrape-marks on the BMW's front fender when he pulled out without looking? The nice man didn't know, but he spent a few minutes looking around anyway. More than enough for the Mole to slip into the basement wearing his NYNEX uniform. And for the Prof to get past the apartment locks and go to work, while Max stood by the door just in case.

Me, I made a couple of phone calls. One to a reporter named Hauser, the other to a cop named Morales.

Morales owed me, and he came through. He found Bondi's girlfriend. Sybil. And she lived in the Village, just like Bondi told me. If this was a scam, there was a ton of truth in it. The mark of a pro.

J ust past midnight the next Tuesday, we got together at Mama's. The joint wasn't closed, but Mama rarely got late customers—she worked at keeping the place looking about as inviting as a TB ward.

"Ante up," I told the crew.

"The Mole says there's three separate phone lines," Michelle said. "I gave you the numbers before. Probably one for her, one for the modem, and the one the watcher uses."

"Good guess," I answered her. "Morales pulled the records. One of the numbers hasn't made a single outgoing call in the past three months. On the other line, she calls this girlfriend of hers, Sybil, every day. Sometimes a few times."

"This Sybil a ho too?" the Prof asked.

"Dancer," I said. "Works the Playpen in Long Island City. Same place Bondi used to work, Morales said."

"They got sheets?"

"No. Not a single fall between them. Only reason Morales had her name, some freak jumped her in the parking lot a couple of years ago, tried to carve her a new face."

"Trick thought he got picked, right?"

"Right," I said. Happens all the time in those joints. Lap dancers, they're not as honest as whores. They make their money off repeaters, let the suckers think they got something going between them besides the cash. A *relationship*, right? Sooner or later, some psycho goes for it, decides he's not a customer, he's the boyfriend. And they hold the wedding in a body bag."

"She get hurt bad?" Clarence asked.

"Nah. Just banged up. She was sitting on her car, smoking a joint, waiting for Bondi to finish her shift. Bondi rolled up just when the guy made his move. They fought him to a standstill. Made so much noise somebody finally called the cops."

"There is a bouncer in those clubs, isn't there, mahn?" Clarence wanted to know. "To protect the girls, yes?"

Michelle's musical laugh was wrapped around a thick vein of contempt. "They're not there to protect the girls, sweetie," she told the young West Indian gunman who had taken the Prof as his father one ugly night—the night I had cleaned out a house of beasts with a gun while the Prof and Clarence waited outside for anyone who tried to leave. "They're there to protect the pimp . . . the guy who owns the joint. You have a problem, you take it outside, that's the end of it."

Clarence shook his head in disgust. He wasn't from the same place as the rest of us. Raised by a mother he still adored from across death's chasm, he couldn't understand how any man could fail to protect a woman. Any woman. Even when he went to work for a Brooklyn gunrunner named Jacques, he did it to get the money to bring his mother some of the peace she never had working three jobs to provide for her only son. A savage-hearted young man, cobra-quick with his pistol, Clarence would take a life before he would disrespect a woman. He was one of us, part of our family, but he was the only one of us who wasn't raised by beasts. He could know what we knew, but he could never feel it as deep. Michelle reached over and patted his hand. "Stay sweet, honey," she said sadly.

"Hauser came up empty," I said. "Whoever this Kite guy is, nobody ever heard of him. Nothing on NEXIS, nothing in the street."

"Not *Hauser's* street," the Prof said.

"You got something?"

"Not yet. But this guy's been walking too heavy not to leave footprints. He can slide, he can glide, but he can't hide."

"Her credit's just like she said," Michelle added. "I had Abe run a TRW for me. American Express and Visa, paid every month, right on the dot. Got a few locals too—she runs a tab with the dry cleaner, beauty parlor, couple of restaurants that deliver, like that."

"Abe look at the banks for you too?"

"Of course, darling." Michelle smiled. "Six large a month. Deposited *every* month. Like clockwork. The watcher never misses."

"She move it out?"

"No. She's got one of those 'private banking' deals. He probably set it up for her. T-bills, a couple of mutual funds, jumbo CD. Nothing risky. I think she knows this isn't going on forever—it scans like she's building a stash, maybe going back to Australia, like she told you. . . ."

"How'd you make out?" I asked the Prof. There was nobody better at vacuuming a joint than the little man. I remember sitting on the floor of his cell upstate with the other young thieves while he conducted his seminars. Find it, take it, and get gone quick. But the Master Class—the one where he taught how to phantom your way all through a house without leaving a trace of your passage—that was reserved for family.

"Bitch got enough underwear to open her own boutique," he said.

"What kind?" Michelle interrupted.

"What kind? How I know what—"

"The *labels*, Prof," Michelle said. "Was it Victoria's or Frederick's?"

"I didn't look at no labels, okay?"

The Prof's disclaimer was about as effective as the War on Drugs—when it came to the subject of lingerie, Michelle was not to be denied. "What colors? Pastel or harsh? Lots of bright-red and black . . . or pink and blue? Did it have lots of straps? Was it what you'd wear under a dress or only by itself? Did you see—?"

"Girl, I didn't see *nothin'*, okay? I wasn't looking for no *souvenirs*, all right?"

"What else?" I asked, trying to take him off the hook.

"Cash money," he said, looking over at me gratefully. "Less than two large. Careless, not in a stash. Bunch of letters, wrapped in a ribbon. All from Australia, all from Amanda . . . some girlfriend, I guess. Gossip stuff: Sara married Sean, Isabelle just had a baby, you know. Joint was *clean*, like she had a maid come in every day. Beds made, dishes done. Bunch of pills in the medicine cabinet, but all over-the-counter stuff except for some Valium. Prescription too—had her name right on the bottle. Money stuff: bank statements, checkbook. Fur coat. White fur."

"What *kind* of fur?" Michelle asked.

"Fucking polar bear, all I know about it," the Prof snapped at her. Turning to me, he continued: "Back of one of the drawers, a vial of crystal. Just the one vial—looked like someone gave it to her and she just threw it in there. Jewel box had a couple of sparklers, looked real to me. But I ain't Mama. . . ." He shrugged.

Mama nodded, acknowledging the respect for her expertise, but she didn't say anything.

"Passport. Don't know if the picture's her, but it's got that name, all right. Bondi. Big fat leather address book. Filofax, whatever the hell *that* is. Pretty full too. Looked straight-up, nothing in code. Pussy doctor, dentist, hairdresser. Lots of addresses in Australia. Number at the club where this Sybil works."

"You see the name Kite anywhere?"

"Not a trace, ace."

"Bottom line?"

"It's a hotel, bro, not her home. She may *play* there, but she ain't gonna *stay* there . . . and she knows it. Had some real nice luggage. Alligator, the real thing. Old-fashioned kind—none of those little wheels on it. I figure she could fill them suitcases, empty out the joint, be in the wind in a few hours."

"You think it's worth me talking to her?"

"She's a ho, bro. She sees the gelt, her heart'll melt," the Prof offered.

Michelle pulled a deep drag from her long black cigarette. When she took it from her mouth, her cherry lipstick was all over the snow-white filter tip. "What you do for a living doesn't make you a whore," she said softly. "Sure, there's women so cold you'd need a CPA to find their G-spot. And maybe that's her, I don't know." She took another drag. "But there's another 'maybe,' Burke. Maybe she told you the truth. Maybe she was in love."

The little round brunette's hair was cut shorter than the watchers like it in the wet-dream joints, but she'd spent enough on the implants to keep them paying attention. Her breasts were right at the tolerance limit for her frame, so stuffed she had cleavage even topless. They tumbled free as she tossed her black bikini bra into the audience; bounced deeply as she reached behind her to the fireman's pole; finally stabilized as she steadied herself. She ground the pole between her buttocks and humped hard to the music, her fingers patting herself between the legs, eyes closed. That last part was a smart move—the audience was ugly.

She worked for the money, crawling along the runway, rewarding every bill stuck into the black garters around her chubby thighs with a lick of her lips or a shake from her elevated butt. The crowd was small, but they gave her a big hand along with the cash. The PA system interrupted the music long enough to say her name was Desirée.

"Hi, handsome," she said to me a few minutes later at my table in the back of the club, bending forward so her pendulous breasts were inches from my face.

"You're a great dancer," I said, stuffing a twenty into each of her garters.

"Ummm," she purred at me without looking at the bills—like her thighs could read. "Would you like me to dance some more? Just for you?"

"Yeah, I'd like that," I told her, laying two more twenties on top of the little table.

Then she was on my lap, facing away, straddling my cock like it was the fireman's pole, humping just as hard. I kept my hands on her waist, away from those flopping breasts, whispered into her ear: "You're a really good dancer, Sybil."

I felt her stiffen against me, heard the harsh intake of breath. "Tell Bondi I'd like to see her again," I whispered. "Tell her Burke wants to buy her lunch. I'll call her, okay?"

She deflated on my lap like someone stuck a pin in one of those rubber sex-dolls. "I don't—"

"Just tell her," I said, shifting my weight. She stood up. Walked away without looking back, heading right for the shaved-head bouncer standing with his arms crossed over in the far corner. She was so shook she even forgot the wiggle.

"**H**ullo?" She answered the phone on the first ring the next morning, more a question than a greeting.

"It's me," I said, my voice shaded just past neutral toward friendly. In case she wasn't the only one listening. "I thought, if you weren't busy, maybe we could have dinner or something."

"Something?"

"If you'd rather do something else, I mean. A movie, maybe a—"

"Could we go to a club?" she asked in a little girl's voice. A little girl expecting to be disappointed, but taking a shot anyway.

"A nightclub?"

"No, one of those comedy clubs," she said, switching to her normal voice. "I've always wanted to go, but I never did. You ever have something like that? Something you always wanted to do?"

"Yeah," I told her. "But I did some things I didn't want to do, too. I guess maybe it balances out."

"I know what you mean. At least, I *think* I do—I don't know you that well."

"That's the part I'm trying to fix," I said.

"Why?"

"I like you," I told her. "I just like you. And I thought, if you knew me better, you might like me too."

"Maybe I know you better than you think," she said softly. "Would you rather just skip the date, come on up here instead?"

"No. I mean, I *would* like to come up there. But I thought I'd let you make up your mind first."

"That's sweet. You know, if I hadn't been expecting your call, it would have been a . . . surprise."

"I know. That's why I—"

"Is tonight too soon?" she interrupted.

"Just right," I replied. "Eight o'clock?"

"Do you mind if I . . . meet you someplace? I'm going to be out—getting my hair done. I don't want to break the appointment. How about Seventy-seventh and Central Park West, on the park side?"

"See you then," I said.

"**W**here'd you get this?" I asked Clarence. I was in the back of a black Jaguar Mark VII sedan—an old one, but it looked and smelled showroom.

"It's my mate's, mahn," Clarence said over his shoulder. "I let him hold my Rover for the night. Heathcliff knows I love my ride like he loves this one. We trust each other with our babies. No problem."

"It's a beauty," I said, patting the oxblood leather seat.

"It is a good one, mahn, that I know. Not as fine as mine, it is true, but very cherry anyway. I know the woman will like it. And mine, you know, it is really too small to play limousine. This one has real privacy," he said. "Try the button."

I pushed the button he pointed at, and a thick pane of frosted glass slid up from behind the front seat. "Can you still hear me?" I asked him in a normal voice. When he didn't answer, I hit the button and asked the question again as the glass slid down.

"It depends on how loud you speak, mahn. Cliff would not want wires running through his pride and joy, now."

"That's okay—it's not about that tonight."

"But this *is* the woman, yes, my brother?" Clarence asked in his honey Island voice. "The one whose apartment my father—?"

"Yeah, it's her. But we haven't got her mapped yet. After tonight, we should know."

"Very good, sir," Clarence said, crossing Columbus Circle, a smile in his voice.

She was sitting on one of those drab green sidewalk benches, waiting. Back straight, legs crossed. Wearing a pair of blue jeans over red ankle-height boots with spike heels, topped by a plain white jersey top, a black leather motorcycle jacket over her lap. Her long chestnut hair was pulled into a ponytail—didn't look like a hairdresser's work.

The Jag glided to the curb. Clarence stepped out, his usual rainbow outfit replaced with a somber chauffeur's uniform, right down to the black cap. He walked over to where Bondi was sitting, said something to her. She got up, followed him to the car. Clarence held the door open for her.

"Hi!" she said, climbing in to sit next to me. "Wow! I didn't expect all this."

"Because we're just going to a club?"

"Because it's just me, honey. This must have set you back a bit."

"You like it?" I asked her.

"Oh, I *love* it!" she said, patting the upholstery. "It's so elegant."

"Then it's worth it," I told her.

Her smile flashed brighter than her rhinestone choker.

You look very pretty," I told her.

"Red, white, and blue," she said, pointing at her shoes, then touching her chest and her thigh. "Our colors too, you know. The bloody Brits had them first, but we made the best of them."

Clarence piloted the Jag like it had a crate of Fabergé eggs in the trunk. But we weren't in a hurry, small talk smoothing the way. Once he hit the FDR heading south, I touched the button, and the privacy shield slid up. I lit a smoke—I'd cleared it with Clarence in front—and leaned back against the soft cushions.

"Well, give us a puff too," Bondi said.

I handed the cigarette to her with my right hand, but she took my wrist and looped it over her shoulders, moving against me. "Give us a snuggle first," she said, a merry tone in her voice.

I slipped my arm around her, held the cigarette so she could take a drag from my hand. Her perfume was light, just this side of the too-sweet edge. Spring flowers after an ionizing rain.

"I haven't had a date since—"

"Ssssh," I said softly. "This is now."

The club was on the East–West Village border, the ground floor of what had once been a small factory. Ten bucks at the door, two-drink minimum, open microphone. We sat through maybe a dozen numbers. Mostly women, mostly talking about relationships. One did a funny riff about working as a temp. Most of them bombed. The best was a girl who imitated an answering machine, doing the voice mail of a stalking victim: "It doesn't matter whether I'm home or not, I'm not answering my phone. If you're calling to promise never to do it again, press One—then go fuck yourself. If you're in therapy and have some insight into your own behavior, press Two—and then go fuck yourself. If this is a death threat, press your carotid artery . . . tight. And leave it there until I call you back." One guy went on and on about Bosnia. Mostly, they were weak, and the people in the audience ignored them, working on their self-images. But no hecklers—it wasn't that kind of a joint.

Bondi loved it, clapping loudly for each one, asking me, "Isn't this great, then?" over and over. I watched the people watching the people, See-and-Be-Seen in full swing at every table. The only ones sitting alone were there for one of the performers—who joined them after their sets and watched their competition.

I looked at Bondi's face for the first time then, really seeing it. A crackle of red in her dark-brown hair, a light bruise of freckles across the bridge of her flat little nose, her wide mouth turning down just a little at the ends, hazel eyes direct and set wide. It wasn't that the parts were so pretty; it was the mix. And when she smiled, it made you want to taste it.

It was past eleven when she wanted to go. I tapped a number into the cell phone, waited for her to finish her drink. When we stepped outside, the Jag was in place.

"**Y**ou want to come up?" she asked on the drive back.

"Yes," I said. "I sure do."

"Honey, would you mind . . . I mean, I know it's tacky and all, but . . . could you drop me off and put me in a cab? And just hang out for a half hour or so? Then I'll buzz you in, okay?"

"Sure."

"It's just that . . . there's no other entrance. And if he sees me come in with . . ."

"Nothing to it," I told her.

"**W**e found a cab stand in the Fifties, just off Fifth. I put her inside, gave the driver the address. She reached a hand behind my neck, pulled my face down. "Here's a down payment," she whispered against my mouth. "See you soon."

"**W**hen she let me in, she was wearing a midthigh black spandex sheath and black spikes. Her hair was down and her makeup was fresh, red lipstick glistening in the reflected light from one of the baby spots. The rest of the living room was dark. "Sit down, honey," she said, pushing me toward the two-person chair.

"You want a smoke?" she asked, bringing over the glass ashtray without waiting for an answer.

She turned her back and walked over to a cabinet that held a stereo and a stack of CDs. The black sheath had a zipper all the way down the back, anchored at the top with a big brass pull-ring. Stripper's gown. The sheer stockings had thin black seams, a faint metallic glitter pattern in the mesh. She slipped in a CD. Heavy, pulsating music throbbed out of the speakers—all bass, baritone sax, and low-register piano—nothing I recognized. She played with the volume control until it was so muted I could feel it more than hear it.

She turned and walked back over to me. Stopped when she was still a few feet away. "Did Sybil dance for you?" she asked softly.

"She danced for the money," I told her.

"Was she good?"

"Good enough, I guess. Good as a lie can be."

"What do you mean?"

"You said it yourself—did she dance for *me*? That's the lie. She's not—in that club, anyway, she's not—a woman, she's a jukebox. You shove the money in, she wiggles and jiggles. The money runs out, the music stops."

"But the men all know—"

"I didn't say she was a crook, Bondi. A lie's what they're paying for. They're not getting cheated."

"Did you think she was pretty?"

"Pretty enough."

"What does that mean?"

"Nothing spectacular."

"Her bloody *boobs* are spectacular, right?"

"Not in a place like that, they're not. You just dial the size you want, right?"

"What did *you* want?" she asked, bending forward like the answer was really important.

"Just to have her tell you I'd be calling. So you wouldn't spook."

"Why would I spook?"

"Because it wasn't about that . . . job you wanted."

"What *was* it about, then?"

"What I told you. A date."

"You wanted to go to bed with me again?"

"Yes. But I wanted to . . . be with you too."

"Because you like me?" a film of sarcasm over her soft voice. "And you thought if I knew you better, I'd like you too?"

"That's right," I said, my voice soft but strong against her mockery.

She turned her back on me, standing quiet for a minute. "And that's not a lie?" she asked, looking over one shoulder. "What you just said?"

"No. That's not a lie at all, Bondi."

She was still another minute, looking at me steadily. Then she started to roll her hips to the music, standing in place, the spike heels riveted to the carpet. She reached back and pulled the zipper halfway down as she turned. Her back was bare.

She did the whole routine, prancing in a tight circle. All she had under the dress was a black thong and the sheer stockings. She moved back so I could see all of her: a graceful swan's neck, small, rounded breasts with tiny nipples sitting high on her chest over a sharp-cut waist, slightly flaring hips, long smooth legs. A model's body with a stripper's curves. She worked it hard, a clear coat of sweat popping out to the soft-pounding music.

It was a real dance—she never left her feet until she dropped to her hands and knees. Then she crawled over to me, head up, purring like a tigress. When she got close enough, she pulled down my zipper as easily as she had her own.

The first time was quick. Hard and quick. She recycled faster than I did, but she was patient. Then we went slower, quieter.

I think I fell asleep then, but I wasn't under very deep.

A couple of hours later, she prodded me awake, her nose rubbing my chest. "You don't . . . *start* things much, do you, honey?"

"What do you mean?"

"Well, we've . . . done it a few times, right? Tonight and . . . before. When you first came here. And I still don't know what you like."

"I told you—I like you."

"I don't mean that, luv. I want you to like what we *do*, too."

"I do."

"But what do you like *best*, honey? I've got . . . toys and stuff. For fun. Stay here."

She got off the bed and walked out of the room, swaying slightly. Not putting on a show—like she was getting her bearings. When she came back, she was wearing a white domino mask, a white leather riding crop in her hand.

"You want to try this?" she whispered, standing next to the bed. "The Brits say they invented it, but some of us Aussie birds like a little touch-up too . . . sometimes."

I reached over, took the riding crop from her hand. Tossed it over my body to the floor on the other side of the bed. "Take off the mask," I said, tugging her down beside me.

When she came around, her face was puffy. Slightly double-chinned, soft and round, with little jowls showing. Her lipstick was gone. Her eyes were slitted. She made a growling sound, like she didn't want me to wake her up. I took one of her tiny tight nipples between my teeth, just holding it there. She locked her hands behind my head, holding it in place, made sweet noises.

Later, she cat-stretched from where she was lying on her back next to me in the big bed in her room. She leaned all the way forward and touched her toes, then turned herself over so she was on her stomach. "Give us a rub, will you?" she purred.

She leaned into the back rub so hard I could feel every vertebra on her spine. Then she nestled into me, arms around my lower legs. I thought she was going to sleep, but she slithered toward the front of the bed, then hooked a smooth hard thigh over me and sat up, impaling herself on me. "See? It pays to be nice to me." She giggled over her shoulder, bouncing into another dance.

Still later, her head on my chest. I thought she was asleep, until she said, "I could have done that too, you know?"

"Done what?"

"The implants. Sybil makes more money than I did, just because of those things. They're way too big, you know. She's gonna have to have them cut out in a couple of years."

"You look perfect the way you are," I said. Thinking about Vyra, an old girlfriend of mine. Vyra with her thin, curveless body. And those enormous breasts that looked grafted on. The breasts were as real as Vyra's sadness about men only liking her for them. I wondered if Bondi would have liked no-implant, all-natural Vyra better than surgically enhanced Sybil. Somehow, I didn't think so.

"No I don't," she said, her voice hard and resigned. "Not for the club life. That's the first thing they look at, you know? 'Take off your top, girlie—let's have a look-see.' That's what they say. I can *dance*, you know. I mean, really dance."

"I know."

"But it doesn't matter, not a bit. They all want the giant boobs. The managers, I mean. Sometimes they strip us all down, like a bloody meat rack. And they'll tell you, right to your face: go get the work done. They all know doctors. Some of them, they'll even front the money for the implants. Let you work it off, you know?"

"And grease a little on the price."

"Of course. All the dancers have to do it eventually . . . except the Oriental girls. They *like* them to be small, like little girls, even. I don't know what that's all about."

"Yeah, you do."

"I guess I do. Maybe that's why Thailand's such hot stuff. Back home, they all take trips over there. I heard you can get *real* little girls in Bangkok."

"Little boys too."

"Ugh! I hate—"

"Me too," I said, stroking the back of her neck with two fingers. She was quiet for a bit. Then: "Burke?"

"What?"

"You're right, you know. What you said. It *is* a lie. I hate lies. That's why I—"

"I know."

"You say that a lot, don't you, honey? 'I know.' But the way you say it, I almost believe you do."

"I'm careful when I say it, Bondi. And it's true when I do."

"Is Burke your first name? That's a Brit name, you know. Or maybe it's Irish. . . . Is it your first name or your last?"

"It's both, actually."

"Oh God, I *heard* about stuff like that. Your mother must have had some sense of humor."

"Yeah, Mom loved her jokes, all right," I said. Thinking about the indifferently typed letters on my birth certificate, the one I'd had to commit a crime to see. In the institution they sent me to when I was a kid. I'd used a screwdriver on the file cabinets in back of the social worker's office. Looking for my father's name—one of the older kids said it would be there. My father's name turned out to be UNK. My mother hadn't even bothered to give me a name. The fucking State had done that: Baby Boy Burke.

Maybe it was something in my voice—she stayed quiet for a while after that. I listened to her breathing. It smoothed out and settled down, but she never flirted with REM.

"Burke?"

"What?"

"Can we tell each other the truth?"

"I can," I lied, holding her closer.

"It's true," she said softly. "He's there. Across the street. Watching. At least, I think he is."

"But . . . ?"

"But it wasn't my girlfriend who told me. That he lets other people watch me, I mean."

"Who was it?"

"A woman. A big, hard woman. Not fat, really. Just . . . muscular. Pushy too. Like a bloody man she was."

"A lesbian, you mean?"

"No, silly. They're women too. This one wasn't like that. She came right to my door. Rang the bell. She said her name was Heather. Heather, huh! Some name for a creature like that, I tell you! She had orange eyes. *Orange!* Can you imagine? Contact lenses, for sure. They looked so . . . I don't know . . . aggressive. She . . . scared me, like."

"Did you ask her how she knew? About what was going on?"

"It didn't matter, honey. She knew. She told me all about it— what I . . . do for him. She must have seen it. Or he told her about it—that's just as bad."

"What else did she say?"

"She just said if I wanted to . . . do something about it, she knew a guy who could get it done."

"Did she say my name?"

"*Your* name? No, baby. She told me about this guy Harry. I called him. Went to his office. He asked me what did I want to do about it. He was playing like maybe I wanted to get him done. My . . . boyfriend, I mean. Bash him up, maybe. Or even worse. I told him I didn't want that. I just wanted him to pay."

"Whose idea was it about the safe?"

"That was Harry's. He said he knew some guys who could handle it. That's what he said: 'handle it.' I should just wait, and he'd give me a call."

"And you didn't hear from him again?"

"Just from you, luv. That one time."

I kept my eyes closed, concentrating on keeping my voice gentle. "You knew it was a wrong number, Bondi. You thought some man was going to come around, you were going to tell him that story, he was gonna go in there, take care of business . . . and mail you your share?"

"No," she said quietly. "I never thought that. I thought something was gonna . . . happen. To him. I didn't much care what. I told you the truth about that part. I'm going home. And I'm not looking back."

"Tell me the rest," I said.

"She came again. This Heather, she came back here. She said a man would come around. A quiet, hard man. You. She didn't say your name, but she described you perfect. She said, if you didn't ask any questions, just keep my mouth shut."

"But if I did?"

She got off the bed again, walked out of the room. When she came back, she had a card in her hand. I knew what it was. I couldn't see the lock, but I could hear the tumblers falling into place.

"**H**e's got to have a couple dozen grand in the setup," I told Mama, sitting in my booth in the restaurant. "He spent all that money, he's got to know where to find me. He knows the connect to Michelle, that's for sure. All this dancing around just to leave me his business card. What's the point?"

"You know my place on Mott Street?" she asked, like she hadn't heard me.

"Sure," I told her. Behind an orange steel door, a series of immaculate rooms, all furnished in duplicates: twin chairs, twin lamps, twin ashtrays. Inlaid mosaic tile tables, teak floors, pristine white walls dotted with framed calligraphy on parchment and old tapestries. Recessed lighting. Heavy dark plum floor-to-ceiling curtains blocking all outside light. Central air-conditioning whispering within cork-lined walls, vacuuming humidity away. A marble slab covered with black velvet, twin stalks of fiber-optic adjustable lights for examining jewelry.

"Showroom," Mama said. "Understand?"

"To show the goods?" I answered tentatively, not sure where she was going. Mama dealt in product. Transportable product. Diamonds, bearer bonds, engraved currency plates. Guns were too bulky, narcotics too shaky-flaky. When I first met her, I realized we were in the same business. Only Mama stayed at the high end.

"Goods not change," she said. "Emerald on velvet is same as emerald on wood, yes? Mott Street not to show the gems, to show the dealer. Face. Very important. Serious business, *take* serious, okay?"

"You think this Kite guy, he went through all this just to show me he was a serious player?"

"Sure," Mama said, shrugging her shoulders to show it was no big deal. "Good investment, maybe."

"I'm small-time, Mama. Nobody needs all that to try and sell me a job."

"Must be big job," is all she said.

C alling Kite was a no-risk—if there was a way to kill someone over the phone, nobody'd work for the Motor Vehicle Bureau. And I always use the phone like it's a party line anyway—with the cops on the other end. But the way this was coming down, even all that didn't make me feel safe enough.

So just before daybreak, I drove up to Hunts Point. The city's supposedly been fixing the FDR for years, but under its lousy overhead lighting, it was even more of a killing ground for cars than usual—busted chunks of pavement cleverly camouflaged the cavernous potholes, broken glass glittered everywhere. Buying a new car in this cesspool of a city is like wearing a tuxedo to a gang fight.

The streets were still slick from a midnight rain, so I picked my way carefully over the Triborough. Rolling north on the Bruckner, I drove by an underpass and spotted a tow truck lurking, shielded from sight, its red taillights the glowing eyes of a carrion-eater, waiting for the next car to die.

I pushed the button for the all-news station. Big bulletin: Seventeen overdose deaths directly attributable to a new brand of heroin on the street called China Doll. That's the kind of crap they call a "public service announcement." Sure. Truth is, they're not scaring the junkies off with that kind of crap—they're running a promotion for the new stuff. Every dope fiend in town is going to want a piece of that fresh dynamite; if it's killing people, it's the real thing, not some cut-sugar lemonade.

The radio said the year-end survey showed subway crime was down. In all areas except homicide—the only crime that self-reports. I wonder why they call it "news."

There's an all-sports station too. They had an interview with the guy who owns the Yankees, Steinbrenner. He was saying how nobody wants to go to the Bronx to see the Yankees, because the neighborhood around the stadium is too dangerous. Not suitable for families. Except for the ones who live there, I guess. Steinbrenner charges a hundred bucks for a pair of tickets and a couple of beers and he says the reason the attendance is so lousy is because of crime. Maybe he means highway robbery.

The rest of the AM dial was all halfass advice: money, love, real estate, food. And the usual hate talk. New York's all black and white now, a sharp blood-red line between the colors. The black radio stations still don't get it—when O. J. Simpson was acquitted, every Klansman in America cheered.

I switched over to FM, looking for some music, but BGO was playing jazz, not blues. And the CBS oldies station was playing disco.

I went back to the news: Some freak took real good care of his girlfriend. Paid for everything, including her implants. When she said she was leaving, he tried to repossess them. With a knife.

A drunk driver's car hit a child so hard they found his license plate inside the kid when they did the autopsy. Happened in Queens—the driver'll probably get probation. Doesn't matter—last guy to run for D.A. there did it on the Democratic, Republican, Liberal, and Conservative tickets. Even if sheep could talk, they'd never ask questions.

An idiot in an iridescent yellow Honda Accord flew past me on the right, huge tires set so far outside the fender line they looked like pontoons. That's what the tires were about—looks. The car wouldn't handle worth a damn. Lot of guys make that mistake, and not just with cars.

I nosed the Plymouth against the razor-wire-interwoven chain-link fence and waited. The junkyard was quiet, like it always is. It's always alive too. The dog pack ambled up to the fence, only mildly interested but on full alert. Then Simba chested his way through the pack: a German shepherd's face on a bullmastiff's body, his single-coated fur a dull gold color, his ears too big for his head. He looked misbegotten, but his carriage was a king's. Not a bloodline king, a warrior king who had taken his throne by combat. He was old now. Slower, maybe, but stronger than ever, case-hardened from years of successful survival. Darwin's Dog. A white pit bull female with a black patch over one eye strode next to him, a step back and to the side. Not deferring, guarding the flank. A harlequin Dane watched from the left, standing alone. To the right, a half dozen of that special breed of lean, dirt-colored, slash-and-burn brothers to wolves and coyotes—the American Junkyard Dog.

Terry walked through the pack, good-naturedly bumping dogs out of his way with a knee when they blocked his progress. "It's Burke, Simba!" he called out to the boss dog, as he unlatched the gate so I could pull the Plymouth inside.

If Simba was impressed with the news of my arrival, he managed to keep it concealed, pinning me with his alligator eyes as I climbed out of the car, his posture telling the pack to hold its ground. I stood there while Terry moved the Plymouth between some junked cars. It merged with the other wrecks, looked right at home.

We walked all the way back to the clearing next to the Mole's bunker. "He's gone out," Terry said, answering my question before I asked.

I raised my eyebrows—the Mole left the junkyard about every three, four years.

"With Mom," he said. Meaning Michelle. She'd taken Terry out of a kiddie-sex freak show years before. Adopted him by force. I was the force, Michelle was the love. She'd never said anything about wanting a kid all the years I knew her, but she took one look at Terry and gave birth.

He was a little one then, performing on command. Sold by his bio-parents, pimped by a smooth-talking psychopath right out on the Deuce. A fast-food service: fresh hot chicken to go, rentals only. I didn't know how old he was, not for sure. Birth certificates aren't required in our family. He looked about sixteen now. A slim, hand-some teenager. He'd be taller than me when he got his full growth. That was the only genetics in him. The Mole taught him science, Michelle taught him art. With those two in him, it was a sure bet the kid would break atoms and break hearts. Someday, he'll walk around the finest college campus, and he'll have lots of friends. He'll look just like them too. Except for his eyes.

Michelle was done with her journey. It wouldn't be long before Terry started his. If that bothered the Mole, he kept it to himself. But Michelle was digging her talons in as deep as any mom who'd raised her baby from the cradle, knowing it was coming, holding tight against it anyway.

"I need the phone," I told the kid.

He just nodded his head, acknowledging the respect I paid him by asking.

I went down the carved-earth steps to the bunker, moving past the machinery, the microscopes, the computers until I got to the phone. It was a blue-box loop job—the signal went into the 800 circuit and came back up, ready to dial, impossible to trace. I didn't know how it worked, but I knew it did. I lit a cigarette, thinking. The Mole tried once to explain the filtration system he had set up down there. I never understood that one either, but it worked perfect. The Mole put it together so he wouldn't kill himself with the fumes from his experiments—the bunker always smelled like an operating theater.

I held Kite's business card in my hand. Noticed for the first time that it flickered in the light. I turned it slightly, looking close. Some kind of pattern punched into the vellum—blind embossing, they call it, kind of like braille. I traced it with my fingers. Something was under the engraving, but I couldn't bring it up. I tried one of the Mole's examining lamps for a couple of minutes before I saw it: a kid's kite, slightly puffed out against the lifting breeze, a long tail dangling.

The number was a Manhattan exchange. Easy to tell now—all the other boroughs are 718. I tapped it out on the keypad, listening to the long series of beeps as the signal went out and looped back around. Then it started to ring. Once, twice, three times, then . . .

"Good morning." A woman's rich, husky voice.

"I'd like to speak to Kite," I said, my own voice as neutral as a heart monitor.

"May I tell Mr. Kite who's calling?"

"Burke."

"Could you hold just a minute, please?"

She didn't wait for a response before switching the line to hold.

"Thank you for calling," a man said suddenly. His voice was thin but strong. Titanium wire.

"What do you want?" I asked him, done with the ceremony.

"To talk. Face-to-face. I have an offer to make. For your services. Your *professional* services. The offer is complicated. I wouldn't feel comfortable making it on the phone."

"I'm retired," I told him.

"Yes," he replied, like he knew what I meant and it made sense to him. "But not retired from *listening*, I'm sure. That's all I want, for you to listen. I know your time is valuable. And I'm prepared to compensate you for any inconvenience involved. But I did go to considerable trouble—"

"That wasn't neces—"

"Actually, I believe it was, Mr. Burke. And I'm prepared to go to much more trouble if I must. May I have the opportunity to explain?"

It was a perfect threat, skillfully delivered. He could find me if he had to . . . and he sure as hell knew where to look.

And he knew about Michelle.

"Sure," I said, like he was being too reasonable to refuse. "How do you want to do it?"

"Completely at your convenience, as I said. I can come to you, you can come here . . . whatever you say."

Telling me he knew where to find me? Mama's? The building where I live with Pansy? Max's dojo?

"I'll come to you," I told him.

"Would tomorrow be acceptable?" he asked. "Anytime after three . . . ?"

"Four."

"Four it is. I appreciate this very much, Mr. Burke. I look forward to seeing you then."

He gave me the address and hung up.

F or some reason I didn't quite understand but still trusted— maybe some tiny tug at the tip of the hyper-vigilance that comes standard with all Children of the Secret—I shaved real close the next morning. Then I combed some of that stupid gel Michelle got for me through my hair. Put on an undertaker-black worsted suit over a cobalt silk shirt with a plain black silk tie. I stepped into a pair of soft black alligator boots with steel toes and hollow heels. One heel held ten hundred-dollar bills wrapped around a handcuff speed key; the other, a little round box like women keep lip gloss in. If you pulled the tab off the top and waited about five seconds, it would blow a door off its hinges. I fitted a smuggler's necklace around my neck under the shirt. Twenty-four one-ounce ingots of pure gold—you could pop them out one at a time, bribe your way free of damn near anything.

A complete set of ID went into my wallet. Not the Juan Rodriguez stuff I used for my license and registration—I wouldn't be taking the Plymouth. Arnold Haines was up-to-date on all his credit cards. He appeared on a few visiting lists in a couple of upstate prisons, but hell, a lot of legit businessmen were on those lists.

I never thought about taking a gun. But under the bead capping the tang to my belt buckle was an alloy needle tipped with a dab of paste the Mole gave me—a little present from one of his pals in the Mossad. And the gold coin I used for a money clip had a half-moon razor I could push out with a thumb without looking.

Pansy watched me suspiciously, somehow knowing she wasn't coming along. "When I come back, I'll bring you something special," I promised her. "No Chinese this time, okay?"

She made her snarfling noise, ice-water eyes regarding me with all the mercy of a polygraph. "I *promise*, okay?" I said, patting her massive head, scratching behind her ears until she shifted to a purring sound, trusting me again.

I wish it was always that easy.

"**O**h be *careful* with it, mahn. *Please*, now. This is not a damn lorry you are driving, all right?"

Max shifted the Rover into second gear as carefully as a surgeon removing a cataract—his huge hand looked like a scarred piece of old leather on the floor knob. His eyes flicked at me in the mirror, asking for sympathy for Clarence's mother-hen attitude. The West Indian hawk-eyed the Mongolian's every move, as nervous as I'd ever seen him.

"He *insisted* on driving, mahn," he told me. "And you know how delicate my ride is."

"So why'd you let him?" I asked.

"Ah, he is my brother," Clarence said. "And he wanted to so badly. . . ."

For some reason I never quite got, Max loved to drive. He wasn't real good at it, especially in the city. It was like he expected cars to step aside for him the same way people did. He'd banged up the Plymouth more than once. But he was handling the Rover like it was a fragile child, keeping a nice cushion of air around him as we wove through the narrow streets of Chinatown. It was just past two in the afternoon—plenty of time to get to the midtown address Kite had given me.

"It'll be okay," I assured Clarence. "Max knows you love your car."

A truck blocked the cobblestoned street ahead of us. One-way street, traffic behind us. There was almost room enough to get past. Max inched the Rover forward. Clarence clasped his hands in prayer. A parked car on our right, the outside rearview mirror of the truck to our left. We were only about four inches short of slipping by, but that still left us wedged in—no place to go.

I signaled Max to stay put and climbed out of the back seat. Three guys were sitting on a loading platform, drinking something out of big white styrofoam cups.

"That your truck?" I asked them.

"Who wants to know?" the guy in the middle asked back, chin up, neck muscles starting to tighten.

"You're blocking the road, pal," I told him. "Just pull over a few inches and we can get by."

"In a minute," he said, dismissing me. The guy on his right nodded approval.

Asshole. I got back in the car, lit a cigarette. Max rapped the dashboard. I leaned forward, caught his eyes. Put my inside wrists together, clapped my hands, making a "yap yap" gesture. I tapped my watch, held up my hand, fingers spread. Meaning: another five minutes, they'll get tired of the game and move the truck—no big deal. Max started to get out of the car. I held my palm out like a traffic cop. No—it wasn't worth it.

"He wants to tell those guys to get a move on?" Clarence asked me.

"Yeah," I said. "But he wouldn't tell them nicely, and I don't want trouble."

"I tell them, mahn," Clarence muttered, his hand snaking under his jacket.

"Chill," I told him. "They're just profiling. Give 'em a minute, they'll move the truck. Nothing to it."

Horns honked behind us. I smoked my cigarette. A red-faced fat slob knocked on my window. I hit the switch to let it down—his sweat-smell flooded in.

"What's the fucking problem?" the slob wanted to know. His face looked like an overripe muskmelon, about to burst from the heat.

"There's no room to get by. The truckers said they'd move out the way in a minute. We're just waiting."

"Well, *I'm* not," Fatso snarled, walking over to the guys on the loading dock.

He came back with the three truckers. All screaming at each other, lots of fingers being pointed. And nothing moving. Horns really blasting now—a lot of them, it sounded like. Someone was going to do something stupid, guaranteed.

Max hit the switch and his window came down. One dark, veincorded hand extended out. He grabbed the mirror on the truck and twisted. There was a crack, and the mirror came free in his hand. Max held the mirror in one hand high above the car. As soon as he was sure the truckers saw it, he flipped it over the top of the Rover in their direction, flicked the gearshift into first, let out the clutch, and pulled away. Slow.

By the time we got over to Canal, Clarence had calmed down a bit.

We were heading up First Avenue, pointed toward Sutton Place, the address Kite had given me. "I'll ring every fifteen minutes or so," I told Clarence, holding up the cell phone. "Don't answer it. Don't do anything. A half hour goes by and it doesn't ring, call this number and ask to speak to me," I said, handing him Kite's card. "You don't get an answer, or they won't put me on the phone, come on up. Both of you."

"Got it, mahn."

"The Prof looked it over?" I asked him.

"My father says it is Old Money, mahn. Very exclusive. No funny stuff in that place, that is for sure."

"And he's in the penthouse?"

"Yes. It has a separate elevator, the last one in the row."

"Security?"

"My father did not go up, mahn. But even when they had to throw him out of the lobby—he had his shoeshine kit—they only had a couple of old men with uniforms. No professionals, not on the ground floor anyway. If he has muscle, it will be inside his apartment, I am sure."

When we pulled up in front, Clarence was out the door before I was, going over his beloved Rover with a chamois cloth, checking for scratches.

Max just sat there, waiting.

I told the deskman my name. He didn't bother to pick up the phone, just pointed at an elevator standing open at the end of a four-car row.

At the top of its ride, the elevator car opened inside a small foyer painted a robin's-egg blue. It was all clean-cut lines in the wood, stark and sharp-edged, without a scrap of furniture. On the far side of the foyer was a narrow opening covered top to bottom with wrought-iron grillwork—it looked like the door to an upscale prison cell. As I walked closer, a dark shape materialized behind the grille. A woman, thick-bodied but curvy, with the kind of pinched-in waist that you can't get from genetics. Another step and I could see she had jet-black hair, straight and thick, curving sharply just past a tiny, pointed chin to frame a fleshy face. Small red rosebud mouth. Heavy blusher on her baby-fat cheeks, eyebrows plucked down to pencil lines, curved to parallel the hairdo. The orange eyes Bondi told me about. There was a hard shine to her face, like a ceramic glaze. Her small eyes were as bright as a bird's, and about as warm. She was wearing a black dress of some shiny material, slashed deeply down her chest, thin black straps crisscrossing the cleavage.

"Mr. Burke," she said, the husky voice of the woman who had answered the phone.

I nodded. She turned a knob—I heard the heavy bolt giving way. She pulled the gate toward her, stepping back as she did. I crossed the threshold, closing the space between us.

"Come with me," she said, moving away in a smooth, flowing motion.

Her hips were wide and rounded, muscular bottom outthrust in the tight skirt. Her heels clicked on the floor as she walked down a hall lined with framed certificates. I stayed a couple of paces behind, hands at my sides.

She turned a corner. When I followed, I found myself in a long, narrow room. The wall to my right was pitch black, empty. A white Formica table ran its full length, its top covered with machinery: three computer screens, only one of them alive, with what looked like a color spreadsheet, fax machine, copier, a reel-to-reel recorder with four separate mikes, each with its own VU meter, a fat box with something that looked like a blood-pressure cuff attached to a standing tube. The wall to my left was pure dazzling white, as blank as its mate opposite, except for a bright chrome picture frame maybe two feet square. The frame was empty, the white wall gleaming from within its borders.

Between the walls was a big fan-backed chair with a diagonal bisected design, white leather on one half, black on the other. Behind it, nothing but windows. Old-fashioned casement windows with small individually framed squares of glass. Behind the glass, the East River.

Next to the chair was a little round café table with black legs, topped with a white marble disk. On the table, a miniature dumbbell, gleaming chrome. I'd seen one like that before. They use them to test for telekinetic power. A long time ago, I met this wild-haired, calm-eyed girl—a graduate student at NYU. She was in the wrong place, a storefront in Bushwick where somebody told her she'd find a psychic who could speak to the dead. The storefront was empty, another Brooklyn burnout. But the rat-packing teenagers who surrounded her thought it would still do just fine for the games they had in mind. They weren't real bright, those little beasts, but they knew what the sawed-off twelve-gauge I was holding would do to their futures, so they backed off quick enough. I stuffed her into the Plymouth and took her back where she belonged. Tanya was her name. She was doing her Ph.D. on psychic phenomena. After we got to know each other better, she got convinced I had this telekinetic power . . . and I spent hours trying to move one of those little dumbbells. She told me I could, if I would only care about it enough. I guess I never did.

"Mr. Burke." A man's voice, the titanium wire I'd heard before, snapping me out of the memories.

I turned slowly. He was moving toward me, coming from around the same corner I'd turned. Short, slim man. Elegantly dressed in a dove-gray suit with a faint red chalk stripe, a white shirt, and a red tie with a black swirl pattern running wild against it. His hair was white. Not gone-from-gray white—no-color white. His face was the same no-color, a faint network of capillaries clearly visible beneath the skin. Pink-tinted glasses covered his eyes. He stepped closer, holding out his hand for me to shake. A white hand, the veins clear blue against the translucence.

An albino.

His grip was moderate—measured, like there was plenty left. His skin was dry; I felt a faint trace of powder. He smelled like lime.

"What sort of chair do you prefer?" he asked, inclining his head toward the fan-backed one sitting under the windows, telling me that one was his. "Straight-backed, armchair, director's . . . I thought you'd be more comfortable with your own preference."

"Doesn't matter to me."

"Please," he said quietly. "Indulge me. It's one of my pleasures to give people exactly what they want."

"An armchair, then."

The woman spun sharply and left the room. He remained standing, hands clasped behind his back, saying nothing. The woman came back in, carrying a butterscotch leather armchair in her hands as easily as if it were a portable typewriter. She held it level, using only her wrists, walking it over next to the fan-backed chair. She moved back and forth, still holding the chair aloft, until she was satisfied. Then she put it down gently, forming a vee between us.

"Please . . . ," he said.

I took a seat just as he did. We were facing each other at an angle. I was looking over his shoulder at the bright windows. His face was in a shadow just past the light. I couldn't see the woman—she was somewhere in the room, somewhere behind my back.

Maybe two minutes passed. I kept my eyes on the lenses of his glasses, my breathing shallow. If he thought waiting was going to make me nervous, he didn't know as much about me as he thought he did.

"You probably think I went to a great deal of trouble," he said, finally.

"Depends on what you wanted," I answered. "If it was just to impress a small-timer like me, you wasted your money."

A flickering just to my left. The white wall. Only now it was a painting. No, a photograph . . . a giant photograph of a child's kite, dark blue against a pale-blue sky, a long tail dangling, strips of different-colored ribbons tied on. The kite seemed to float on the wall, moving in a breeze I couldn't feel. A hologram? It was hypnotic, pulling me into it. I turned my eyes back to the man, focusing on the lenses of the pink glasses.

"What I wanted," he said, like he hadn't noticed me looking away, "was to prove to you that I am a fellow professional. A serious person, with serious business."

"What business is that?" I asked him, getting to it.

"I'm an investigator," he answered. "Like you. In fact, we investigate the same things."

"I'm not a PI," I said. "I may have looked into a few things for some people over the years. But that's not what I do. That's not me. You've got me confused—"

"No, Mr. Burke. I don't have you confused with anyone else. Confusion is not a problem for me. Not in any area. I had thought—what with all the trouble I went to—that perhaps we could dispense with the need for all the tiresome fencing about and just talk business. As professionals."

"Professionals get paid," I reminded him.

"Yes. And if you accept my offer to . . . participate in what I'm working on now, you will be paid, I assure you. You and I will have no financial problems, Mr. Burke—there is money in this for you. And more, perhaps."

"More?"

"Perhaps. What I need from you now is a quality you have already demonstrated amply. Some patience, that's all. I went to all this . . . trouble, as I continually refer to it, to set the stage. Not out of any sense of theatricality but to make a point. I have an offer for you, but it will take some time to explain. If you'll grant me that time, you will be rewarded."

"How much time?"

"Say, an hour," he said, glancing at the wafer-thin watch with a moon-phase chronograph face he wore on his left wrist. "Perhaps ninety minutes. Right now. All you need do is listen . . . although you are free to interrupt, ask me any questions you wish."

"And the reward?"

"The reward is down the road, Mr. Burke. And like all rewards, it is not guaranteed. But professionals don't talk about rewards, do they? Professionals talk about compensation. Payment. Will you agree to, say, a thousand dollars. For listening. One hour. That's a better rate than any lawyer gets."

"I'm not a lawyer."

"I am. Do we have a deal?"

"Yeah," I said, tapping one of the tiny buttons on the cell phone in my pocket to auto-dial the phone in the Rover. The audio had been disconnected—the little phone didn't make a sound—but Clarence would get the ring at his end.

I heard the tap of the woman's spike heels, felt her come up behind me on my right side. Smelled her thick orchid perfume, felt a heavy breast against the back of my shoulder. A small, chubby hand extended into my vision. Her manicure was perfect, the nails cut short and blunt, burst-orange lacquer matching her eyes. Her hand was holding what looked like fresh-minted bills. I took the bills, slipped them into my inside pocket. Her breast stayed against the back of my shoulder for an extra couple of seconds, then she moved back to her post, somewhere behind me.

"Would you like to smoke?" he asked, tilting his head to look at the woman.

"Smoke?" I asked, a puzzled look on my face.

"Oh. Excuse me. I thought you . . ."

I looked at him blankly. The faintest tremor rippled across his face. He was a man who relied on information. *Needed* it to be right—because he was going to use it.

He cleared his throat. "Very well. As I said, I am a lawyer. Law school was a great disappointment. A simple-minded exercise—not exactly an intellectual challenge. You know what excites law students—those budding sociopaths? The great apocryphal stories: like the man who paid his lawyer a fortune to create an unbreakable will . . . and was later hired by the same man's widow to break it. And the professors—those pitiful little failures with their practiced little affectations. The older ones bombard you with pomposities, the younger ones act oh-so cynical, so blasé. You know: 'A trial isn't a search for truth; it's a contest to determine a winner.' Well, it was then I decided: my career would be precisely that—a search for the truth."

I shifted position in the armchair just enough to show him I was listening, counting time in my head.

"But it was *all* a lie," he said, the titanium wire clear in his voice. "Ninety percent of all cases are over as soon as the jury is picked. Juries today are over-amped on their own power. They're treated as celebrities—the garbage press waits with bated breath for their 'revelations,' as though the morons actually have something of value to contribute to our collective store of knowledge. Ah, the sacred 'impartial' jury . . . with each member trying to outpace the others in getting their story to the media first. It's *all* media now. Haven't you ever seen them walk out of the courtroom holding up their index fingers, doing their stupid 'We're number one!' routine because they just awarded some mugger ten million dollars . . . some poor soul who was shot by the police trying to escape? It's disgusting."

I shrugged my shoulders. Me, I was never in front of a jury. Like most people who live in my part of the city, I had the opportunity plenty of times . . . but that was one chance I never took.

"Do you understand the concept of jury nullification? Where the jury just decides to *ignore* the evidence and substitute its own will?"

"What's to understand?"

"What's to understand, Mr. Burke, is how the concept has become so perverted. Classically, jury nullification applied when the *law* was the problem, not the facts. So a father shoots and kills two men who had raped his daughter. The jury hears all about how he had no right to defend his daughter *after* the attack took place, but it decides to disregard the law in favor of justice, and they find him not guilty, yes? Today, jurors nullify the *facts*. If they don't like the way the police investigated the case, if they don't like the way the prosecutor presented it, if they don't like the way one of the witnesses spoke on the stand . . . what*ever* . . . they simply refuse to convict.

"It's a disgrace. A foul, disgusting perversion," he spewed venomously. "It makes me sick to my stomach. Did you know there are actually 'Jury Clubs'? And that they lobby for what they're calling 'Jurors' Rights' now? It's as though some demonic trickster had rewritten the Bible: '. . . and a pack of imbeciles shall lead us.'"

"That wouldn't be a major change," I said. "What with Congress and all."

"It's not a source of humor to me, Mr. Burke," he said quietly. "With Congress, there is at least some sense of reviewability, do you understand? But once a guilty man is set free by jury nullification, that's the end. The injustice is permanent."

"Yeah, okay. So then you . . . ?"

"First I tried matrimonial law," Kite said, brushing aside my interruption like I hadn't spoken. "I thought that would be a way to make a difference. So many divorces. So many children cast adrift. But the practice of matrimonial law requires you to be morally malleable when it comes to those children. Everyone in the courthouse whines about the 'best interests of the child,' but if you ever put a child's interests ahead of your client's, that would be malpractice. Some people are perfectly willing to destroy their children's lives to gain a financial advantage in a divorce. Or to play out some personal, neurotic script. And when you're their lawyer, it's your job to help them do it. That's no problem for most lawyers. When I was in school, there was a lot of rhetoric about 'ethics.' I remember the stupid ethics exam I took. An idiot could have passed it . . . but I saw some students cheating on it anyway."

"There's other kinds of law," I said, playing the role like I gave a damn about this guy's moral dilemmas. A red stone set in a heavy silver ring sparkled on his right hand—I hadn't noticed it before. I'd never seen a ruby sparkle like that, pulling at my eyes. . . .

"Of course," he said, interrupting my thoughts. "Have you ever watched one of those odious talk shows? That steady parade of damaged people: children molested by their fathers, rape victims, psychotic females who think they're in love with serial killers. You know what they have in common? Look closely at those shows— you'll always see their lawyers hovering near the camera. They sell their clients to obtain publicity . . . for them*selves*. Because the average dolt who suddenly needs to hire a lawyer only remembers he saw the lawyer on TV or read his name in a newspaper. It doesn't matter if the lawyer lost every case. Actually, it doesn't matter if the lawyer ever *tried* the case. There are whore lawyers in this town whose names are household words simply because they 'cooperate' with the press. They do some chest-beating public display like the performing seals they are, then they go into court and plead their clients guilty. And the public laps it up."

I shrugged my shoulders again. Some wet-brain who wanted a divorce might hire a lawyer he saw on a talk show, but in my part of the world, we knew the kind of operator we needed when they dropped the indictment. Some wars are better fought by mercenaries.

"I switched to entertainment law," he continued. "That was about as intellectually stimulating as Saturday morning cartoons. So I invented a software screen for movie contract boilerplate. It picks out certain language, references the user to the case law in the field, alerts them to the mousetraps. I sell it privately. It saves lawyers a ton of hours."

"Which they still bill for, right?"

"I'm sure," he said dismissively. "The law is such a common, low-class profession. You've had some . . . experience with it yourself. Don't you agree?"

"I haven't had much experience with any *high*-class professions."

"Well said." He smiled thinly. "And sometimes, if there is no path to follow, you create your own. That's what I did. My own search for truth. I started out as a debunker."

"Like the UFO stuff?"

"No. When it comes to alien activity, the real challenge is to prove that it actually exists, not that it doesn't. No, my interest is in a particular phenomenon. It's still in development. Provisionally, I am calling it the Fabrication for Secondary Gain syndrome."

"Lying is a syndrome now?"

"Not lying, Mr. Burke. Lying without apparent motive. Oh, there *is* a motive, that's true. But a motive only a specialist could detect. For example: a man who sets fires. Not for the insurance money, not because he's a pyromaniac . . . but so he can put them out and be a hero. Or a woman who writes threatening letters to herself . . . so she can stand up to the 'stalker.' Understand?"

"Sure. I just don't see where you come in. You can't make a living at it, right?"

"If you mean financially, perhaps not. At least, I didn't necessarily believe so at the time. I don't need money—the software brings in more than I could ever spend. And I have new versions in development all the time." He leaned forward in his chair, eyes behind the glasses right on me, dropping the lofty tone for tight-voiced intensity. "But eventually I found my way down a new path. To a branch of the syndrome with profound implications not just for individuals but for our entire society."

He paused, waiting for me to respond. I stayed flat as a dead man's heartbeat. I recognized him now.

"Do you believe that self-righteous bilge that 'kids never lie about child sexual abuse'? Surely you understand that children are no different than anyone else—they can lie quite convincingly if there's something in it for them."

I played it in my head: kids lying when there was something in it for them. That was true—who knew it better than me? Remembering all the lies I told just to live to see another day of pain. I kept my face in audience-mode, not saying anything.

"Allegations of child sexual abuse," Kite intoned. "The nuclear weapon in divorce cases, the staple of talk shows, the darling of the tabloids. Absolutely pandemic. And when those allegations are *false,* a greater threat to the fabric of our culture than AIDS, cancer, and cocaine combined!"

I hit the button on the cell phone in my pocket, still waiting.

Kite took a breath. "Do you have any . . . reaction to what I just said, Mr. Burke?"

"I heard it before," I said. "That backlash stuff has been around for years."

"It's *worse* than that now," he said, still leaning forward. "In America today, what's going on is nothing less than the Salem witch hunts! Am I right or wrong?"

"You're wrong."

He snapped back in his chair, tapping his fingers on his knees. "How so?" he asked, the superior tone back in place, a law professor dealing with a not-too-bright student.

"In Salem," I said softly, "there *were* no witches. And child sexual abuse isn't the nuclear weapon in divorce cases—lying is."

He went quiet, watching me. I felt the hologram shift form somewhere to my left, but I kept my eyes straight on him. A minute passed. "Yes," he said finally, the superior tone vanishing. "That's right. And that's the problem. That's why I asked you to come here." He stood up suddenly, turned his back to me, looking out the window. "Now we can talk. Would you like a cup of coffee or something?"

"A glass of water."

"Certainly," he said, still looking out the window. "Heather!"

I heard the tap of her heels as she exited the room.

She was back in a couple of minutes, holding a brass tray in one hand. On the tray, a glass tumbler, a bowl, and a pitcher, all in the same shade of pale blue. The bowl was full of ice cubes, the pitcher held what looked like water. She bent so sharply at the waist that she had to look up at me from under her eyelashes, showing me a flash of orange and some remarkable cleavage. "Ice?" she asked.

"Please."

She plucked three cubes from the bowl with her fingers, orange fingernails catching the light from the window. Then she carefully poured from the pitcher until the glass was full.

"Thank you," I said.

She took the full glass off the tray, held it to her mouth, tilted it back, and drained it dry. "It's very good water," she said in that husky voice. "Good for you." Then she filled the glass again and handed it to me.

I took a sip just as Kite pulled a thin silver tube from his jacket pocket. He nodded at Heather. I heard the clack of a slide projector, and a giant color photograph appeared on the flat black wall over the computer display. An infant, maybe a year old? Facing away from the camera, wearing a diaper. On the baby's back, two heavy lines parallel to his spine. And radiating from the spine, heavy dark marks—as though a giant had placed his thumbs on the baby's chest, wrapped his hands around the little body, and *squeezed*.

The silver tube was a laser pointer. The hair-thin red line pointed out the marks, tracing their path down the baby's back. "What do you see, Mr. Burke?" Kite asked.

I told him.

He made a sound like a contemptuous snort. "What you are *in fact* seeing, Mr. Burke, is the result of an Oriental practice known as 'cupping.' It is called *cheut sah*, or, occasionally, *cao gio*. The practitioner, usually an elder, takes a coin—often coated with Tiger Balm—and scratches specific patterns in the skin. Notice how dramatic and symmetrical the marks are?" he said, using the laser pointer to emphasize his crisp words. "This is a time-honored treatment for infant illness. The opposite of child abuse. What you see is a centuries-old cultural practice, but the amateur—some *caseworker*, for example—would certainly conclude otherwise."

Kite walked back to his chair like a defense attorney who had just scored a major hit on cross-examination. As he basked in the glow of Heather's admiration, I used the opportunity to glance at the white wall. Now the image was a bird, a raptor of some kind, hovering high above a seascape, hunting with its eyes.

Suddenly, he looked up to face me. "A child, a boy, four years old. He says a man down the street, a neighbor who has lived in the community for years, told him he had a puppy in his house and would show it to him. The man took him into his basement and fondled him," Kite said suddenly, looking at me. "Medical examination is negative. A therapist says the boy is suffering from some form of depression. He's blunted, mopes around, doesn't like to play with his friends anymore. Mother says he has nightmares, wakes up screaming. The man says he's talked to the boy a few times, but he never took him into his house. And never laid a hand on him. They ask you to talk to the boy, find out what really happened. What's your move?"

"That's all the information I've got?" I asked him, my voice as flat as his.

"That's all."

"You want me to go through the whole routine? Winning the kid's confidence, making him feel safe, taking my time . . . all that?"

"No. In fact, let's make it you get to ask him one question. One question only. What would that be?"

I took a minute, pretending I was thinking about it. Finally, I tilted my head back so I was looking at the ceiling. A pure, uniform off-white, as seamless as a sociopath's story. " 'What did the basement look like?' " I said.

"Yes!" Kite said, clenching a fist. "Didn't I tell you?" he challenged, looking over my shoulder at the woman. "Mr. Burke is our man. Good research never lies."

The woman bowed her head, like she just heard the Truth.

"I have been told you are a master interrogator," he said, turning his gaze back to me.

"By who?" I asked him.

"Mr. C.," he said smoothly, laying down a trump card with a

flourish. Mr. C., the Mafia don who paid me ten thousand dollars once. Just to come to a meal, listen to what some man I didn't know said. And tell Mr. C. if he was saying the truth. He wasn't.

"Anyone else?" I asked him, not showing he'd scored a hit. Not on my face anyway.

"Oh yes, Mr. Burke. *Numerous* others. Heather . . ."

I heard the tap of her spike heels again. Another tapping then: computer keys. Then the quiet whirring of the laser printer. I worked the cell phone signal again. The woman walked briskly past me, a long piece of paper in her hand. She handed it to Kite, not bending over this time. Stood standing next to him, hip-shot, arms folded under her breasts. The backs of her arms were thick with muscle, her legs were power-curved, calves bulging hard against her stockings. He glanced over the paper, gave her a curt nod. She walked off. When I heard her heels stop clicking, I knew she was back in position again, somewhere behind me.

He handed the paper to me. A list.

A baby-raper sitting in the Brooklyn House of Detention. His 18-B lawyer thought he was innocent. Asked me to come along on an interview so I could get the facts, start looking around. I talked to the freak. And he finally told the lawyer all about what he'd done. A sick man, he said he was.

A Teflon-slick pedophile, computer-networked. In a lovely brownstone, safe and secure. We danced and dueled. Ended up trading. I got what I needed. He got what he thought was a free pass the next time he fell.

A guy who hired me to find out who raped and killed his wife. He thought he could trust me—after all, I was working for him. Twice stupid.

A long list. And you couldn't get that stuff just by having a friend on the force or bribing some clerk.

"Good job," I said, not pretending.

"I always do a good job," he said.

"Say what you want," I told him, glancing at my watch, making sure he saw the move.

"Can't you guess?"

"Somebody said they were sexually abused. Some kid, I guess. And you want me to prove they're lying."

"No, Mr. Burke," he said, talking in measured tones, making sure I heard every word. "I want you to prove they're telling the truth. I know your time is valuable. And I've used a good deal of it this afternoon. Heather will give you a representative sampling of my work on the syndrome. I'd like you to look it over. When you're ready, give me a call. Then we'll talk again. Fair enough?"

"Yes."

"Thank you for your time," he said formally. He got to his feet and walked out of the room.

I sat there, waiting. The woman came over to me, handed me a thick red folio, its flap anchored by the string looped between two circular tabs. "It's all here," she said.

I got up, followed her to the wrought-iron door. She didn't say goodbye.

"**Y**ou okay, mahn?" Clarence asked, as I climbed into the back seat.

"Yeah," I told him, not sure myself.

"What did the man want, then?"

"Offered me a job. At least, that's what he said."

"Our kind of work?" the West Indian asked. Meaning: did he want something stolen or someone scammed. Or shot, maybe.

"I don't think so," I said. "Hard to tell. But I think I know who to ask."

I never opened the red file folder. It sat on my desk like an ashtray a kid makes for his mother in school—a mother who doesn't smoke. No point reading the stuff until I knew who wrote it.

It took four days to set up the meet. Wolfe wasn't chief of City-Wide Special Victims anymore. Couple of years ago, three college boys slipped a little chloral hydrate into a sorority girl's drink at a frat party. When she passed out, they took her down to a basement they had all fixed up. When she came to, she was tied up, penetrated by all three of them at the same time. The games went on for a long time. Thirty-six minutes, to be exact. Easy enough to prove that. Easy enough to prove it all—the boys had it on videotape.

When they were done, they dumped her on the front lawn of the sorority house. Naked. Bleeding a little bit from where they used the broomstick. The house mother called everybody except the police, but one of the other girls finally got the victim to a hospital.

The rape kit came up aces. Lots of sperm, and the boys were all secretors. The hospital took nice close-up photos too. You could see the bruising and the inflammation so clearly that some freak would probably pay a good price for it—good torture-porn stuff is always in high demand.

Nobody thought to test the victim's blood. They figured she'd been drunk, never suspected anything else. Everything was quiet until one of the rapists' frat brothers saw the video at a beer party. It didn't turn him on. It made him sick—he had a sister. He took it to the cops.

Wolfe played the video for a grand jury. The boys were indicted for the whole boatload: Rape One, Sodomy One, Aggravated Sexual Abuse, Unlawful Imprisonment. . . . They were looking at about a thousand years apiece on paper—maybe eight and a third to twenty-five in real life . . . if some whore judge didn't give them probation.

The boys said she was a nympho. Begged them to do it. Hell, told them *how* to do it. The video . . . well, they had that lying around, sure. But making the movie, that was her idea. Even asked them for a copy. SHE ASKED FOR ROUGH SEX, SAY COLLEGE BOYS! screamed the headline from the same paper that called a thirty-five-year-old teacher "Classanova" for having sex with one of his fourteen-year-old students. New York: No jungle was ever so savage. Or so cold.

The boys' parents put together a whole team of lawyers—a white-shoe firm to negotiate a civil settlement, a couple of hardball criminal defense guys to explain what was going to happen to the girl if she was stupid enough to take the stand. They offered a sweet package—let the boys plead to a bunch of misdemeanors, take probation, do some community service, maybe even some sensitivity training in "gender boundaries." And they'd pay for whatever therapy the girl needed, say a quarter-million dollars' worth. After all, she was a sick kid, but the boys were still willing to take responsibility for their part in the whole sad affair.

Wolfe had the girl with a therapist. A good, strong therapist who was a warrior in her own fashion. She got the girl ready to face it all—ready for war. Wolfe told the pack of lawyers she was going to do to the boys what they'd done to the girl. Only it was going to last a lot longer.

Then Wolfe got taken off the case. In fact, they pulled the whole thing right out of her unit. Gave it to a kid who'd never tried a sex case before. A kid who'd gone to the same school where it all happened.

Wolfe told them they were tanking the case. They told Wolfe to shut up. Wolfe told them where to stick it and went to the papers.

Accusations flew.

Wolfe got fired.

The case went to trial.

The boys were acquitted.

Wolfe was the best sex crimes prosecutor anyone had ever seen. Every cop in the city knew it. They all said if Wolfe had handled the Simpson case, O.J. would be working on a life sentence instead of his golf game. But nobody would hire her after the unpardonable sin of standing up. If you work for the DA's Office, you can be a drunk or a fool, a moron or a pervert. You can be late to work, screw up cases, have sex with your secretary . . . it doesn't matter, if your hooks are good. But you have to go along to get along, fall to your knees when the bosses snap their fingers.

Wolfe wouldn't do that, so they threw her whole life in the garbage for payback.

The rest of the staff got the message. None of the others in her old unit stood up except her pal Lily, the social worker, who only worked there as a consultant anyway. Wolfe formed a new crew. Started working campus investigations: date rape, sexual harassment, stalking. The schools hire her on a per-job basis—she'll never have another boss besides herself.

But there was something else. Something I'd picked up from the whisper-stream that flows just under the city's streets. The word said she'd gone outlaw after being fired, running her own intelligence cell, picking stuff up from the deep network she'd established when she was head of City-Wide . . . and selling it.

You can't trust everything you hear from the underground—the whisper-stream vacuums up everything, gold to garbage.

But I knew who to ask.

"I can place the face," the Prof said to me out of the side of his mouth, "but the crew is new."

We were on a bench in the park next to Grand Army Plaza in Brooklyn. A beautiful fall day, late September but still warm enough for the "Look at me!" crowd to display a lot of skin. The Prof was looking across to a parking lot, where a tall woman with long curly hair was getting out of a battered old Audi sedan. She was wearing a white jumpsuit, a white beret set on her head at a jaunty angle. It was a good fifty yards away, but I could make out the distinctive white wings in her hair. I recognized the barrel-bodied Rottweiler she held on a short leash too. Wolfe. And the infamous Bruiser.

"You got them all?" I asked.

"One on the left," the Prof said. "With all the kids."

I took a glance. A small girl with straight dark hair, surrounded by a pack of children. She was wearing a baggy pair of red-and-white-striped clown pants and a white T-shirt with some writing on the front. Big words, red letters. A beret on her head too; red. She had the kids bouncing around in some kind of snake dance, all of them laughing and waving their arms, following her lead. Black kids, white kids, Latino kids, Oriental kids . . . dozens of them, it looked like. The girl took a quick run-up and launched into a cartwheel, bounced up and clapped her hands. The kids all tried it at once, a riot of color tumbling over the grass. Adults stood back and watched, respectful of the magic.

"Catch the backup?" the Prof asked, tilting his chin at a rangy-looking man in jeans and a cut-off black sweatshirt, his long light-brown hair tied in a ponytail. He had an athlete's build, stood with his hands open at his sides. Moving to the back of the watchers, rolling his shoulders, his hands empty, the man never took his eyes off the girl in the clown pants.

"Karate man?" I asked.

"Or boxer," the Prof replied. "Something like that. He ain't strapped, but he's got the broad wrapped, no question."

A young woman came down the path, a mass of dark-blond hair spilling out from under a purple beret. Lemon-yellow bicycle shorts were topped by a white T-shirt with red lettering, same as the girl in the clown pants. She had a cell phone in a sling over one shoulder, a vanilla ice cream cone in the other hand. At her side was a light-tan dog with a white blaze on its chest—looked like a pit bull with uncropped ears. The dog moved with a delicate, mincing gait, its big head swiveling to watch anyone who got close.

The blonde stopped, dropped to one knee, held the ice cream cone inches from the dog's snout. The beast didn't move a muscle, feral eyes somewhere in the middle distance so it wouldn't be tempted to break the command. Then the blonde said something, and the dog snapped the entire head off the ice cream cone in one happy snatch. The blonde stood up and kept walking, nonchalantly munching on what was left of the cone.

The girl got near enough for me to read the lettering on her shirt: the same DON'T! BUY! THAI! I'd seen on the woman at Boot's joint. I knew what that was about—I'd seen the same shirt a dozen times since. There's been a boycott going against anything made in Thailand for a while now. They sell babies for sex in Thailand. "Kiddie sex tourism," they call it. A whole lot of folks figured it out a long time ago: They sell babies for money; you choke off their money, maybe they'll stop it. Me, I'd rather choke off their air supply, but their neck's too thick.

The young woman stopped a few feet away from us, the dog halting next to her, regarding us with that flat, disinterested stare all the really dangerous ones have. The dog's short, muscular body was wrapped in one of those layered workout shirts, pink on top with just a hint of white around the neckline. When she sat up, I could read what was printed on the chest of the jersey. IF YOU CAN READ THIS, CALL 911.

"What kind of dog is that?" I asked her.

"She's an AmStaff," the woman said. "An American Staffordshire terrier."

"Looks like a pit bull to me," I told her.

"They were originally the same," she said, like she had all day to explain. "Petey, you remember, from the Little Rascals? He was the first AmStaff. They're like the show version of the pits. Sweeter too, right, Honey?" she cooed.

The dog responded to her name with a soft snarl. The woman stepped closer. Her face was lovely: huge eyes, peaches-and-cream skin. But her mouth was straight and serious—I didn't need the beret to tell me she was with Wolfe.

"You have something for me, Mr. Burke?" she asked.

"Just a message," I said, not reacting to her knowing my name. "For Wolfe. You can do that, right?"

"Yes."

"I'm interested in somebody. Man named Kite. Think she could help me?"

"That depends."

"On . . . ?"

"We're in business, Mr. Burke. Just like you."

"I'll pay what it costs," I said. "When can you do it?"

"Maybe now," she answered. "I have to make a call. Just stay here, all right? Pepper will come over and tell you."

"Pepper?"

"You already spotted her," the young woman said, glancing over to where the girl in the clown pants was showing the kids how to twirl long thick ribbons on sticks.

I opened my mouth to say something, but the young woman walked off. The dog she said wasn't a pit bull looked over her shoulder at me without breaking stride, a clear warning.

I t was another fifteen, twenty minutes before the girl in the clown pants broke away from the mob of kids, waving goodbye. Half of them tried to follow her—it took her a few minutes to get clear. The guy in the black sweatshirt stayed right behind her, about twenty feet back. I watched Max pick him up on an angle, moving fast but so smooth you couldn't tell unless you referenced him against the stationary trees.

She rolled up on us with a springy dancer's walk, flashing a smile bright enough to light up a suicide ward. "Hi!" she called out.

"You're Pepper?" I asked by way of greeting.

"That's me, chief!" she said, throwing a mock salute. "At your service."

The guy in the black sweatshirt settled in behind her, hands still at his sides. Max settled in too, maybe four paces to his right—he must have made the guy for a southpaw.

"Tell your friend to relax," I said to Pepper. "We're friends too."

"My friend? Oh, you mean Mick? He's fine where he is, okay?"

"Sure. You're gonna fix it? For me to talk to Wolfe?"

She stepped closer. Her eyes were as dark as her hair, deep and lustrous, shining with some inner happiness I'd never know. "You know the big statue? In the plaza?"

"Yes."

"Go on over. Walk slow. By the time you get there, you can talk to her."

"Thanks."

"You get what you pay for," she said, flashing another smile.

Clarence caught up with me and the Prof before we got halfway to the statue. He was wearing a mango jacket over a black silk shirt buttoned to the neck. His pants were black too, ballooning at the knees and tapering down to a narrow peg at the cuff. The saddle-stitching matched his jacket, right out of the fifties. His shoes were midnight mirrors.

"Max went with the big guy, followed him right out. He hooked up with the Pied Piper girl. He's got a beautiful old bike, mahn. A Norton Black Shadow. British, you know. The girl just jumped on the back and they took off."

"What about the other one? The blonde with the pit bull?"

"Ah, *that* one. She is a piece of work, mahn. I was walking behind her. Just slow, ambling, like. You know the pull-over spot? Where the cops park to watch everything?"

"Yeah. By the library, right?"

"Yes, mahn. There are two cops sitting there in a prowl car. You know, kicked back—not cooping or anything, just chilling. So this blonde girl, she walks up on them. And the pit bull, mahn, it stands up on its hind legs and sticks its snout right inside the car. And when it comes out, it has a doughnut in its mouth! I could not believe it, mahn—that damn dog must think the police car is a vending machine. I never saw such boldness."

"Ah, the cops were probably just trying to make points with the blonde."

"No, mahn. It was not like that, I tell you. It was the dog. I believe it does that all the time, like a regular thing. Amazing."

We found a piece of railing just across from the statue. Wolfe was nowhere in sight. The Prof hoisted himself up onto the railing, dangling his short legs free, basking in the sun.

Girls walked by. On parade. Every size and shape and color on the earth, it seemed like. The railing was lined with young men, some not so young. All fishing off the same pier, but using different bait. Some smiled shyly, some fiddled with cellular phones self-importantly, like they were making some big deal. One guy did an ostentatious series of stretches, like he was getting ready to run a marathon. Some crooned "Baby!" some snarled "Bitch!" Some of the girls smiled, some of them looked away. None of them stopped.

Clarence just watched. A woman with high cheekbones and glowing dark-chocolate skin approached. She had on a white halter top and white shorts, cornrowed raven hair swinging with her step. She passed right in front of us, close. Her butt looked like a bursting peach. "Oh, God has *blessed* you, girl!" Clarence called out, sincerity lacing his voice like honey in tea.

"Might be He could bless you too, you act as sweet as you talk," the girl called back over her shoulder, not breaking stride.

Clarence catapulted off the railing, falling into step next to the woman like he was going to walk her to church. We watched them until they were out of sight. The Prof extended an open palm for me to slap. "That boy can *go*. And I taught him everything he know."

"He learned from the master," I acknowledged.

"Too true," the little man replied. "Only thing, I can't figure out why he likes them so skinny."

I didn't say anything. The girl had been maybe five six, and she'd trip the scales right around welterweight. If every man in America had the Prof's taste, anorexia would vanish overnight.

A few minutes went by peacefully. Then the Prof said, "The Queen's on the scene, Schoolboy. Get it done, son."

I started across to the statue. Where Wolfe waited.

The years hadn't changed her. Pale gunfighter's eyes set wide apart in a cameo of fair, unblemished skin, all surrounded by a mass of heavy brunette curls. Standing tall on black spike heels, her carriage proud and straight. "It's been a long time," she said softly, "but I keep hearing about you."

"I hear about you too," I told her.

"And that's why you're here," she said, getting right to it, like always.

I just looked at her. Years ago, she'd told me the truth: "You and me, it's not going to be," she'd said then. Reading the menu, changing restaurants before she got a taste. I didn't blame her—Wolfe crossed the border once in a while, but she didn't want to live there. "You know about a guy name Kite?" I asked her finally.

"You want pedigree?"

"I want whatever you got."

"Past, present, or future?"

"You do that? Surveillance?"

"Not twenty-four-seven. But we can pull agency stuff every day. And he's on the Net too."

"What's the toll?"

"You can have a voice bio for a deuce, paper package for five. A cross-check, right up to today, that's another five, unless he's webbed and you want the whole thing run."

"And the updates?"

"A grand for every hit, voice-notify. Half that just to keep the watch on."

"You must be rich, girl, you getting prices like that."

"I've got heavy expenses," she said, flashing her gorgeous smile. But her eyes stayed hard.

"You trust me for the voice bio?"

"Sure," she said. "But I know you wouldn't hit the street without at least that much cash. The kind of bail they'd put on you, you have to be carrying a much bigger piece just for case money."

"You want it here?" I asked, not denying her diagnosis.

"Tell one of your people to throw it in the car," she said, nodding her head in the direction of the Audi.

"Nobody's getting that close to your beast," I told her. I knew how Wolfe parked her car: passenger window wide open, the Rottweiler in the front seat, praying for invaders. He was a legendary killer—rumor is he even has a Judas cat who lures other felines into the yard so the Rottie can munch on them.

"Bruiser doesn't eat money," she said, giving me another smile. "I said *throw* it in—it'll be okay."

I held up two fingers, like I was testing the wind. "Consider it done," I told her.

Wolfe slit a pack of cigarettes with a long red fingernail, tapped one out. I fired up a wooden match, cupped the flame for her. She leaned against me, slightly, just barely making contact. I could smell her lemon-jasmine perfume. Sweet and sharp, like she was.

"He's a lawyer," she said softly. "Yale. Class of 1975. Full scholarship. Law review, top five percent. He did matrimonial, then entertainment."

I nodded. Like I was listening, not like I'd heard it before. Wondering how she had all that in her memory bank—was she working Kite for someone else?

"He gave that up, years ago," she continued. "Now he's a freelance hit man on child abuse cases. Specializes in blowing up testimony. He's damn good at it. Smart, thorough. Plugged in too. He gets really good information. Mostly pays for it, but he trades too."

"Bent?"

"I don't know," she admitted. "I'd like to think so, the side of the street he works and all. He plays hard. Even dirty, sometimes. I don't know where he gets some of his stuff, but I never heard of him manufacturing evidence."

"He's a science man?"

"*Soft* science. Psychology, not DNA or fingerprints. And pseudo-science too. Garbage like the 'False Memory syndrome.' He stays in the shadowland. The kind of cases where you never *really* know the truth, understand?"

"He never got burned?"

"Not badly. He doesn't testify himself. I know of at least three different cases where there would have been a finding if it hadn't been for him."

"A 'finding'? You mean a conviction?"

"No. In Family Court, in a child abuse case, they call it a 'finding' if they decide the abuse really went down. He works the civil side too. You know, lawsuits—"

"Yeah," I interrupted. "But if he doesn't testify . . ."

"One time, he found out the testifying therapist was in the middle of her own case. Trying to bar her ex-husband from visits, claimed he had molested their daughter."

"So? That doesn't mean—"

"He found out she'd done a couple of dozen evaluations. And she *always* concluded the child was molested. Every time. And she always said certain things were done to the child. Every time."

"She made it up?"

"Or she was so spooked she kept seeing ghosts, projecting her own kid's life on the ones she interviewed. No way to know. But when the jury heard she never interviewed a kid who *wasn't* abused, not even once . . . that was the ball game. Another time, he found out that the therapist had been abused herself when she was a kid."

"That's not so amazing, right? A lot of people go into the business because they—"

"Sure," Wolfe said, holding my eyes. "But this particular therapist, she'd never said a word until she was all grown. In her thirties. And when she came out with it, nobody believed her. So the way the jury got to hear it, the therapist was obsessed with believing whatever a child had to say, see?"

"One of those 'kids never lie' people, huh?"

"You got it. And that was the ball game right there."

"The information he had, it was righteous?"

"Absolutely. But that doesn't mean he always shows you the whole deck."

"So if he had information that would hurt the defense, he'd sit on it?"

"I don't know. He says not."

"You talked to him?"

"Once. Years ago. He was trying to get me to drop a case. He came to the office. We talked. He's got a real true-believer rap. Says it's all a witch hunt. Kind of like the lawyers who say every time a black man's accused of a crime, it's racism. I couldn't tell if he bought his own speech or not—he doesn't give a lot away on his face."

"What happened with your case?" I asked her.

"It was a day care center. Molestation. We got a conviction. Reversed on appeal—the Appellate Division said the initial questioning was too suggestive."

"Your office?"

"No." Wolfe bristled. "The first caseworker on the scene. And the therapist they referred the kids to."

"You buy it?"

"The questioning could have been cleaner," Wolfe admitted. "But there was a ton of other evidence. It's like the AD was looking for an excuse."

"There's a lot of that going around," I said.

"Yeah," she said dryly. "Anyway, this Kite's a strange bird, all right. He said to me—actually, he *swore* to me—that he's just after the truth. That if he ever found a real stand-up case, he'd go to the mat with it. For the kid, not the defendant."

"And you've heard that before. . . ."

"I have. Lots of times. But with this guy, I wouldn't swear to it. Either way."

"Thanks."

"You want the documents?"

"Yeah. Whatever you have. And maybe the watch too."

"Are you in something?" she asked quietly.

"I might be. I don't know. But if I go down the tunnel, I'd like some light."

"Chiara—you talked to her before—she lives around here. Goes for a run every afternoon around five. She'll have the documents with her tomorrow, okay?"

"The blonde girl with the pit bull?"

"That's an AmStaff," Wolfe said, smiling.

"Sure," I told her. "Whatever you say."

"Give her the money," Wolfe said by way of goodbye. She turned and walked away. Suddenly, she pivoted, stepped back toward me. I walked up to meet her. She stood very close, voice low, hardly moving her lips. "He's got a lot of friends," she said. "If something happened to him, there'd be a lot of people looking."

"He got a lot of enemies?" I asked her innocently.

"Those too," she said.

"**A**nything happening?" I asked Mama from the pay phone on the fringe of the park.

"Woman call. Say you call Kite tomorrow morning, okay?"

"Okay. Anything else?"

"No. Burke . . ."

"What?"

"Woman very angry."

"Why? What did she say?"

"Say nothing. What I tell you, that's all."

"So?"

"*Under* her voice. Very angry."

"At me?"

"I don't know. But *very* angry. Maybe you—"

"I'm always careful, Mama," I told her.

When someone at Kite's social level says "morning," they mean: anytime past nine. Me, I was raised different. You knew it was morning by the PA system blaring in the corridor. That was prison. Before that, it was the juvenile institution, with the boss-man sticking his ugly head into the dorm room and screaming at you. Most of the time, in the juvie joints, I was awake anyway—hard to sleep when it could cost you so much to close your eyes or turn your back.

I never heard an alarm clock when I was a kid, not even in the freakish foster home they sentenced me to that first time. They woke me up there with a kick or a slap. Once with a pot of scalding water. I told the social worker it had been an accident—told her I tripped right near the stove. She didn't believe me. I didn't *want* her to believe me. But she acted like she did, and nothing ever happened.

If it hadn't been for the fire, they would have left me in that place.

I watched the darkness lift, sitting with Pansy on my rusty fire escape, smoking a peaceful cigarette, scratching her behind her ears the way she likes. I had the cell phone with me, complete with a newly cloned number good for at least another few days, but time wasn't pressing, so there was no need to risk it. I heated up a pint of roast pork almond ding Mama had insisted I take with me last visit. Pansy's the only dog I ever heard of who loves almonds. But until I run across something she *won't* eat, I'm not going to be too impressed with it. Me, I had some rye toast, dry, and some ice water.

I ate slowly, reading the paper. The usual mulch of crime and whine. Another little girl tortured to death. Child Protective Services couldn't comment on the rumor that they'd returned the kid to her mother after the last abuse and never bothered to check up on her again. After all, their records are confidential. To protect the kids. Lying maggots. Politicians promised an investigation as the usual babblers ranted on: *If you're a parent and you feel like hurting your kid, seek counseling.* Yeah, that ought to do it. Next thing you know, they'll be telling incest victims to Just Say No.

Of course, a spontaneous memorial sprang up outside the building where the little girl died: handwritten poetry about how much everybody loved her, pictures cut from newspapers. Flowers as dead as that baby. But that's okay—it'll make the late news on TV. And they'll have an open-casket wake, so there'll be plenty of photo ops too.

All that concern for dead babies, none of it for the living ones. Everything as empty as a President's promise.

I felt a shudder of hate, like someone had pulled a string of broken glass right through my spine. I stared for a long time at the red dot I'd painted on my mirror, breathing deep through my nose all the way down into my groin. . . .

When I came out of it, it was almost three hours later. I didn't think about where I'd gone, but I didn't like the fear-stink in the room.

I took a shower and tried to start over. I worked on my mail for a while, keeping the lines out, trolling for freaks. They're the easiest to sting, especially the stalkers who want kids. But the Internet has changed the game a bit—they all want samples now. I know this guy. Everyone calls him Spike. Doesn't leave his house much, and doesn't say why. But he hates the baby-rapers, and he's real good with software—you lock modems with this boy, your hard drive's going to fry.

Spike lets me use one of his machines for an E-mail drop, but I only tap it for big scores, not the nickel-and-dime stuff I usually work. It's all anarchy on the Internet now. Makes me nervous. I'm more comfortable when I know the rules—it's easier to cheat.

"Mr. Kite's office." It was the woman, a tightness in her husky voice.

"It's Burke," I said. "Returning his call."

"Thank you. Can you come over? There's some information you need to have. Before you make up your mind."

"Come over now?"

"Yes. If that's convenient."

"I need about an hour, hour and a half."

"That would be fine."

There was enough of a snap in the air to justify my putting on a leather jacket over a denim work shirt and a pair of cargo pants. I laced up a pair of work boots, patted myself down to make sure I had everything else, tapped Mama's number into the cellular, told her where I was going. Now that Wolfe had confirmed Kite was a major player, I wasn't worried about his pulling up stakes. And Max knew where to find him if he was going to be stupid.

It didn't feel like that, though.

I walked over to Foley Square, taking my time, and grabbed the 6 train uptown.

I found a seat next to a white kid with the sides of his head shaved and center-parted long hair flopping down each side of his narrow face. He had a pair of headphones tight on his head, but I could still hear the bass line pounding through. He was nodding to himself, playing Russian roulette with his eardrums.

I got out at Fifty-first. The streets were quiet—still too early for the two-hour-lunch crowd. I snapped a half-smoked cigarette into the gutter and stepped into Kite's building.

The doorman opened his mouth to say something about the service entrance, but I beat him to the punch with Kite's name. He picked up the desk phone, announced me, listened for a second, then waved me into the private elevator with no change of facial expression. He was a professional ass-kisser, reserving his special talent for members only.

The ancient elevator car's hydraulics were as well-greased as Congress—it rocked slightly but didn't make a sound on the way up. The door opened to show me the woman, Heather, standing behind the grille. She was wrapped in a gauzy piece of red chiffon, heavy makeup masking her face. Her hair was sleek and shiny; in the faint light, it looked the same color as the black-cherry soda I used to love when I was a kid.

She stepped back so I could swing the grille open. The chiffon wrap was open to the waist, cinched tightly with a belt of the same material. Her breasts looked artificial in the dim light, jutting huge and rigid, the nipples so heavily rouged they almost disappeared.

I closed the grille behind me. When I turned back to face her, she was already walking down the hall, without a word. I stepped behind her, not too close. Her hands went to her waist, came away with the sash. She shrugged her shoulders, and the wrap slid off.

She kept walking, barefoot, naked except for a red garter high on her thick right thigh. Released from the bondage of the corset she'd been wearing the last time, her body was still curvy, but soft and fleshy, shimmering with every bouncy, assured step she took.

As she turned the corner into the big open room, she suddenly stopped dead in her tracks. I stopped too, just in time to keep from blundering into her. She spun on her heel and whirled to face me, a left hook coming up from around her hip, catching me right under the cheekbone. I dropped with the punch. As I hit the ground, I whipped my left leg around on the slick hardwood floor—the toe of my heavy boot cracked hard into her ankle. Her leg wouldn't hold her, and she fell forward, right on top of me. I took her face into my chest as I fired a two-finger strike into the side of her neck. She gasped in pain and tried to claw at my face, snarling some foulness I couldn't understand, but I had my forearms crossed and she never got through. I turned under her, just in time to take her knee on the outside of my thigh, pulled my right hand free and hit her with a sharp, digging punch just under her ribs—I felt her breath go. I spun with the punch, got her facedown on the floor, and rammed my knee into her spine as I reached forward and locked her jaw with both hands. "One snap and you're in a fucking wheelchair for life, bitch!" I whispered in her ear.

Her whole body shook, but she didn't try to break the hold. "You done?" I asked her.

"Yes," she said quietly, her body limp.

I backed off her, carefully. She stayed facedown on the floor, pulling in ragged breaths. A muscle jumped right over the red garter on the back of her thigh.

A minute passed. I slipped my right hand into my jacket pocket, palmed a roll of quarters, made a fist. Waited.

She slid her knees forward so her hips were elevated, but she kept her face on the floor. It was a submissive position, like an animal calling off a territorial fight. "Can I get up?" she said.

"Do it slow," I told her.

She tried to put some weight on her left leg, but it was no go. She gave it up and turned to face me on her knees, eyes on mine, gazing up. She didn't look submissive any longer—her orange eyes were as cold and watchful as a lizard's.

"What the fuck was that?" I asked.

"A warning," she said, still short of breath, but her voice hard. "It was supposed to be a beating. Just to show you. I thought if you saw me naked all of a sudden, you'd be . . . frozen. And I could get the first shot in, before you realized . . ." She gulped down another breath, eyes still steady on mine. "I thought you'd take it—I didn't think you'd hit a woman."

"You had bad information," I told her.

"No," she said. "I had good information. But I didn't listen. He always warns me about that. Not listening."

"You're *still* not listening. I asked you: What *was* that all about, jumping me?"

"A message. That you better not play him wrong. If you do, I'll kill you."

"You don't have to worry about that, you crazy bitch—I'm done with this."

"You *can't*," she gasped. "He'll . . ."

"What?"

"He doesn't know anything about this. I mean it. He's not even here. He didn't know you were coming today. This was all mine. I read your file and I was . . . afraid for him. This is important. *Really* important. You'll never know how much. It means everything to him."

"You got a funny way of—"

"And he means everything to *me*," she cut in. "*Everything*, you understand? I did it wrong, okay. You want to kick my ass now, that's okay too. Go ahead—I won't say anything."

"I don't care *what* you say," I told her, meaning it.

"You *have* to do it," she said, looking down at the floor, her voice soft. "Please."

"I don't have to do anything."

"I'll make it up to you. I promise. I'll make it worth your while. Just tell me what you want. . . ."

I stepped carefully around her, kept going all the way to the front door. She called something softly at my back. I closed the door be-hind me, leaving her there.

I could feel my face swelling under the skin, but I didn't think the cheekbone was broken. Putting my fingers to the pain, I couldn't feel my pulse in the damaged flesh. Not too bad, then.

The subway glass reflected back my image, just starting to go swollen and discolored, the eye already closed. Nobody but me was interested—straphangers see worse every day.

I spent the rest of the ride reading the posters. My favorite was from a law firm:

BABY BORN BRAIN-DAMAGED?
YOU MAY BE ENTITLED TO A LARGE CASH AWARD!
FREE CONSULTATION—NO FEE
UNLESS WE GET MONEY FOR YOU!

Back at the office, I cracked open one of those Insta-Cold packs they sell in drugstores, squeezed it in the middle until the liquid formed inside, and held the artificial ice against my cheek while I reached out for Mama on the cellular.

"That woman call. Call twice. She say you call her, okay? Very, very important. Call right now."

That was quick. "Anything else?" I asked her.

"Girl call too. Bondi. Say to call her too. Very important also, okay?"

"Okay."

"You need Max?"

"I'm all right, Mama."

"I get him here. You call later, okay?"

"Okay."

"Okay?"

"*Okay*," I told her.

"That's a beauty, isn't it?" Bondi whispered, looking at my face under the gentle reflected light from one of the baby spots. I was lying on her couch, shoes off, a pillow under my neck, darkness just coming outside through the closed blinds of her showcase window.

"It's okay," I told her. "Not too bad."

"Ah, a tough boy you are, huh? You let them X-ray it?"

"I didn't go to the hospital. It was a punch, that's all. An amateur punch."

"What happened to the other guy?"

I watched her face to see if she knew something, but her grin was innocent—impish, just playing. "It's all done," I said. "Finished. Don't worry about it."

"She called here. Heather . . . that big fat woman I told you about."

"So?"

She leaned over me, eyes narrowing in concentration, working hard to make sense out of whatever she was going to say. "She said there was money for me. A . . . bonus, like. What I needed, I mean, what I needed to *do*, I had to get you to meet with her."

"Meet with her where?"

"*Anywhere*, luv, that's what she said. Said it just like that, too. But it had to be soon."

"Soon?"

"Tomorrow," she said softly.

"And how much is your . . . bonus?"

"Five thousand, she said. In cash. And Burke . . ."

"What?"

"She said she'd give it to you. For me, I mean. She'll give it to you when you meet with her."

"So she knows—"

"Oh, I don't know *what* that damn witch knows!" Bondi snapped at me. "I'm not a player, am I? Never a player. Me, I'm always the goddamned game."

"Why you biting at me, girl? This isn't mine, and you know it."

"I'm sorry," she said quietly. "I know it's not you. It's not even just . . . men now. Not with . . . her in it. I wish I'd never started with that miserable bastard."

"The guy—"

"Yes! The man across the street," she said, voice hardening. "That's right. Him."

I closed my eyes, drifting with her rhythm. "How're you supposed to tell her?"

"She's going to call. At eight tonight. I told her I'd reach out for you. But I couldn't be sure if you'd—"

"It's all right, Bondi. Tell her I'll do it, okay?" Then I told her about a certain park bench.

It was eight on the nose when the phone rang. Bondi left the couch, punched one of the lines on the phone console.

"Yes?"

. . .

"Yeah, I did that."

. . .

"Tomorrow, then. Seven in the morning."

. . .

"Yes, in the morning—that's what he said."

. . .

"I don't *know*, do I? He just said seven in the morning, that's all." Then she told the voice I couldn't hear where to come.

"Maybe cats have the right idea," Bondi said, her face so close to mine it was out of focus. In her bedroom, the queen-size bed walled in with suitcases, all packed and ready.

"About what?"

"About licking their wounds," she purred, coming close, her pouty breasts brushing my chest, tongue flicking across my cheek where Heather had hooked me.

"Bad idea," I said, wincing from the little stab of pain.

"No," she whispered. "Just a bad place." She licked my stomach. Gentle, tip-of-the-tongue licks. "See?" she said softly.

'm leaving tomorrow, honey," she said later. "I hate this place. I hate this life. I'm going home."

"The man across the street—"

"—doesn't matter to me anymore. It was a bad idea. Maybe just someone else using me the way they always do. I don't know. But if you want to mail the money to me—her money, what she's going to give you tomorrow—I'll leave you my address at home. If you . . ."

"I want it anyway," I told her, the words coming so smoothly out of my mouth that I didn't stop to think if they were true. But they bought me a smile, her small white teeth flashing in the darkness.

The phone rang, a sharp intrusion. My eyes blinked open. The digital clock on the nightstand said 12:44.

"It's him," she said, wide awake, not moving.

"So fucking what?" I asked her. "Guess he's gonna miss his little show for once."

The phone rang again. Three times more. Then it stopped.

"Ah, it's my fat bum he wants tonight," Bondi said, an ugly edge on her voice. "I never liked that one."

"What difference—?"

"I know how I can do it," she said, suddenly sitting up in the bed. "I know what would square it. How I can get him. Right now."

"Bondi . . ."

"Will you help me, honey?"

"I'm not going over—"

"No," she said softly, her lips to my ear. "I know a better way. Please . . ."

When the mini-blinds opened a few minutes later, whoever was watching saw Bondi's last performance. She put everything she had into it, doing it all.

Only this time, she had a co-star.

"You pick up the stuff?" I said into the cellular. It was about four-thirty in the morning. The city was still dark through the windshield of the Plymouth as I worked the West Side Highway downtown.

"Made the call, got it all," the Prof came back. "Heavy package too. When you need it?"

"Couple of hours, if that's okay. I need something else too: a triangle. At the park bench. Can you do it?"

"I can do two, that's always true. But has the third heard?"

"I can do that part, I think."

"What time does it rhyme, bro?"

"I made it for seven. Got to shade it at least a half hour."

"How many for breakfast?"

"One. *Better* be one. Any more than that, it's a red zone, got it?"

"Dead and buried, Schoolboy. What's the rules? Got to keep hands showing, what?"

"It's not like that. Just watch, okay?"

"Yeah. One person, you said. Looks like . . . what?"

"A woman. Big woman. And she'll be limping."

I got hold of Mama, wondering for the thousandth time if she ever slept. And where. She said she'd get Max to the spot in plenty of time. The Mongolian would eyeball Clarence and the Prof first, then he'd fit himself into the triangle.

Pansy was glad to see me. And overjoyed at the cold filet mignon Bondi insisted I take from her refrigerator. "I'm not one to let good food go to waste, honey. And when he comes over here, he's not gonna find anything except the bare walls, I promise you. And I plan to leave him a little something there too," she said grimly, an uncapped red lipstick in her right hand.

It didn't take us long to say goodbye. Sharing secrets doesn't always make you close.

I took a quick shower, changed my clothes, checked with Mama to make sure Max got the message. Almost six by then. Time to start my walk.

Battery Park is a pocket of green at the very southern tip of Manhattan, on the far side of the Brooklyn Battery Tunnel. The bench we always use faces out toward the Hudson River. There's a couple of ways to get to it, but no cover for the approach. And watching is real easy down here. At seven in the morning, you still got joggers and bikers and lurkers and drunks and wrongly discharged mental patients and drug dealers and the occasional tourist killing time until they open the ferry to the Statue of Liberty—no way to tell who's who, no matter how suspicious you might be.

I was in place by six forty-five. Had the bench to myself, so I didn't have to pull any of the various disgusting moves in my considerable repertoire to clear the space. I thought Clarence and the Prof would be working their shoeshine routine, but I couldn't spot either of them. Even if someone else could, they wouldn't see hardware. Clarence isn't just fast; he's magic. One second you see his hand, the next, it's full of nine-millimeter heat—like the pistol just materialized.

Max was easier. He was standing right by the water's edge, performing a slow-motion kata, a lengthy one that looked like t'ai chi if you didn't know much about it. Passersby watched him with mild curiosity—the routine wasn't interesting enough to make them stop and didn't look threatening enough to make them hurry past.

On the back of one of the other benches, graffiti-splattered in bright yellow: SCHIZOPHRENICS ARE NEVER ALONE!

She came up the path a couple of minutes before seven, gimping along slow but steady, a black walking stick in her left hand and a white leather purse that looked like a horse's feed bag slung over the opposite shoulder. She was wearing a hot-pink sweatsuit, her body back in harness underneath. Her breasts jutted like heavy weapons, not a trace of jiggle anywhere. She halted a few feet from me, tentative, making sure she caught my eye. I nodded, not greeting her, just acknowledging her presence. She came over to the bench, raised her pencil-line black eyebrows. I took a deliberate glance at a spot next to me, still not talking.

She turned her back to me and sat down butt-first, the way you get into a low-riding sports car. Then she unslung the purse, put it gently on the wood bench between us.

"That's yours," she said.

"For what?"

"For nothing. I mean, not for *doing* anything. It's an apology, that's all. Go ahead, take a look."

"I don't have X-ray eyes," I said. "And I don't open strange packages myself."

She nodded as if that made sense. Reached down and pulled the zipper on the bag, using two hands to hold it wide open, like she was spreading the jaws of a giant clam. I looked inside. Banded cash. A lot of it.

"Twenty-five thousand dollars," she said, looking at her hands in her lap. A big diamond glittered on her left hand. An engagement ring? "Hundred-dollar bills," she said. "*Used* bills, no consecutive serial numbers."

"That's a big apology."

"I fucked up big time. Twenty of it's for you, five for the whore."

"The whore?"

"You know who I mean. Bondi, whatever her name is."

"And she's a whore?"

Her orange eyes caught the early morning light. "I did a stupid thing, but I'm not stupid," she said. "The research wasn't wrong. I was."

"So . . . ?"

"So I know what she does. For money."

"I do things for money too."

"Would you let somebody fuck you for money?"

"Meaning you wouldn't?"

"No. I wouldn't. I would never do that. It's wrong."

"So you don't just punch people out; you're a goddamned judge too?"

"If you like."

"No, I don't like. I don't like you. A woman takes money for sex, she's no good according to you, right? But you, you want to do some bodywork on me, bang me around, scare me into doing something you want . . . that's okay?"

"I *said* I was wrong."

"No, bitch. You said you *guessed* wrong, that's all. It worked for you before, didn't it?"

"What?"

"Slapping people around."

"You chipped a bone in my ankle," she said, a little-girl undertone to her voice. "It *hurt*, what you did."

"You hurt yourself," I told her. Thinking of an ancient aikido master standing in a dojo years before, talking to a student who was moaning and holding his broken hand, telling him it was the student's desire to hurt another that caused him so much pain.

"I cop to it, okay?" she said flatly. "When you do something wrong, all you can do is apologize and take what's coming to you."

"And what's coming to you is paying me off?"

"I asked you if you wanted something else."

"When?"

"I said you could kick my ass if you wanted to. You still can, if it would make things right. Or . . ."

"What?"

"Or you can . . . have me. Any way you want."

"Instead of the money?"

"Yes."

"But *you're* not a whore, huh?"

Her face flamed. "You can keep the money too, all right?"

"I don't want you."

"You would if I was . . . nice," she said softly. "I know you would—it's in your eyes."

"You need a translator," I told her.

"Am I too fat for you? Or maybe you just like whores."

"Maybe I just don't like liars."

She took a deep breath, squeezing her hands together in her lap. Max was still into his kata, never breaking the flow. If she'd brought friends with her, they weren't close enough to do much. Not with their hands anyway. I've seen Max move—he was a hell of a lot closer than he looked. And whatever she planned to do, she couldn't run away.

"I'll give you one more thing, then," she said. "The truth. How's that?"

"Say it. Then I'll tell you what it's worth."

She turned to face me, quickly ran her tongue over her lips. It wasn't a come-on—she was getting ready to talk. "When I was thirteen years old I was already . . . built like this. I looked like I was twenty, at least. And I dressed like it too. I met a man. A famous man. He was a writer. A serious writer. He wrote books about economics. And social theory and politics and stuff like that. We were . . . friends. He thought I was older, but he never tried anything with me. Just . . . holding hands and stuff. I told him I was a salesgirl. In a record store. I knew a lot about that—I used to spend all my time in one. We were together a lot. Mostly in this coffeehouse in the Village. An old-style one. Little tables, checkered tablecloths, you could sit there for hours and nobody'd bother you. . . .

"But sometimes we went to his place. He had an apartment, the first floor of a brownstone on Bank Street. It was mostly books. Real quiet and peaceful. He'd give me books to read, and we'd talk about them. I wanted him to love me. And I think he did, maybe. . . ."

Her voice trailed off. I closed my eyes so I could hear her better. Waited.

"I had a key to his place. I got there before him one night. I wanted to surprise him. I took my clothes off and took a bath. A bubble bath. In his tub. Then I put on this negligee I bought. I thought it was real sexy, but now I know it was just cheap and tacky. I was going to be a surprise package for him when he got home. So he could unwrap it, you understand?"

"Sure."

"But when he walked in the door and saw me, his face got all red, like he was real mad. I asked him what was wrong. And then he asked me how old I was."

"I lied. Like I did before. But he wasn't going for it. I showed him my fake ID and everything, but it was like he . . . knew something. I took off the negligee. I stood right in front of him. Naked. But he didn't budge, just stood there with his arms folded. And then I told him the truth. His face went white. He was scared, I could tell."

She went quiet for a minute, her head bowed. A tear tracked her cheek, cutting a soft river through the heavy makeup. I turned my detector on full, but the signals were still scrambled. I swept the field with my eyes without turning my head, but the ground all around me was bland. Max was still in place.

Maybe a minute passed. If she was waiting for me to say something, she was out of luck. Finally, she looked up. "That's when I . . . did it. I told him he had to make love to me. He *had* to. Or I'd tell everyone he did."

I made some neutral sound, encouraging her to talk, not judging.

"He just stood there with his arms folded. I got dressed and I left. I called him after that. A lot of times. After a while, he just used his answering machine to screen the calls. It made me so mad . . . knowing he was right there and he wouldn't even talk to me."

"What could he have said?" I asked quietly.

"I don't *know*," she answered. "Something . . . But he didn't. Nothing. Nothing at all. So that's when I did it."

"Did what, Heather?"

"I told on him. I told my mother. But she said that's what I deserved, dressing like a slut, not listening to her and all. She called me a fat fucking cow. She always called me that. My father . . . they're divorced, he lives in L.A., I never see him. So I told a teacher. A guidance counselor. And then *she* went to my mother."

"What did you tell the counselor?"

"That we were lovers. That we had sex. Not . . . real sex. I was too smart for that. I mean, I was a virgin. And I knew there were ways they could tell. I knew what to tell them. I told them we did . . . other things. My mother was real mad. Not for what happened— what I *said* happened—but because I embarrassed her. She went and got the strap. But I told her if she ever raised that thing to me again, I'd break her fucking arm for her. She knew I could do it then—I was almost as big as I am now. Strong too."

"So what happened?"

"She didn't do anything. Just left me alone. But she told her boyfriend. A lawyer. And he told her she could make money if I sued him. So that's what we did."

"Did you go to the police too?"

"No. At least, not at first. Her boyfriend, he told us we should ask for money first. In a letter. But he wouldn't pay. He wrote and said I was a liar. And I was."

"How did the case . . . ?"

"It made the papers. They even took my picture. My mother's boyfriend had me dress up like a little girl. No makeup, a big loose dress and everything. We sued him for five million dollars. I looked just like I really was—a fat, ugly, sad little girl."

"He ever pay it?"

"No," she said, her voice strangling on grief. "He never paid it. He killed himself. With a gun. In his apartment. In that same room."

"Ah . . ."

"He left a note. Not for the papers, for me. He mailed it to me—I got it after he was gone. It said: 'Your lies took my life.' That's all."

"What happened then?"

"I went . . . nuts. My mother put me in a hospital. I was there almost five years. I wanted to kill myself too. So I could apologize. So I could be with him and apologize. It took me a long time before . . ."

"Before . . . ?"

"Before they let me out. Then I went to college. I went to high school in the hospital, so I was ready. When I got out, I just drifted. Waiting for something, I didn't know what. And then I met him."

"Kite?"

"He gave a lecture. It only cost ten dollars. He talked about the climate. The American climate. How we have witch hunts all over again, only this time, about child sexual abuse. After the lecture, I went up to him. And I told him the truth, like I just told you."

She clasped her hands under her breasts, lifting them up like the offering she'd made to the man she killed so many years before, her voice rapt with true-believer lust. "He didn't shun me. He listened. He explained to me why I did it. He said if the climate was right in America, I wouldn't really have caused that much damage. Nobody would have been hurt. The right people would have asked the right questions, and the truth would have come out. That's what he does. That's his work.

"He told me something else too," she said softly. "How I could make up for what I did. Helping him in his work. That's what I've done ever since. Almost ten years now. And when he told me about you, I was scared. I read your file. You're a criminal. You went to prison. I think you even killed people—it says you did in your file.

But he was sure you were the right man for this. It's so important to him."

"What?"

"The *truth*—don't you understand? He always says the people who say it *never* happens are just as crazy as the ones who say it *always* happens. He believes this wom— In this case, I mean. I do too. And he says you're the man to prove it for him. . . . If *you* can't break a story, it can't *be* broken, that's what he says."

She turned her head toward the river, looking at the dark water as if it would give her strength. "He says you would have broken me. That if you had been on the job, I never would have gotten away with it. Oh God, I wish that had been. But you're a . . . mercenary; that's what he calls you. I was afraid you wouldn't play square. That you'd take money from the other side and betray us. He's not a . . . strong man. Not physically, I mean. I was afraid you'd take his money and then just go away and laugh at him."

"So you thought you'd . . . what? Scare me?"

"I thought if you knew . . . that I'd kill you if you betrayed him, maybe you'd . . . I don't *know*! I wasn't really trying to hurt you. Not hurt you bad. If I wanted to do that, I would have used these," she said, one pudgy little hand going to the waistband of the sweatsuit. She moved slow and careful, taking out a pair of brass knuckles. Not fitting them over her fists, just showing them to me. "I know how to use them," she said. "I learned to do it in . . . there. Some of those attendants, they . . . I wanted you to know, if you did that to him, I'd kill you."

"I believe you'd kill me, Heather," I told her. "That's why I'm walking away. I got enough enemies."

"You *can't*!" she cried, grabbing my hand. "*Please!* He *needs* you. I do too. I'm sorry for what I did. Sorry for what I did to . . . him. And to you too. I don't care if you hate me. I wouldn't even blame you. I hate me too. Please, please . . . just take the money. And . . . whatever else you want."

I had no map for this, so I went with the only thing I knew. "Tell Kite I'll call him in a couple of days," I told her, scooping up the feed-bag purse as I got to my feet.

I didn't look back.

The Prof was standing next to Clarence's Rover as I approached, a lawyer's black leather attaché case in his hand. "She rolled in alone, home," he said. "In a big beast. All white, smoked glass—a high-glide ride."

"You get a look inside?"

"Just a glimpse, when the door opened. I tried to sneak a peek, but I couldn't see nobody else. She was behind the wheel."

"Think Kite doesn't know?"

"No way to tell, Schoolboy. She parked a *long* way down. Bitch had to gimp it for a good quarter mile."

"Yeah. That the stuff from Wolfe?"

"That's the true clue, babe. Pickup went smooth. Clarence copped it from that blonde with the doughnut-snatching pit bull. She was right on time."

"Thanks," I said, taking the attaché case from him. "How's this scan to you?" I asked, running down what happened in Kite's apartment, what Heather just told me too.

The little man listened close, head cocked so I didn't have to speak up, a habit that marked him as clear as a jailhouse tattoo. "She knows how it's done, son. Stripped to freeze your eye, dropped the sucker punch before you could catch the lie. Can't be the first time she played that tune."

"Yeah. Felt like she was going for it too. I hadn't stopped her, she was gonna hurt me."

"You think pain's her game?"

"No."

"You sure?

"No. And I'm not gonna find out either. That's a freaky, dangerous broad. I think she was telling the truth. She wants this. Wants it *bad*. I think she's used to bulling her way through things. She's real . . . I don't know . . . *physical*. Maybe she works the bad-cop thing with Kite. When he does questioning . . ."

"If rough-off's the tool, she's a fool," the Prof said. "You got to check out the canvas before you paint."

"I know," I said, remembering. It was one of the first things he taught me.

"You gonna play it?" he asked me, not pushing either way.

"Man went to a lot of trouble," I said, thinking it through out loud. "Time and money both. It's me he wants. For this job anyway. I don't know what he'd do if I pulled out, but there's no reason to risk it. We're gonna get paid, right? And some of that money's gonna buy us the same gun he's pointing at my head—information."

"Yeah," the little man agreed. "I wouldn't want that Wolfe woman getting me in her sights either."

I reached in the feed-bag purse, counted out five thousand, and pocketed it for Bondi. Then I handed the purse over to the Prof. "There's twenty in here. Five apiece for you, me, Clarence, and Max. Hush money, bitch thinks it is. I'm gonna *stay* hushed for a while. Near as I can tell, Kite wants me to talk to someone, see if they're telling the truth. I'm gonna do that. Then . . ."

"You backed, Jack," the little man said.

I drove away slowly in the Plymouth, enclosed in the steel but looking out through the glass. Thinking about how safe the Prof always made me feel.

I'd come into prison a rookie thug, pulling armed robberies cowboy-style, ready to risk a life sentence for a payroll. The prison economy produces entrepreneurs the same way the Outside does. Pressure extrudes. There was this guy who was always just one beat off from the crime music the rest of us lived by. The Prof called him Einstein, and after a while, we did too. Einstein was always coming up with great ideas. One was books-on-video for the deaf: On the screen would be a person signing the whole book, like closed caption. Another move was Mother Nature's cigarettes: organically grown tobacco, no pesticides, rolled in recycled paper. He was going to sell them in health-food stores. The flash of his ideas always blinded him to the one little problem with them.

Einstein was out in the World once and finally hit on a winner—selling special limited editions of books by authors who never made the best-seller list but had real followings among collectors. He did it right: leather-bound, ribbon markers, marbled endpapers ... everything. First time he tried it, he ran off a printing of five hundred, and he sold every single one. Then, of course, the genius figured he was on a roll, so he went back for a second printing. Couldn't figure out why that one flopped.

See, Einstein was a citizen in his heart. Only reason he kept coming back to prison, he was always using a gun to turn banks into his personal ATM, grabbing R&D money for his next project.

Einstein read a lot. I mean, a *lot*. He was always looking for the Answer. Anyway, one day he comes out on the yard, sure he'd finally found It. He'd just finished some book on the Civil War—it was all about how rich men avoided the draft by paying poor men to fight in their place. So Einstein figured this time he had the perfect scheme: why not let rich men who got convicted of crimes pay other guys to do their time?

He ran it down, all excited, the way he always did. The first guy to respond was a stone fool named Vinnie. "I wouldn't do that for a million bucks," he sneered, superior.

But the Prof wasn't going to let anyone riff on Einstein. "Yeah, right. You too slick for that trick, huh? Naw, you wanna keep sticking up your goddamn bodegas for chump change! How much you pull from your last score, Dillinger? Few hundred bucks? And what you doing on this bit, another nickel-and-dime? My man Einstein may be loco, but he ain't stupid!"

By the time the Prof was done with my education, I knew a dozen slicker, safer ways to get money. All crooked.

I knew this was one of them—but I didn't know how to do it yet.

I sent the money to Bondi in a plain little box, tightly duct-taped inside the brown paper wrapping. It's a big-time felony to ship cash into Australia, so I put the package together as carefully as a letter bomb—if the cops opened it at the other end, it wouldn't bounce back to me. I did all the lettering with a pantograph—no handwriting, no hands. For a return address, I used a sex-dance joint in Times Square. Maybe they'd figure some old customer was sending her a present.

I used the main post office on Eighth, the busiest one in the world. As I walked out, I stripped the surgeon's gloves from my hands, tossed them in a Dumpster, and disappeared into the subway.

Back in the office, I went through the package I'd paid Wolfe for. Kite was born in 1951. Weighed six pounds three ounces. No prior live births listed to his mother. Pediatric records showed regular visits. Nothing remarkable except a bout with whooping cough and surgery to correct an undescended testicle.

Parents both dead, car accident. Drunk driver took them out when Kite was eleven years old. Raised by mother's sister and her second husband, a lawyer in Spokane, Washington. Tonsillectomy, age thirteen. Pretty late in the game for that—must have been painful. Straight-A student in high school. Chess club, debate team, drama society. SAT score of 1540. Full scholarship to college.

In 1970, his aunt's husband was arrested for a series of highway rapes near the Idaho border. The rapist was a cripple-hunter, cruising the side roads in bad weather, looking for cars that had broken down . . . cars with women drivers, alone and stranded. He wore a stocking mask, never left prints. They caught him with an undercover operation, used a woman decoy cop standing next to a car with the hood up. Found the stocking mask, heavy pair of leather gloves, and a lead pipe wrapped in black friction tape. When they let him out on bail, he called a press conference. He said all the evidence had been planted—they had the wrong man and they knew it.

But two of the victims ID'ed him. The mask didn't help—he hadn't been circumcised until he was an adult, and the penile hood had a distinctive flap of darkened flesh where the surgeon had left a piece.

He pleaded guilty on the eve of trial. The prosecutor agreed he was suffering from a "mental disease or defect" and prison wouldn't be appropriate. He was committed to a closed psychiatric facility for an indefinite period, his status to be reviewed periodically.

Three months into his term, he was stabbed to death in the shower room.

His mother's sister remarried a year later. Kite never returned to Spokane. I glanced over the law school stuff—just a flesh-out of what Wolfe had already told me. Law Review, Order of the Coif, American Jurisprudence Award in Contracts. Admitted to the New York Bar in 1975, Federal District Court in 1976.

Never married. No indication he was gay. The Sutton Place address was the only one anybody had. No driver's license. Premises permit for a SIG-Sauer P230 semi-auto.

He had a SEP account at a major brokerage house. Started in 1988, rolling over the 401(k) from the last law firm he'd left. Present value: $588,644.22. The Sutton Place joint was a co-op. Mortgage of $860,000, this after a down payment of $750,000 flat. Monthly nut, mortgage, carrying charges, and taxes: $13,100.29. Paid perfectly, auto-EFT from his business checking account. The unit he owned included a basement garage. A 1996 Cadillac STS sedan was registered to him at that address. A white one.

Kite was listed as the sole stockholder of Screentest Supreme Software, a closely held corporation based at the Sutton Place address. Its only asset was a series of copyrights and trademarks. His 1994 IRS 1040 showed a net income of $801,444. Nothing looked cute about the tax return on the surface: no exotic deductions, no tax shelters. No employees either—he paid everything on a contract basis, from word processing to an occasional chauffeur. Heather received checks totaling almost forty thousand in 1994, all marked "research."

Bank accounts, T-bills, a smattering of stocks, mostly technology issues. His real estate portfolio was heavy: five co-op apartments in the city, from a three-bedroom high-floor to a couple of studios. A management company was handling them, and it looked like it was doing a good job—they were all rented. They all had mortgages too; he was carrying most of them flat, showing a slight profit on the biggest unit, making his profit off the mortgage deductions and depreciation.

American Express, VISA, MasterCard . . . all paid-to-date, no balances. Except for the mortgages, he didn't owe anyone a dime.

Wolfe's papers estimated his net worth at $4.3 million, "conservative."

The package also contained photocopies of various briefs and motions he'd submitted when he'd worked as a lawyer, a couple of contracts he'd drawn, even a transcript of oral argument on an appeal. The briefs were more science than law: charts and graphs, citations to articles in psychiatry journals, complicated logic chains, painstakingly and elegantly drawn.

One of them was a custody case, Kite representing the father. The mother said she had discovered the man was sexually abusing his son. She wanted him barred from visitation. Kite argued that she'd made the whole thing up, proved that she'd been abused herself as a child, said she was "spooking at shadows" and that she was a "secondary victim of an incompetent therapist." His deposition of the therapist was a masterpiece. He questioned her about the protocols she used, showed she had no special training in the use of anatomically correct dolls, pointed out a few minor exaggerations on her résumé, asked why she never videotaped her sessions with the child. And his own brief was full of citations to studies by psychologists pointing out the damage to any child forced to carry the burden of a false allegation.

He won that case. The court said the mother's conduct was so egregious that it warranted an outright change of custody: the mother was allowed to see the boy only under supervision. The decision was upheld on appeal.

A year later, the mother was arrested for trying to kidnap the kid. She was all set to flee—had fake ID for them both. They bagged her at the airport, tickets to France in her handbag.

Kite had an AV rating, the highest, from Martindale-Hubbell. He was listed in *Who's Who in American Law*. Except for a half-dozen brief mentions in the *New York Law Journal* over the years, the newspaper search had come up empty—he wasn't a publicity hound.

No. He was a hover-hunter: a bird of prey who didn't need a perch to work from.

The last document was a double-spaced list of all the lawyers Kite had consulted to since he went into solo private practice. It ran four pages, went coast to coast. I recognized a couple of the names—media-slut matrimonial bombers—but most I never heard of. Wolfe had annotated the list, breaking the names down by specialty and type of case. Mostly custody and visitation, but a good many civil lawsuits and a few criminal cases.

In the matrimonials, Kite worked for whoever hired him. In all the others, he was always for the defendant.

I read it all through, then I read it again, looking for a pattern. The only one I could think of didn't pan out: although most of his clients—or, actually, the clients of the lawyers who hired him—were male, almost a third were female. He wasn't one of those "father's rights" guys.

Wolfe was good, and her microscope went deep. But I didn't see any cracks in the wall.

I took a break. Piled Pansy into the Plymouth and drove down to one of the abandoned piers on the West Side and let her run around a bit.

When I got back, I made us both some lunch. Then I opened the file folder I'd taken from Kite.

Articles by psychologists. Briefs by lawyers. Stories by journalists. Every one about false allegations of child sexual abuse. None of them written by Kite. But then I noticed the highlighting—neon-bright see-through colors splattering almost every page, sometimes several colors on the same one. At the end of the packet, I found a neat chart marked KEY. Each color was represented by a bold slash from the highlighter. Next to each slash, some tiny, crabbed handwriting in jet-black ink, so hyper-precise that at first I thought it was a computer font.

[Red] An "unfounded" allegation of child abuse does not mean the allegation was "false." The "unfounded" designation also applies to cases in which the investigation could not be completed because the suspects left the jurisdiction, etc. And many "founded" cases are never made the subject of a Child Protective Petition.

[Blue] The "statistics" cited are not "statistics" at all. They are extrapolations based on estimates. No scientific validity.

[Yellow] (1) Expert witness for the defense was quoted in an interview in which he defended "pedophilia" as an "alternate lifestyle." (2) Individual testifying here not recognized as "expert" by courts in three separate jurisdictions. (3) The term "validation" is a misnomer: "valid" means "true _this_ time," while "reliable" means "true _over_ time." (4) "Expert" cannot testify as to whether child is telling the truth—this invades the province of the jury.

[Orange] Unsound research (sample too small, insufficient controls, et al.).

[Green]: Financial interest in outcome. Hidden agenda. Undisclosed connection to foundation named as principal in lawsuit. Settlement forced on defendant by insurance company.

[Purple] Does not meet DSM-IV criteria for "syndrome." No data collected. Never submitted to refereed journal. Not scientific—merely the carefully packaged pronouncements of a merchant.

[Tan] Case reversed on technical application of the Confrontation Clause. Media reports as "vindication" inaccurate.

[Magenta] Statute of Limitations alert!

[Cyan] (1) "Protective Parent" label entirely self-awarded, meaningless. (2) Diagnosis of Post-Traumatic Stress Disorder is <u>not</u> axiomatic indicator of child sexual abuse. Pressure to carry a false allegation could induce stress in a child.

[Pink] Journalists ranked on "Loyalty Index," set up a prediction model. 100% accurate: journalist's name a perfect predictor of the article's "findings."

On the next page, still in the same tiny handwriting, more notes:

Hechler, <u>The Battle and the Backlash</u> . . .
APSAC protocols . . .
Salter, <u>Treating Child Sex Offenders and Victims</u> . . .
"Expert" cites own articles as "source material" . . .
NAMBLA member . . .
501(c)(3) criteria precludes lobbying . . .

And then the coda, all caps, double underlined, centered exactly at the bottom of the page:

<u>A TRUE DEBUNKER OPERATES WITHOUT AGENDA.</u>

Kite's religion?

I let it simmer a couple of days, waiting to see if Heather turned up the pressure. But the phone at Mama's stayed silent. Okay.

"I'm ready to talk," I told her when she answered the phone.

"Thank you so much," she whispered into the phone, an undercurrent of promise in her voice. "When can you do it?"

"Tomorrow morning?"

"I'll have to check—no, I know it'll be fine. Is ten all right?"

"Yes."

I docked the Plymouth in an outdoor lot north of the Fifty-ninth Street Bridge near the FDR and walked to Kite's building. I was dressed the same as I was the last time. Not because I thought Heather would pull the same stunt—I just wanted to make sure her memory was refreshed.

She stood on the far side of the grille, wearing a black bustier under a transparent white blouse over black Capri pants anchored with a wide red belt. Her black-cherry hair was a lacquered helmet. Her eyes were little circles of orange glass in the dim light, bright even against the thick makeup. When she turned her back on me to lead the way, I saw she was back to spike heels. The left ankle was wrapped in tape—it must have been painful. I ignored the sway of her powerful hips, my eyes on her shoulders, but she stepped smoothly to one side to usher me into Kite's chambers without a hint of aggression.

The butterscotch leather armchair was in place next to Kite's fan-shaped chair. He waved me over like he was an old pal who'd been waiting for me in our regular saloon. I took my seat. He didn't offer to shake hands. If he noticed anything different about my face, it didn't show on his.

I heard the tap of her spike heels behind me. She leaned over with a glass of water, but she kept her head high, her nose almost in my hair. I heard a faint sniff, probably because I was listening for it. She was checking for cigarette smoke, her ankle reminding her not to relax her guard around me, but between the strong shampoo and the heavy gel, she didn't have a chance. I'd washed my hands in rubbing alcohol too, just in case.

"I won't insult you by asking if you read the material I gave you," Kite said by way of opening. "I'm sure you wouldn't be here if you hadn't."

"Okay," I said, staying inside myself. Thinking of that Zen rock, polished by years under the waterfall until it was as seamless as the water itself. Like Kite's rap. Prison is full of raps. Glassily ceramic, keeping your focus on the surface so you never looked inside. The cons who call themselves Aryans say blacks are mud people and whites are sun people. And the cons who call themselves Africans say blacks are earth people and whites are ice people. Two sides of the same smooth stone. And not a speck of truth under the sleek surface.

"Do you have any reaction?" he asked, white eyebrows raised behind the pink glasses.

"Liars lie," I said indifferently. "Guy rapes a woman in Dallas, he says it was consent, okay? Another guy rapes another woman in Chicago, he says it was consent too. That doesn't make it a national conspiracy. But some whore psychologist writes an article about some bullshit mental disorder that makes women who actually consented to sex scream 'Rape!' and all of a sudden, it's a fucking 'syndrome,' and defense attorneys have a field day."

"It cuts the other way too," Kite said, leaning forward. "A gang of pedophiles sexually assault a child in Sweden. On the videotape, they're all wearing black. The same videotape shows up in the house of a collector in the United States. He's got a black shirt in his closet. So the police tell the newspapers they've cracked an international ring of child molesters."

"Like I said: liars lie. So?"

"So idiot therapists who do their incompetent 'validations' of child sexual abuse start adding 'Did he have a black shirt?' to their stupid checklists. And when they get an affirmative answer, as they inevitably will in some cases, there's their 'proof.' The first thing any charlatan needs is nomenclature. A special language. Trappings. That's the true genesis of psychobabble terms such as 'disclosure' and 'in denial.' Every good con man needs plausibility. . . ."

"People see what they want to see," I said. "Whatever pays their bills or races their motors. You pointed it out yourself, in the stuff you gave me."

"And so what's missing?" he asked, making a temple of his fingertips, gazing out at me between them. "I'll tell you, Mr. Burke: objective, damn-the-consequences *investigation*. The entire problem with the so-called system is lack of objectivity. Prosecutors want to prove their cases, not find the truth. And defense attorneys . . . obviously, most of the time, it's their job to *avoid* the truth."

"What about caseworkers?" I asked, knowing the answer. "Like for Child Protective Services?"

"*Please,*" he sneered. "Search as you may throughout this country, you will not find more undertrained, undersupervised, understaffed, and underpaid individuals. They operate entirely without protocols, without standards. Tell me this: Why should a case of suspected child abuse not be investigated the precise same way in Detroit as it is in Denver? In some jurisdictions, they use actual social workers. MSWs. In others, any college degree will suffice. Do you know what the Star Chamber was, Mr. Burke?"

"England, right? Three, four hundred years ago? A little room where they dragged you in and told you you were guilty."

"Close enough," he acknowledged. "For the child, for the putatively *abused* child, every single little caseworker is a personal Star Chamber. If that caseworker decides there is probable cause to proceed, so be it. But if he or she does not, then what? Nothing. Nothing at all. If the caseworker is a bigot, or a moron, or an overzealous do-gooder, *that* determines the result, not the facts. The true investigator is, first and foremost, a skeptic. He does not operate under superstition or myth. But if you have a caseworker who doesn't 'believe' incest occurs, any investigation that individual performs will be fatally flawed . . . and the poor child won't have a chance."

"And if they see incest under every bed . . ."

"Yes! Then the poor parents won't have a chance. In America, the predominant factor in the outcome of *any* child abuse case isn't the truth itself. No, it's the quality of advocacy on either side. An incompetent prosecutor, or even a lazy one, will result in more acquittals than even the most brilliant defense could provide."

"Yeah, and—"

"Of course"—he cut me off—"a sufficiently skilled defense can shred even the truest case. It happens all the time." He leaned back in his chair, folding his arms across his chest. "Mr. Burke, I live in the crossfire between two armed camps: the 'Believe the Children!' lunatics and the 'False Allegations!' fanatics. My only weapon is the truth. And if my syndrome is to achieve *genuine* professional acceptance, I must avoid the personal stigma of being associated with either group. My credentials as a debunker are impeccable when it comes to child sexual abuse. I have exposed case after case of incompetent, shoddy, or outright fabricated allegations of child sexual abuse. But I have never taken the position that such things do not, in fact, occur . . . and I personally find every single such occurrence abominable. Most cases, if you work them diligently enough, are susceptible to actual proof. And if the law were brought into the twentieth century, that proof would be much more widely available."

He took a short breath. When I didn't say anything, he rolled on like there had been no pause. "For example, the law should be that every single abortion performed on a minor must include the preservation of fetal tissue for DNA analysis. You could not ask for better, stronger proof of incest, if it actually caused the pregnancy. But the anti-abortion crowd, those so-called 'pro-family' people, they are bitterly opposed. And they have enough clout in Congress to keep such a law off the books."

"Kids don't vote," I said softly. Thinking: *They don't carry guns either. Until they get older. And then they almost always shoot each other.*

"Politics doesn't interest me," Kite replied. "The political process is tawdry, as whorish as anything you could find in Times Square. I'm not an organizer. I don't speak at conferences. I don't go to demonstrations. I'm not even an activist. I hunt . . . the truth. My contribution will be the FSG syndrome," he said, voice thickening. "And I do not intend to have all my years of research and investigation trivialized by snide little comments about my objectivity. My syndrome has validity only through *contrast*," he continued, his no-color complexion blotching red. "That is the very *essence* of investigation: friction creates heat, and heat creates light. The light of truth."

"And I come in . . . where?" I asked him, calling a halt to the flow. I could hear a harsh, resentful intake of breath somewhere behind me. Heather, angry that the minister's sermon was interrupted by some fool talking in church.

He took a deep breath. I heard the tap of spike heels. Heather brought him an earless white china cup, holding it in both hands like a precious offering. He sipped from the cup, inhaling the fumes as he did, pulling in calm. "Forgive me," he said quietly. "I am not normally a˙passionate man. This . . . my syndrome . . . is the one thing that inspires me to emotionalism. Your question is a fair one. I should have anticipated it—and answered it—first. Mr. Burke, I am not usually publicly associated with the cases I investigate. I have no desire for the spotlight; quite the contrary, in fact. But I realize that all causes need publicity if they are to capture the imagination—and the support—of the public. An hour on *Oprah* is, regrettably, worth more to a cause than a hundred articles in the most prestigious journals.

"Indeed, I will be completely honest with you: Miss Winfrey is one of my objectives. She combines a massive audience with a high degree of personal credibility. And on this particular issue, child sexual abuse, she has been a leading figure in American consciousness."

"I still don't get it," I told him. "You can't just call up and book a spot on *Oprah*. She doesn't do Siamese-twin lesbian dwarf adultery stuff the way the others do."

"Mr. Burke, believe me, I have thoroughly researched *all* the available television talk shows. In fact, I've made poor Heather monitor them every day for months," he said, glancing over my shoulder. She made some little sound, too faint for me to recognize. "The sexual abuse industry has made it impossible for a straightforward victim to tell her story. Simple incest won't even get you a booking on the trash shows anymore. It isn't good theater. But in a short time," he said soberly, "a young woman is going to come forward with the most shocking allegations concerning a major figure in a religious organization. She will have *no* conventional proof other than her own word. She will be immediately embraced by one end of the continuum . . . and immediately attacked by the other. I plan to stand with her, right in the middle of that firestorm, because every word she will utter will be the *truth*. I expect to defend her against all the so-called investigators who will try to tear her story apart. For the first time in my career, I will personally handle a case," he said, voice gathering momentum. "As her attorney, I will sue not only the perpetrator of the crimes against her; I will sue the organization which spawned him and tolerated his predatory conduct. I will fight them when they raise the statute of limitations; I will fight them on the law; I will fight them on the facts." He took a deep breath. "And I will prevail. The *truth* will prevail."

"So this is all about a lawsuit?" I said.

"No, Mr. Burke," he said sharply, "this is *not* about a lawsuit. It is about the launch of a new era in the investigation of child sexual abuse. This case will be my credential, my entrée to the rarefied air of public credibility. You see, I do expect to be on *Oprah*. But without my client. The show will not be about this one case, it will be about my syndrome. Before I can establish a new method of investigation, which will disprove false allegations, I need to establish that some allegations are true. Yes, this one case will get me on the show. But I will use the time to illustrate dozens of other cases. Cases in which my syndrome was employed as the ultimate litmus test."

"Yeah, all right. But I still don't see where I come in."

"Because I have to be *sure*, Mr. Burke. Everything is resting on that one foundation. And unlike others in my profession, I will never fall victim to arrogance. I am convinced to a moral certainty that this young woman is telling the truth. But I cannot take chances, not with an undertaking of this magnitude. I want you to step in now. I want you to do anything you can, and I mean *anything* at all, to break the young woman's story. If there's a defect anywhere, I want you to find it."

"But if I did find one . . . ?"

"Then there is no case," he said flatly. "And I will wait patiently for another which appears to meet all my criteria. This isn't about money for me, not at all. In fact, I am taking this case *pro bono*, waiving my fee entirely, including expenses. But I know I will come under fire, and I simply cannot risk being wrong."

"How do you expect me to—?"

"I don't *care* what you do, Mr. Burke. I hope I made that crystal clear. I want the truth. Wherever it may be found and whatever it turns out to be. My client has pledged full cooperation. She will answer any questions you have . . . and do whatever else you want."

"You polygraphed her?"

"Yes. Two separate examiners, with impeccable credentials. No deception was indicated."

"She saw a psychiatrist?"

"And a psychologist. Both agreed: Post-Traumatic Stress Disorder. The psychologist's diagnosis included child sexual abuse as proximate cause. The psychiatrist wouldn't go that far . . . but they never do."

"Medicals?"

"Inconclusive. You'll see for yourself."

"Independent corrob?"

"Same answer."

"How much time would I have?"

"As much as you need," he said. "I am not going to move forward until I'm absolutely certain. You are the last piece of the puzzle, Mr. Burke. My own investigation is completed—the lawsuit awaits only your own."

"You went to a lot of trouble," I said quietly.

"I always do," he replied.

I could feel Heather behind me, the sheer intensity of her pushing against the cushion of air between us. "How would we work it?" I asked him.

I couldn't read his eyes behind the pink glasses. A tic jumped in his face. "We both know paying someone by the hour leads to potential corruption," he said calmly. "The same goes for paying by the result. I propose a flat fee, open-ended. I will be buying your complete investigation, for as long as it takes. And your *confidential* report."

"I won't—"

"Not in writing, Mr. Burke. You report to me. Verbally. Your name never comes into this."

"And you wouldn't expect me to testify?"

A smile snaked its way from one corner of his mouth, disappearing when it reached the far end. "No offense, Mr. Burke, but your record makes you something less than an ideal candidate for courtroom testimony."

"None taken," I assured him.

"Then there's only the matter of your fee."

"I don't know how to estimate a job like this," I told him. "Could take a long time to—"

"I understand. Still . . . I was thinking, say, thirty thousand dollars. In cash, of course. Payable one-third now, one-third as you progress, and the final third when you tender your report."

"I was thinking seventy-five," I said, taking the traditional gangster lawyer's route: more than double your asking fee, get the biggest chunk you can right then, and expect the client to stiff you for the rest. "Half up front, half when I'm done."

"Yes, I'm sure," he said smoothly. "Perhaps a compromise is in order. Heather!"

I heard the tap of her heels, caught a glimpse of her black-sheathed hips as she brushed past me to my left. She was back in a minute, carrying a slim black anodized-aluminum case. She bent forward, her back to Kite, and put the case in my lap.

"There's fifty thousand dollars in there, Mr Burke," he said. "In a form I'm certain will be acceptable to you. Will you take that as payment in full?"

I took it as a signal we were done playing this game. "Yes," I told him.

He nodded as solemnly as if we had just signed a cease-fire treaty. "As soon as my client is available for your first interview, I'll call you."

I got to my feet, the aluminum briefcase in my hand. If Kite was surprised I hadn't opened it, his face didn't give it away.

Heather led me to the grille. When she got a few feet away, she stopped, slowly enough so I could see it coming. I stopped too. She backed up, one little step at a time, until her bottom was pressed hard against my crotch. The thick corset made it feel like a side of beef. "Thank you," she whispered, shifting her hips.

"Your ankle must hurt in those shoes," I said.

"I'm real good with pain," she said, twitching her bottom against me again. "And I still owe you. Don't forget."

The next morning was a Sunday. The blue dragon tapestry was in the window of Mama's restaurant. Cops inside. I wasn't worried about it—cops were always dropping in, wasting their time asking questions. There was plenty to ask about. The Chinese youth gangs had pretty much given up trying to get a toehold on the gambling industry. Their elders had been at it too long, had too many connections. And the young ones had decimated their own ranks in bloody turf wars that made the old Colombian kill-crews look like Quakers.

The new crew was mostly Fukinese, and their latest game was kidnapping. They weren't any good at it. The wild kids snatched shop owners right out of their houses, dragged them to some abandoned apartment building, tortured them into calling their families. The snatching was easy, but the vicious amateurs never mastered the art of the ransom exchange. Though they mostly got nabbed, the body counts kept going up, and the business community was pressuring the cops hard.

When I was a kid, one of my foster homes was right on the Chinatown border. The old border, next to Little Italy. Some of the kids I knew had real mothers, not the State-paid ones I got. I always listened to what real mothers said, trying to hear the difference in their voices, to see how come they had wanted *their* kids. The real mothers always pointed to the Chinese kids as role models. So studious, hardworking. So polite and respectful. You wouldn't see *those* kids hanging out on street corners or in some stupid gang. No, not then. We let immigrants build this country, then we leave our mark on them for gratitude.

Mama wouldn't touch rough stuff, and the cops knew it. They knew she wouldn't talk to them too, but they kept coming.

I had time to kill, but I didn't want to leave the neighborhood, so I drifted over to a sidewalk kiosk.

"You got the Racing Edition?" I asked the Chinese woman, pointing at the comics section that covers the Sunday *News*.

"Not ready yet," she said, nodding her head at various stacks of the different sections waiting to be assembled into one edition. "You need coupons?" she asked brightly, holding out a colorful sheaf.

"No, thanks," I said.

The woman deftly flicked the coupons sideways into a large carton without looking and went back to her work. A little girl, maybe nine years old—her daughter—was sitting at a makeshift desk inside the kiosk. Someone had jury-rigged a single bare lightbulb for the child to work by. Behind her was a perfect cardboard imitation of the wall of slots they use for mail at hotel desks. The scissors in her small hands flashed as she snipped the brilliantly colored sheets of coupons into individual units, sticking them in the pigeonholes without looking.

I stopped by the door to light a cigarette. A white woman wearing a quilted green parka pushed past me, asked the kiosk operator: "You have any for Pampers?"

"Sure, we got. How many you need?"

"Twenty?"

"Pampers?" the Chinese woman called out to the little girl.

"Yes," the child said gravely, handing over the coupons.

"Twenty coupons, fifty cents off, two dollars," the Chinese woman told the customer.

"That's . . . what? Twenty percent?" the woman in the green parka said. "No. I'll go a dollar, okay?"

"Dollar fifty," the Chinese woman said, holding out the coupons.

The white woman reached in her purse.

The little girl made a mark in her schoolbook, adding to a neat column of figures.

The old woman was a good poacher. Most people don't give a damn about the coupons, so she pulled them out of every paper. If somebody bitched, she could always give them back. And the white woman had just saved herself some real money. Even with her Sunday paper costing an extra buck and a half, she was still way ahead of the game. If you know where to shop, you can buy anything in this city.

When I walked by the second time, the white dragon was in the window. I went around to the alley in the rear, slapped my gloved palm against the door. One of the thugs let me in. I took my booth in the back. The soup arrived about the same time Mama did. She serves it around the clock, always keeps a giant pot bubbling in the kitchen, throwing stuff in from time to time as the mood seizes her. It's the only thing she ever cooks herself.

"You had visitors?" I asked her.

"Not me," Mama said. "You. Bull cop."

That wasn't slang for Mama. Only one cop it could mean. Morales, the human street-sweeper. A while back, he'd been stalking me—some unsolved homicides inside a house of child-molesting beasts in the Bronx. I was guilty, all right, but he couldn't lay a glove on me no matter how many rounds we danced. Then I got caught between him and a psychotic woman detective fronting for a serial rape-murderer. At least that's what I thought, right until the end. She shot Morales, I shot her. She died. He took the shooting for himself, ended up a hero in the process. Morales always hated me. Probably still did. But he was a man, and he paid his debts.

"What'd he want?" I asked.

"He say, 'Kite is dirty.'"

"That's all?"

"Yes. He wait for you. Long time. Order plenty food."

"He eat the food?"

"No."

"He pay for it?"

"Yes. Leave money on table. Right there," she said, pointing to a corner table.

"He say he want me to call him?"

"No. Say, 'Kite is dirty. Tell Burke. Kite is dirty.' Then get up and go."

"Okay. Look, Mama—"

"You not like soup?"

"Oh. Sorry," I said, spooning up a mouthful. "It's perfect, Mama. As always."

"Yes. Max be here soon, okay?"

"Okay. And the Prof, you found him too?"

"Everybody come. Before ten, okay?"

"Thanks. Mama . . . ?"

"What?"

"Is there any such thing as a sparkling ruby?"

"Sparkle?"

"Yeah. Like a diamond. But red."

"Not ruby. Ruby not sparkle. Red diamond."

"A red diamond?"

"Sure. Yellow diamond too. Call 'fancies.' But not so much."

"Not so much what?"

"Money. Fancy diamond not cost like pure white."

"But not cheap?"

"Oh no." She chuckled. "No diamond cheap."

I ate some orange-glazed duck with roast pork fried rice and snow pea pods, washed it down with ice water as I read the paper. I checked *Parade* first, always do. Whoever thought up the idea of a free stand-alone magazine in Sunday papers all over the country was a genius. I heard their advertising rates were the highest in the world.

Another subway rape in Jamaica. Another drive-by murder in Washington Heights. Another racial assault in Bensonhurst. Another woman beaten to death by her estranged husband, died with an Order of Protection in her purse. Another baby-raper pleaded guilty and got probation. They don't need to hire reporters in this city—the stories are all written; all they have to do is fill in the names and dates.

Max showed up before I could get to the race results. We still had some time, so I didn't argue when he pulled out a score sheet from our life-sentence gin game. One of the alleged waiters brought a fresh deck of cards, and we got down to it.

It was Max's lucky day. I never saw the cards fall so good for him. Even as bad as he plays, even with Mama hammering him with incompetent advice, he hit me with back-to-back triple schneids, something he'd never accomplished in the thousands of games we'd played until then. Max has got a natural poker face. And the card sense of a chimp. But when the Prof showed up, the little man took one look and said, "My man ain't grinning, but he doing some *serious* winning, ain't he?"

I nodded to acknowledge the obvious reality of the situation and set my teeth, praying for the cards to change. It wasn't the money; even at the tenth of a cent per point we always play, Max was into me for almost a quarter of a million dollars over the years. We'd agreed when we started that we'd settle up wherever we ended up, after this life was done. But I knew there was no way on this planet I was getting up from *this* game with Max on the streak of his life. The Mongolian would sit there until I started winning or Cuba started holding elections, whichever came first.

The Prof knew it too. He sat down next to me and started in on a stream of criticism that would have cracked concrete. Clarence sat next to Max, a smile flashing broadly in his ebony face as the warrior drew bonanza after bonanza. Hell, I fucking *dealt* him gin twice in one hour. It didn't matter who held the cards—I passed my turn to deal over to the Prof with no change in the result.

"You got one humongous hoodoo, Schoolboy," the little man intoned. "The double-jinx maxi-mojo curse. Ain't nothing to do but let it do its worse."

Max kept glancing to the heavens, as if wondering when the sky was going to fall, but he never so much as shifted position, superstitiously keeping everything exactly as it was for as long as the magic moment lasted.

It was almost one o'clock before I turned the tide. And it was two-thirty before he was convinced that his incredible run was actually over. He stood up, bowed deeply . . . and snatched the score sheet from the table so fast I saw a vapor trail behind his hand.

And it was getting close to four in the damn afternoon by the time Immaculata showed up, with Flower in tow. Max quickly signed to them both, explaining in painstaking—and painful—detail how he had accomplished the ultimate gin destruction of his own brother.

And then we had to have supper.

By the time we got down to business, it was dark enough for it.

Heather called Tuesday night, leaving a number I didn't recognize. It was after midnight when I got the message from Mama, but I called anyway.

"Hello?" Her voice was wide awake, buoyant.

"It's Burke," I said. "You called?"

"I wanted to . . . thank you again . . ."

I didn't say anything, waiting.

". . . and to tell you it's all set. Either tomorrow or Thursday, whatever you want. Anytime, day or night."

"What's all set, Heather?"

"The *interview*," she said, a throb in her voice now, telling me how important this was. To her? "He says to tell you you'll have as much time as you want, okay?"

"Okay. Let's make it Thursday, all right? First thing in the morning okay with you?"

"With me? Oh! You mean with—"

"Yeah. Nine okay?"

"Yes. Absolutely."

"See you then."

"Burke?"

"What?"

"Would you want me to maybe come over and . . . see you?"

"I already said I'd do it, Heather. I made a deal; I'll keep it. Don't worry about it."

"Not for . . . that. I know you'll do it. I know you're a truthful person. That's all I care about, you know. The truth. It's holy to me. I'm just . . . sorry about what happened. And I thought I could maybe . . . make it up to you."

"We're square," I said.

"Well, if you ever change your mind . . ."

"You'll be the first to know," I said, and cut the connection.

Then I called the precinct and asked for Morales.

I met him at the dead end of Old Fulton Street in Brooklyn, a few blocks from the Federal Court. Outside of territory for both of us. When I pulled in, he was already there, still driving that fire-engine-red Dodge Stealth, convinced it was the perfect undercover vehicle. Like every player in the city didn't know it was his.

"You all healed up?" I asked him.

"Like new," he growled, smacking his chest where Belinda's bullet had taken him hard enough to crack a rib a while back. He looked the same: ball-bearing eyes in pouchy pockets of flesh, a round face with a pushed-in nose and a thin scar of a mouth sitting on a tree stump of a neck. Stood a couple of inches shorter than me, short arms, big chest. Morales looked like a not-too-bright pit bull, but the first part was all wrong.

"Thanks for the stuff," I said.

"No problem. Like I left word, motherfucker's dirty."

"Meaning . . . ?"

"He did work for Aiello. You know, the greaseball who took over for Sally Lou on the Deuce."

Sally Lou had been a fringe player for the wiseguys. Not a made man, but what they call an "around guy," sniffing at the edges, doing whatever. His game had been rough-stuff porno. In the freak sheets, he peddled it as "extreme, not terminal," but street talk was that he could find you a snuff film if you hauled enough green. No question about kiddie porn, though—Sally Lou specialized in video of hairless little girls. He was gone now, part of the fallout in a mess I got into a long time ago. And like always, some other slime seeped in to fill the void. Crime's like nature—it hates a vacuum.

"What kind of work?" I asked Morales.

"I don't know exactly," the cop said with a "what the fuck does it matter?" shrug. "Legal research, it said on the bill. A *big* bill, I know that much."

"That's not dirty."

"Yeah, it is. Anything for that maggot Aiello is dirty. But I think it was something else. Word is, this Kite, he knows a lot of people. Political people."

"Like senators?"

"Like judges. Aiello was on the hook deep. A video studio, in a basement off Forty-fourth. The usual whips-and-chains stuff, no big deal. But there was little girls in there. *Little* girls. There was some kinda legal bullshit, like could we prove he *knew* they was under-age? Fuck, you just *look* at the stuff, you know they wasn't grown. Anyway, the judge tosses it. Said the search was bad too. The CI spooked. Disappeared. Or maybe got done. But we couldn't produce him in court. That was just the excuse, though—the whole thing was juiced from jump."

"Kite was the lawyer?"

"Nah, Aiello had a regular mob mouthpiece. Your old pal Fortunato. Remember him? Like I said, wired like a motherfucking Christmas tree. Fortunato put out the word Kite did the research, like I said. But the way I scope it, the only research he did was knowing a bent judge."

"Okay."

"I wish Wolfe was still on the job. Wouldn't have happened if she was there—too much media heat. I love that bitch."

"Me too," I said. Then I caught his look. "I mean, I wish she was still working too."

"Yeah. Right. Anyway, watch your back, Burke. If this Kite motherfucker knows judges, he knows cops too, you understand me?"

"Sure. Thanks."

"Anything else I could . . . ?"

"Run a phone number for me?"

"You got it."

Early Thursday morning, I let Pansy out to her roof. Then I cut a fresh semolina bread at the two-thirds mark, scooped out the interior from the one-third, and painted inside the crust with a light coating of cream cheese. That was mine. I put the two-thirds piece and the guts from mine in Pansy's steel bowl. Then, on the hot plate, I heated up some Mongolian beef with scallions I took from Mama's and I poured the whole thing over the bread. When she came back downstairs, she snarfed it up like it was a vitamin pill.

I had mine with some cold ginger beer. To settle my stomach.

I dressed carefully that morning—I figured this woman had already seen enough lawyers, but I didn't want to look like a hood either. Or a cop. When I told her the problem, Michelle had come over the night before and picked everything out. "The alligator boots, babe. They're always perfect. Casual class—that's our look, okay?" She put together a pair of gray flannel slacks, a black-and-white-striped shirt with a button-down collar, and a dark-purple silk tie. From a garment bag she carried over her shoulder, she pulled a soft charcoal wool sports coat. "This is perfect, honey. It's semi-structured. See, no shoulder pads. Lots of room, very comfortable. It *whispers* money. Put it on, let's see how it works."

"I'm sure it'll be—"

"Put it *on*, honey."

It fit perfect. Michelle's eyes were micrometers. "How much?" I asked her.

"Thirteen hundred—"

"*What?*"

"Oh, that was *retail*, honey. I got it for only six. Some bargain, huh?"

"Six hundred dollars?"

"Yes, six hundred dollars," she said, in the tone you'd use on a moron. A stubborn moron. "I do not buy at Bloomingdale's, baby. And you'll need this belt too—it'll go perfectly with the boots. Now give me some money, honey."

I couldn't wait for the clash of wills when it came time for her and the Mole to outfit Terry for college.

Pansy insisted on rubbing against my leg and being petted goodbye. So instead of cologne, I hit the subway wearing eau de Neapolitan mastiff. And carrying the black aluminum briefcase, empty.

Heather was on her side of the grille when the elevator arrived. This time she was wearing a modest plum-colored silk blouse and a black pleated skirt. But her dark stockings were seamed up the back, and the skirt was six inches too short. I could see the faint outline of an ankle chain surrounding the bandage on her left foot. Her spike heels were the same color as her blouse.

"Hi!" she said brightly.

"How you doing?" I responded.

"I'm *great* . . . now that it's finally happening. Come on, they're waiting for you."

I followed her down the hall, listening to the rasp of nylon as her thick thighs brushed together under the short skirt. She turned the corner, ushering me in ahead of her.

"Mr. Burke," Kite said, getting to his feet. "Thank you for coming."

"Like we agreed," I replied, shaking the bony, blue-veined hand he offered me, going along with the show.

"This is Jennifer," he said, nodding toward a young woman seated in a straight-backed teakwood chair. "Jennifer Dalton."

I walked over to her, held out my hand. "Pleased to meet you," I said.

"Me too," she answered, not getting up. Her eyes were too big for her thin, pinched face. Her hair was mouse brown, thin at the temples. She was dressed in a slate-gray business suit over a fussy white blouse with a small embroidered collar, modest black pumps on her feet, sat with her knees pressed together.

"Would you prefer I . . . leave you alone?" Kite asked.

"Up to you," I said to the woman.

"I'd rather you stayed," she said to Kite. Her voice was low and reedy, but very clear, every syllable articulated.

"As you wish," Kite said, taking a seat in his fan-shaped chair.

I took the leather armchair. Heard the tap of Heather's heels, but this time, she wasn't going to stand behind me—she took a position between the woman's back and the hologram, standing with her hands behind her, chest outthrust, orange eyes steady on me.

I settled in, investing thirty seconds in observing the woman's composed face. "How old are you?" I asked.

Her face twitched. It wasn't the question she'd expected. "I'm, uh, twenty-seven. Twenty-eight in November."

"Were you born here? In New York?"

"In Queens. In Flushing. But we moved around when I was little."

"Where?"

"New Jersey. Teaneck, then Englewood Cliffs. Then to upstate New York. But I really grew up in Manhattan. On the Upper West Side."

"You went to private school?" I asked her.

"Yes. How did you know?"

"Just a guess. You have any brothers and sisters?"

"I have a brother. Robert. He's two years older."

"What does he do?"

"Do?"

"For a living."

"Oh. He . . . doesn't do anything, I guess. He's in rehab."

"For . . . ?"

"Drugs."

"He ever do time?"

"Time?" she asked, her face confused.

"In jail."

"Oh. No, he was never in jail. I mean, just once. A couple of weeks, that's all."

"Did you go and visit him?"

She shifted slightly in her chair. "Why are you asking all this?"

I looked over her shoulder. Heather was in the same spot, standing stony. "Just background," I said.

The woman glanced to Kite. He didn't respond, watching her as though she was a chemical experiment, waiting for the result.

It was quiet for a long minute. "No, I didn't visit him," she said quietly. "We're not close."

"Are your parents still together?" I asked.

"No. No, they're not. Is that 'background' too?"

"Yes, it is, Miss Dalton," I said smoothly. "These are . . . delicate matters. I want to establish a foundation before we explore the central issues."

She took a breath through her mouth, her shallow chest not involved in the process. "Go ahead," she said finally.

"Your turn now," I said, switching gears. "Just tell me about it."

"He—"

"From the beginning," I said softly. "From *before* it started, okay?"

She gulped another breath. "Okay. When I was twelve . . . I know that's when it was because it was just after my birthday, that's just before Thanksgiving. . . . School was already started. I was doing all right there. Not great or anything, mostly B's and C's on my report card. And I was never any trouble. My teachers liked me. I had friends and everything. But my parents thought I should be doing better."

"Your grades?"

"Not just my grades. I was a puller."

"Trichotillomania?"

"Yes!" Her eyes rolled up, settled back down, focusing on my face. "How did you know about that?"

"I had a friend who had it," I lied. "Did they send you to a doctor?"

"No. They didn't know it was a . . . disease then. They just thought I was strange, I think."

"So what did they do?"

"My parents were very religious. Psalmists—do you know it?"

"No. It sounds fundamentalist."

"Well, it's not," she said primly. "The official name of the church is the Gospel of Job's Song. And its prophet is Job, not Jesus. It was founded in the sixteenth century by John Michael, a man who suffered terrible misfortunes—he had epilepsy, and he underwent a crisis in faith. When the revelations came to him, he started the church. Eventually, the Psalmists had to emigrate to America to escape persecution. They settled in upstate New York. Some say their teachings were an influence on Joseph Smith."

"The Mormon prophet?"

"Do you know his work?" she asked, a faint look of surprise playing across her face.

"Only what I've read," I told her. I had no idea what Kite had told her about my background, so I didn't tell her *where* I read about religion—prisons get more missionaries than tropical islands. "You were raised in the church?" I asked.

"We both were, me and my brother. But we didn't shun others. Psalmists aren't a cult or anything."

"So they turned to the church for help with your . . . problems?"

"They said I needed lessons. Religious lessons. So they sent me to Brother Jacob. Psalmists believe you have to pay with your own labor for what you receive. So I had to clean Brother Jacob's house in exchange for the lessons."

"Tell me about the lessons," I said, leaning forward. Heather was a rock in the middle distance, the hologram winking behind her, shape-shifting in the morning light.

"The lessons were all about loving myself. Brother Jacob said if I didn't love myself, I would keep hurting myself. He said that's what people did when they were drunks, or drug addicts. Or even murderers. They hurt themselves. That's why I pulled my hair. And I had to stop or I would never be happy."

"Lessons from the Bible?"

"From Psalms. The Psalms are the truth, the real truth in the Bible. Brother Jacob said the Bible was *written*. By people, not God. But the Psalms were songs that had stood the test of time way before anyone knew how to write."

"So he taught you the Psalms?"

"The *meaning* of the Psalms."

"And how did he teach you, Jennifer?"

"First with the ruler," she said, face tightened as her skin bleached slightly. "He said the ruler was for learning rules."

"A wooden ruler, like for measuring?"

"It was for correction, not measuring," she said in a mechanical voice. "First I would get it on my palm. He would ask me, every time, if I was pulling my hair out. If I told him yes, I would get the ruler. It stung at first, but I got used to it. After a while, he'd have to hit me really hard to make me cry."

"But he did that?"

"Yes. I always had to cry."

"When did he switch?"

"Switch?"

"To someplace else. Besides your palm?"

"How did you *know* that?" she asked, dry-washing her hands, looking at her lap. "How could you—?"

"Just a guess," I said. "Maybe an educated guess."

"One day, I didn't want to get hit. So I lied. I told him I wasn't pulling my hair out. I used to sleep with gloves on. Even with a ski mask on my head—so I couldn't get to my hair. It didn't work. But when he asked me, I lied."

"And then . . . ?"

"He used it on my thighs. He made me lift my dress and he hit me on the back of my thighs with the ruler."

"And it hurt worse?"

"Yes! Not just my . . . legs. It made me feel all . . . crawly inside."

"So you stopped lying?"

"Yes. I mean, no. It didn't matter. He started asking me if I had learned to love myself. Every time I said I *couldn't*, he would hit me. Sometimes with my pants down. After a while, he made me take all my clothes off to be hit."

Heather had shifted her stance slightly, leaning forward with her back arched, like a ship's figurehead cutting the wind, mouth set and hard. "Did you ever tell your parents, Jennifer?" I asked her. "About what Brother Jacob was doing?"

"I . . . tried. But when I started, my mother told me I had to trust him. He was from the church, so I had to trust him. Whatever he was doing, *whatever* it was, it was for my own good. I never told her any more after that."

"What happened next?"

"How did you know there was a 'next,' Mr. Burke?" Her voice hardened with suspicion.

"There's always a 'next,'" I told her. "The only question is what it was."

"Don't you know?" She leaned forward in her chair, a sly, challenging look on her face.

"You learned to love yourself."

She put her face in her hands and started to cry. Heather stepped close behind her, putting her hands on the woman's shoulders, unblinking orange eyes steady on mine.

Kite didn't move.

If I was a therapist, I would have stopped it then. We'd been going a long time; it was a natural place for a break. But if anything was going to break, it was going to be Jennifer Dalton. "Tell me about it," I said.

She looked up at me, her thin face framed by her hands, too-big eyes blurry from the tears. "It sounds like you could tell *me*," she said. "How did you know? I need to know how you knew!"

"I didn't really know anything," I assured her. "But when you hear the same material over and over again from different people—"

"You think I'm lying? That I made this up?"

"No. I don't think that."

"Then you believe me?"

"Not that either. I'm just listening, okay?"

"When do you make up your mind?" she asked me, her hand twitching near her hair.

"When I'm done," I said, going along patiently, letting her take me wherever she wanted me to go.

"Could I have—?"

Heather was already in motion, her heels tapping a faster rhythm than usual. She was back in a few seconds with the heavy brass tray, this time loaded with two small bottles of Coke, a heavy-bottomed clear glass tumbler, and a chrome ice bucket. She used a pair of tongs to drop three precise ice cubes into the tumbler, screwed the top off one of the Coke bottles in one long twist, and poured carefully. She held the tumbler in her left hand, watching it closely, like measuring medicine. Satisfied, she handed it to Jennifer Dalton—a bartender serving a regular customer the usual.

Dalton took a long, deep drink, wrinkling her nose from the bubbles' tickle. She smiled up at Heather. "Thank you."

"Sure, baby," Heather replied, picking up the brass tray in one hand, patting Jennifer on the shoulder with the other.

Jennifer cleared her throat, facing a task. When she spoke, her voice was flat, just-the-facts uninflected. "He told me to . . . touch myself," she said. "First my chest. I mean, I didn't really *have* a chest then, but it was . . . enough. So you could see it, I mean, enough. I had to smile while I did it. A *real* smile—he would always know. Then I had to do it . . . other places. *Every* other place."

"Were you still pulling your hair?"

"Yes. But mostly my eyebrows by then. He was giving me a drug—"

"Brother Jacob?"

"Yes."

"Was he a doctor?"

"No. He sent me to a doctor, is what I should have said. A Psalmist doctor. Psalmists love the natural sciences—it's part of the teachings. The doctor prescribed the drug, but Brother Jacob gave it to me the first time."

"You only took it that one time?"

"No, I took it every day. Once with each meal, and one more time before I went to bed."

"So you had to take them yourself, right? You weren't with Brother Jacob all day. . . ."

"He told my mother," Jennifer said, as though that settled it. "He told her I had to take it. She made sure I took it."

"What was it, do you know?

"A capsule. Orange and white. That's all I remember."

"Do you think it helped? With the hair pulling?"

"In a way, I thought it did. But I thought the . . . other stuff did more."

"Touching yourself?"

"Yes. Like a good medicine that tastes bad, you know?"

"Were you still getting hit?"

"When I did something wrong, like lying. But not very much. I didn't touch myself . . . down there," she said, nodding toward her lap, "the right way. But Brother Jacob didn't hit me. He said he would show me. To help me."

"Did it help you?"

"Yes. Yes, it did," she said earnestly. "He did it . . . better. It was . . . it made me feel . . . warm. And safe. When he did it, I mean. It was safe when he did it."

"Why was that so safe, Jennifer?"

"Because he was in *charge*. He was in control. When he was in control, he could make me do things. Things for my own good. I never pulled my hair in front of him. Never. He told me that once I got my period, I would never pull my hair again. Because he had prepared me. But he wasn't finished. . . ."

She was quiet for so long that I tossed her a question to snap her out of the trance. "He wasn't finished with preparing you . . . ?"

"For my period. He said I had to be a woman *before* it came. My period, I mean. He did it with his hand. His thumb, I mean. He was very gentle. It took a long time. And he was right."

"About what?"

"About everything. He stopped hitting me after that. He just . . . prepared me. We were in love by then. Both of us. I mean, he was older, but he truly loved me. He said we would be together forever. First in spirit. Then in body. Then in wedlock. In the church. We were already together in spirit. But we couldn't join in body until I became a woman. He loved me, so he said we had to wait for that. And we couldn't wed until I was through with college; that's when it would be right."

She went quiet again, but this time I didn't prod her, warned off by a sharp glance from Heather. "It came when I was a couple of months past my thirteenth birthday," she finally said. "That was late, everybody said. I couldn't stand the waiting, but Brother Jacob was a rock. We did . . . other things. But he never came inside me until I had my period that first time. I couldn't wait to tell him."

"How long did it last?" I asked.

"That first time?"

"No. The . . . situation. With you and Brother Jacob?"

"Oh. Until I was fifteen. Almost sixteen."

"What happened?"

"They transferred him. To another community. In Buffalo—all the way on the other side of the state. We wrote to each other. I still thought it was okay. But then I found out—he had another . . . girl-friend, I guess it was. Whatever. She was much younger than me. Just a baby."

"How did you find out?" I asked softly, needing her to tell me the whole thing before she shut down again.

"I went to visit him. A surprise, it was supposed to be. I took the bus. I told my mother I was going on a school trip. It took all day. By the time I got to his address, it was late afternoon. When he opened the door, I could see the shock on his face."

"Did he let you in?"

"Yes. He *had* to. It was cold outside, and getting dark too. He told me he was angry with me for just showing up like that, but he said he wouldn't tell anyone. He took me into a front room and told me to sit down. He said he was seeing somebody, but he'd only be a lit-tle while. That's when I saw her. That's when I knew."

"What did you see, Jennifer?"

"I heard a door open," she said, hands clasped together so tightly they were mottled with bloodless white patches. "I heard him walking down the hall. Away from me. I heard another door close. That's when I knew what he was doing. Going to the bath-room. He always used to do that, just after . . ."

Her voice trailed off. I let this one go, warning Heather with my eyes to stand where she was.

"She was about ten years old," Jennifer finally said. "I snuck down the hall while he was in the bathroom. I looked in and I saw her. Skinny little girl. She was . . . playing with it. With the ruler. I used to do that too. That's when I knew."

"What did you do?"

"I just left. I walked out. I don't even remember going to the bus station. I just went home. And then I just forgot about it."

"What do you mean, forgot about it?"

"I mean *forgot* it," she said. "Blanked it out . . . I don't know. But I never thought about it again until . . ."

"Until . . . ?"

"Until I tried to kill myself. The last time. Psalmists have a prohibition against suicide. A powerful, strong prohibition. Job *wished* for death, but he never tried to take his own life. His refusal mocked Satan and so made Job great. I knew I could be shunned for trying to kill myself, and I was afraid. But the church counseled me. First a neighbor—"

"In the hospital?"

"A 'neighbor' means a member. All Psalmists are neighbors. They can't do pastoral counseling, but they can be . . . supportive, I guess. But it was a minister who did the real counseling."

"Why did you try and kill yourself, Jennifer?"

"Because it was all . . . nothing," she said, just above a whisper. "Just nothing. No matter what I tried to do, I failed. I flunked out of school. College, I mean. The work wasn't hard, but I just never did it. I drank. A lot. And I smoked marijuana. I took pills too."

"The orange-and-white capsules? Too many of them?"

"How did you . . . ? I *did* do that, but that wasn't what I meant. Uppers mostly. Speed. The church helped me with that too. When I flunked out, they got me a job. In an AIDS hospice. Psalmists are the leaders there," she said proudly. "The church has an encyclical condemning anyone who says AIDS is God's punishment for sin. Job's suffering was multiplied by his neighbors' belief that he committed some hidden sin. But really it was Satan who had tricked God into testing Job's faith. Job passed, and God has never tested any of us that way since. AIDS is a plague, not a punishment."

"But the hospice job didn't work out either?" I asked, guiding her back to what I needed to know.

"*Nothing* worked out," she said, hollow-voiced. "I had a boyfriend. We were engaged. But he broke it off. I never knew why—he just came over to my apartment one day and told me. It was hard. Very hard to tell my mother . . ."

"She knew the man? The one you were engaged to?"

"No. She didn't really know him. But he was a neighbor. And his father was a 'son.' That's like a deacon in another church. His whole family was very highly respected."

"And after that?"

"After that, I suffered. But not like Job. Not from illness. And not heroically either. Just . . . suffered. I got pregnant. And I didn't even know who the father was. I had an abortion. And I got . . . hurt when they did it. I can never have a baby now."

"Did you think—?"

"I *knew* it wasn't a punishment," she interrupted. "God doesn't do that. It was a mistake, that's all. Another failure. Like me. I worked sometimes. I was a waitress. And I did office temp too. But I was always bad at it. Bad at everything. I knew I wasn't stupid, but I just . . . didn't care, I guess. I knew I would always lose whatever job I had, so I always got lousy jobs so I wouldn't care when I lost them. I did the same thing with men. Do you understand?"

"Yeah, I do," I told her. Stone truth that time.

"I started pulling again," she said. "All the time. Even in public. I never did that before—I never went so far. Then I realized I couldn't even stop *that*. And I knew I *had* stopped it once. So I would never get better. I had no friends. No *real* friends. Nobody to talk to. I started to cut myself. Not to die; so I could *feel* something. See?" She pulled up the sleeve of her blouse, showing me the perfectly parallel cuts on her left forearm, as neat as tribal markings. "I have them on my legs too. It always made me feel better. . . . I can't explain it."

"Do you ever poke yourself?" I asked her. "Like with the tip of the knife, or a pin or anything?"

"Yes. I did that too. I did *everything* to myself. And one day, I cut myself and I didn't feel anything. Nothing at all. I watched the blood run down my leg and I didn't feel anything. I was going to cut my throat. The artery—I know where it is. But I . . . couldn't. So I found a vein."

"Did you leave a note?"

"Who would I leave a note to? There was nobody."

"How did—?

"I failed at that too," she said quietly. "I passed out, but I didn't die. I was supposed to pay the rent that afternoon. The landlady always came by to get it—she wouldn't take checks; it always had to be cash. When I didn't answer the door, she just opened it up. She had a key. She called the paramedics, and I woke up in the hospital."

"A psychiatric hospital?"

"No, a regular one. Later, I went to a . . . home, I guess it was. It didn't have bars on the windows or anything, and it wasn't a hospital. I don't know what to call it."

I could feel Heather's eyes, but not Kite's—like he wasn't giving off any heat, was just a piece of furniture. When I looked past the woman, Heather had turned her back to me. She was looking at the hologram, standing hip-shot, one hand under her chin, like she was studying a painting. I looked where her eyes were trained. The child's kite was gone. Now there was a bird, hovering high, face to the wind. A hawk, maybe, watching the ground. I couldn't see where the hawk was looking—Heather's hips blocked that part.

"All that time," I asked Jennifer, "you never—"

"All what time?"

"From when you walked out of Brother Jacob's house in Buffalo to when you tried to kill yourself. How long was that?"

"Nine, ten years."

"You never thought about what happened? Never thought about Brother Jacob?"

"No. If I had, I would have gone to a judge."

"Sued him?"

"No, the church has a judge. Every congregation has a judge. Any neighbor can file a complaint against any other neighbor, even a minister. Judges have to investigate the complaints, and then they report to the Council."

"That's still in the church."

"Yes. The Council is always seven: three judges, two deacons, and two neighbors. They're elected. If the judge files a report, the Council decides if there's guilt. And if there's guilt, the Council decides on the punishment."

"Which can be what?"

"You can be fined. Or suspended. Even banned from the church, depending on what you did."

"But you never—"

"No. I never thought about it. Not about going to the judge. I mean, about . . . it."

"You never called Brother Jacob, or wrote a letter?"

"No. I mean, not after that time when I found out—"

"And he never contacted you."

"No. I just went into a void, I guess. I don't really know—I don't understand that part so well."

"So how did you—?"

"When I started the counseling, I just told them the truth. I failed at everything, and I didn't know why. After a while, they said there were . . . gaps, like. That's when I went for hypnosis."

I could feel Kite stiffen next to me, but he didn't make a sound. "By yourself?" I asked her.

"Yes. Oh! You mean . . . No. I mean, it wasn't my idea. They found the therapist for me. The hypnosis, that was just part of it, not the whole thing. And it was a doctor. A real one, I mean. Not a Ph.D. doctor, like I have for my regular therapy."

"How long were you in—?"

"I still am," she said, cutting into my question. "I guess I will be for a long time. It was . . . months before I even *started* to remember."

"But then it all came out?"

"I don't know if it's all out," she said, her voice resigned. "I don't know . . . yet. I remember stuff more and more all the time. But what I told you, that much I know is true."

"We've been doing this for a while," I said, glancing at my watch. "I need some time to absorb everything before we talk again. All right?"

"Yes," she said. Her eyes confronted mine. "Do you believe me?" she asked, her voice so thickly veined it vibrated a little.

"I don't think you're lying," I said carefully.

"Heather will show you out," Kite said to her, suddenly coming alive. "And I'll call you as soon as we have another appointment."

"All right," she said quietly, getting to her feet. Heather was at her side instantly, a pudgy hand on the woman's forearm. I heard Heather's heels moving away on the hardwood floor. Closed my eyes.

I heard a faint rustle from Kite's direction—he was getting to his feet. He moved away, soundlessly. I kept my eyes closed.

The tap of Heather's heels, coming close. Blood-orchid perfume. Sharp intake of breath.

"Are you okay?" she asked.

I could feel her voice on my face. I didn't open my eyes. "Yeah," I told her. "Just . . . processing it all."

"He's an evil man," she said.

"Brother Jacob?"

"Yes. An evil man. A liar. That's the worst thing you can be."

"The worst thing?"

"Lying is the root. Every time. But he wasn't just lying for himself, was he? He made her a liar too. He changed the truth for her."

"Heather, have you ever talked to her?"

"Well . . . sure."

"I don't mean here. Anyplace else? Just you and her, alone?"

"No. I mean . . . when would I?"

"I don't know. I was just asking."

"I'd tell you if I had. I'll tell you everything, if you want to know."

"When?"

"Someday," she whispered, leaning so close her lips were against me. I felt the kiss on my face. Right under my cheekbone, next to the bruise. Then I heard her heels tap away until she was standing behind me, waiting for Kite.

When I opened my eyes, they were on Kite's reposeful face. He'd slipped back into his chair as quietly as a bird landing on a branch.

"It bothers me too," he said. "The whole hypnosis thing. You know about the so-called 'false memory' controversy?"

"I heard about it," I said, neutral.

"The water is very murky. There is no question but that the recovery of repressed memory is a documented, scientific fact. Repression? Of *course* it exists."

I listened to him. Wishing some of my memories were repressed. Maybe there wouldn't have been that dead kid in that basement in the Bronx . . .

"You can't 'remember' pain," Kite went on. "You'd go stark raving mad if you could. Not physical pain anyway. But some memories certainly can be repressed . . . and then surface without warning. Take the 'Vietnam Vet' syndrome. I actually provided some help to the defense in one such case—a man who committed a series of rapes while reexperiencing combat in Vietnam. Flashbacks caused him to—"

"That guy was convicted, right?" I said. I remembered the case. One of Wolfe's, before she got fired. The perp said he'd been flashbacking, believed he was back in Vietnam when he committed the rapes. But he'd robbed the women after he was through with them every time—and he came unglued when Wolfe asked him how many gold chains he'd snatched in Vietnam.

"Society is not always alert to scientific advances," Kite replied, undisturbed. His face shifted into harsh lines, and his voice tightened. "But that does not change the truth. We will *never* succeed as professional debunkers, we will *never* be able to testify credibly in a court of law, we will *never* be able to make a real contribution to society . . . to the *world* . . . if we persist in the overheated rhetoric that *none* of those with recovered memories are telling the truth!"

I heard the tap of Heather's heels behind me, but she wasn't moving, just shifting her weight, caught up in Kite's jury-summation voice.

"I realize I may be dismissed from the movement for this," he said, letting a deeper organ-stop into his voice, as though he realized it was getting shrill. "But I will *not* be humiliated in court the way I have seen it happen to my colleagues. 'Have *all* the cases you've investigated turned out to be false allegations, Mr. Kite?' he said in a sarcastic imitation of a woman's high-pitched voice. 'And if you ever found out an allegation was true, you'd go right to the police, wouldn't you, Mr. Kite?' I will *never* go through such an experience. I need one victim, one *real* victim, one whose memories are just resurfacing. And now I've found one. At least, I believe I have. . . ."

"A legit—?"

"Trauma is scar tissue over memory," he said, his voice changing to a reasonable tone. "There have been cases of violent bank robberies, for example. A woman teller is terrified, goes into traumatic shock. She can't identify the robbers, not even their age or race or height. She undergoes clinical hypnosis at the hands of an experienced, trained professional. And she recovers her memory to the point where she can describe the robbers perfectly. The defense says that you can't trust memories like that—too many other factors might have interfered with the 'picture' the woman's getting. But the *videotape* from the bank surveillance camera shows her description of the robbers was dead accurate. So we know it *can* happen. But . . ."

"You don't always have videotapes."

"No. And there seems to be no question but that charlatans with agendas of their own can implant memories. Especially when the subject is in a highly confused state. Or drug-impaired. Or suffering from a delusional disorder. With certain disorders, there is an enormous need to confabulate. Do you know what that—?"

"Fill in the blanks," I said. "Some people lose time. They can't account for whole blocks of it, sometimes even weeks. It's scary to them."

"Multiple personalities especially," Kite said, an intensity to his voice. "But they test perfectly. A multiple would survive any conventional psychological screen. The MMPI, for example. That could explain accounts of alien abductions."

"Multiples who need to fill in the missing time?"

"It *could* be; that's all I can commit to at this time. But it remains a possibility, one that cannot be discounted."

"You think she could be a—?"

"No. She's been tested. And there's other evidence."

"Such as?"

"We took her down the same road."

"Hypnosis?"

"Sodium amytal. She went right back to it. We had her in the room. Brother Jacob's room. When she was a little girl. She even remembered his cologne."

"A twelve-year-old girl knew his—?"

"Not the name," Kite said, anticipating. "The smell. She described it. And the next time, we brought samples, a whole variety. She picked it right out."

"It happened a long time ago," I said. "Can you—?

"We know we have a statute problem," Kite interrupted, answering the question he thought I was going to ask. "New York has been a strict jurisdiction, very hostile to delayed discovery."

"What's delayed discovery?"

"Ah," he said, changing tone, finally on ground where I didn't know the way. "The analogy is to medical malpractice. An operation is performed and a surgical instrument is left inside the patient. She doesn't discover the error until a long time later. Perhaps when she has other medical problems as a result. The statute of limitations doesn't begin to run until she actually *knows* malpractice was committed."

"But Jennifer *did* know . . ."

"She knew it when it was happening, yes. But the perpetrator's own conduct—the shock of the sudden knowledge that she was a victim—literally drove it out of her mind. She was in a psychiatric coma. She didn't *discover* it until later. And that's another doctrine we plan to utilize: equitable estoppel. It simply means a wrongdoer cannot profit from his own bad acts. Do you understand?"

"I hit someone in the head with a tire iron. He goes into a coma. Years pass, he's still in a coma. The statute of limitations runs out. He wakes up. Remembers it was me who did it. It was me who took his memory, so I don't get a free pass for doing it."

"Yes! Not the most graceful explanation, but certainly a cogent one."

"But that was *physical*," I said. "This was . . ."

"Emotional. Of course. The hardest thing to prove in law is the so-called soft-tissue injury. Any lawyer representing a car accident victim would rather have a broken finger than the worst whiplash. And the human heart is the softest tissue of all," Kite intoned in that jury-summation voice.

"So how are you going to . . . ?"

"Laws change," he said. "Some cases actually *make* law. I have never heard of a better case to prove the viability of the 'delayed discovery' doctrine than this one. And times are changing. Many states recognize that a *child* may not have the internal resources to come forward in a case of sexual abuse, especially when the perpetrator is a powerful figure in the child's life. Connecticut has already extended the statute. So has Vermont. And California. I don't fear the odds. In fact, I look forward to the opportunity."

"Okay. You said there was other proof. Could I—?"

"Take this with you," he said, handing me a pile of paper. And a bunch of letters, neatly tied in a black ribbon. I put them into the aluminum case.

At the grille, Heather said goodbye in a soft voice. When I turned toward her, she put her forehead against my chest, whispered, "Could I have another chance?"

"Who knows?" I lied.

I didn't want to use my Arnold Haines ID for a plane ticket, in case something went wrong out of town. And I knew better than to pay cash. Michelle booked me a round-trip on USAir through a travel agent she knows. Now that the *federales* finally figured out that any crew of drooling dimwits with a rental van and enough money to buy a few tons of fertilizer can level an entire office building, they want photo ID at airports. What they haven't figured out is that anyone with the coin and the contacts can score a complete set of papers in a couple of days. When I showed the uniformed woman at the ticket counter a driver's license that matched the Stanley Weber name on my first-class ticket, she didn't give it a second glance.

I couldn't contract the job out, not in Buffalo. In a few cities, you still have old-time thieves working. Guys who'll do a house as fine as pouring it through a strainer and turn over whatever they find— never even *look* at what they lift, much less make copies. The old-timers have a professional's pride: "If I take a fall, I take it all," the Prof used to say—no rats allowed in that exclusive club.

But those kinds of burglars are a dying breed. Hell, burglary itself is a dying art. Today, it's mostly smash-and-snatch punks, junkies and fools, amateurs who think a fence is what you climb over to get to the window . . . which you break with a brick. They don't know how to bypass an alarm, don't even know enough to start at the bottom of a chest of drawers. They leave their trail like it was blazed in neon, counting on the cops' being too busy to do anything but give you a complaint number for your insurance report. And if they ever run into a dog, all they're going to get is bit.

There're no standards now, the way there used to be. I remember a guy who wanted to join our crew years ago, when we were stealing all the time. Hercules, we'd called him in prison, a big, handsome kid, strong as the stench from a two-day-old corpse. He had a deep weakness for the ladies, but he was stand-up—if he got popped, he'd go down by himself, the way you were supposed to. Still, the Prof had nixed him off. "He's a stone amateur, bro—gets his nose open like a subway tunnel. Never keeps his mind on business. Old Herc, he's a hopeless pussy-hound. The boy can't run with us—he's a rooster, not a booster."

So I was never tempted, always stayed with a true-pro crew even if I had to pass up something that looked luscious. And I can still get it done in a few cities. Chicago has one of the best thieves I've ever known, almost in the Prof's class. There's a real slick guy who works San Francisco, one of those small, compact boys who can move like smoke. And in New Orleans, there's a double-jointed woman who could find a diamond in a vat of zircons with her nose. But they're few and far between, an aging class. And every prison jolt thins the ranks.

In Buffalo, I didn't know a soul. I wasn't going to trust some secondhand recommendation—and without a local bondsman and a good lawyer already lined up, it's not righteous to ask your own people to take a risk.

Besides, whatever Brother Jacob had lying around that might help me was probably in his head, not in some desk drawer. I decided this was a one-thief job.

The flight took under ninety minutes, nonstop. I fly first class because it's more anonymous. The seats are separated—the whole setup doesn't encourage the guy next to you to get into a conversation. And you can board the plane after everyone else but still be first off when you land. If you don't check luggage, you can slip on and off the plane like it was a taxicab.

I ate a little bit of the blah food they served, watching the letters Brother Jacob had written to Jennifer Dalton come up on the screen in my head. They were all fun-house mirrors, tricky reflections, bending your vision. The handwriting was strong, with a confident right-hand slant. On heavy, cream-colored, watermarked paper, each letter only one sheet, one side. No return address, no monogram. Expensively anonymous.

> Dear One,
>
> I know it's hard for you, Jennifer. It's hard for me as well. But there is a right way to do everything, even the most difficult tasks. Patience doesn't come easily to someone your age, but the greatest joys in life are always worth the investment.

And another . . .

> Most things in life are all a matter of perspective. *How* you look at something is more important than what you're looking at. You've seen this for yourself, haven't you, dear?

All the same . . .

> Remember, Jennifer, your feelings are your own. They are private, special things, unique to you and you alone. And you are always entitled to them. They are always yours. The best things in life are always *investments*. You have to wait for them to pay off. And this takes patience. I know things are hard for you now, but they'll get better, I promise.

I thought about promises. In the hands of an expert, they're like razor cuts—so sharp the target never feels them until he sees the blood.

And when the target trusts you enough, sometimes he doesn't even see the blood. Until it's almost all gone.

I rented a bronze Taurus sedan at the airport and used the City Planning Commission maps to find him. It wasn't hard—the house was in Brother Jacob's name, and I had a pretty good photo that came with the file Kite had given me.

A pearlescent orange Jeep chugged up next to me at a light. The sun blazed on the Jeep's wheels—masterpieces of sculpture with hand-set centerpieces, gold-plated. Wheels like that can set you back a few thousand dollars. Useless—you're paying for the flash. Like two-hundred-dollar sneakers. And like the ultra-sneakers, there were more people stealing them than working for them. And not even real stealing—the robot mutant psychopaths don't have the brains to boost a car or shoplift some shoes, so they rough it off face-to-face. Your stuff or your life—either one gratifies the urban punk killing machines.

It was late afternoon by the time I found the place. A freestanding house of weathered white wood on a short block in what looked like a middle-class neighborhood with aspirations. A matching one-car garage stood at the end of a driveway, no fence around the small front yard. The house looked well tended, but whoever owned it wasn't obsessive about it—the lawn could have used a trim, and one of the trees had branches that wouldn't last through the fast-coming winter.

I parked across the street and settled in to watch. A trio of kids flew past on fat-tired trail bikes, shouting each other's names. A woman walked by with a chocolate Lab on leash. It was an active block, probably had its share of housebound watchers too. But I wasn't worried about it—if I got out of there without being arrested, the license plate would dead-end with the Stanley Weber ID.

I pulled around the corner and waited. It stayed quiet until evening dropped black-edged gray over the block. Lights snapped on in houses as kids went back inside. Suppertime. I dialed the number I had for Brother Jacob on the cellular phone I'd brought with me. If a housekeeper answered, I'd have to think of another way.

"Hello?" A man's voice. Middle-aged but vigorous without being aggressive.

"Could I speak to Brother Jacob, please?"

"Speaking."

"My name is Weber, sir. Stanley Weber. I wonder if I could have a few minutes of your time. I—"

"I don't ever respond to telephone solicitations," he said. "If you'd like, you can mail—"

"This isn't a solicitation, sir. I'd like to talk to you about a matter of mutual interest. In a way, I guess you're right: I am a salesman. But what I have to sell isn't to the general public—you're the only one who would be interested, I think."

"I don't understand."

"I could explain better in person, sir. I have some documents you might be interested in purchasing."

"Documents?"

"Yes. I'd rather not go into it on the phone, if you don't mind. I believe it's in your interest that we speak. Privately."

"Look, I don't know who you—"

"It concerns a former . . . student of yours, Brother Jacob. A young lady. Miss Jennifer Dalton."

The phone went silent, but he hadn't hung up. I listened to him breathing—I couldn't tell if the hook was set. Finally, he said, "I'm not sure what you're talking about, actually. But if you would like to—"

"Just a few minutes of your time, sir. At your convenience."

"Yes. Very well. Do you know where I—?"

"I can be at your house in, say, fifteen minutes. Would that be convenient?"

He went back to breathing. Then: "All right. But I don't have a lot of time. I'm expecting—"

"I'll be right over," I said, cutting the connection.

I gave it ten minutes. Then I locked up the car and walked around the corner to the white house. The door was painted a dull red, with a switch for the bell set into its center. I turned the switch to the right and heard the ding-dong sound inside.

A medium-height white man opened the door. He had thick dark hair set unnaturally low on his forehead. A toupee, and an expensive one. He was about my height, with a soft round jowly face, and he wore a red flannel shirt over a pair of old putty-colored corduroy pants, brown blunt-toed brogans on his feet. His eyes were pale blue, set deep into their sockets.

"Mr. . . . ," he said.

"Weber," I finished for him. "May I come in?"

My midnight-blue suit and white silk shirt reassured him slightly, but he still looked spooked. Maybe because I wasn't wearing a tie.

"Uh . . . certainly," he said, stepping aside.

The living room was just past the foyer, furnished in what I guessed were antiques: heavy, solid dark wood, light chintz upholstery. I took the couch. He thought about sitting next to me, then passed in favor of a straight chair with padded arms.

"You said . . ."

"Jennifer Dalton," I told him again, looking at his mouth, avoiding his eyes. I was there as a salesman, not an interrogator. "I have some . . . documents which I thought might be of interest to you."

"Documents?"

"Letters," I said gently. "Your letters, I think."

"Why would you . . . ?"

"Miss Dalton has been seeing someone. A therapist. In the course of their . . . work together, she brought the letters in."

"I don't understand," he said, his voice fibrous with tension.

"It's quite a common thing," I said smoothly. "When a patient is trying to . . . recapture the past, a therapist often asks for . . . keepsakes. To reconstruct events."

"But I don't—"

"I understand," I told him. "Maybe this was a bad idea. If I wasted your time, I apologize."

"Well," he said, clearing his throat, "I don't know. I mean . . . I can't say."

"You tell me," I said, opening the black aluminum attaché case and taking out one of the letters. I handed it over to him, then busied myself looking through some other papers, keeping my eyes down.

He took the letter. I could hear him turning the single page over in his hand. "This is . . . this appears to be something I . . . might have written a long time ago."

"Yes."

"A letter of encouragement. To a young woman with many personal problems."

"Yes."

"Why would you have this?" he asked, breathing through his mouth.

"I'm a businessman," I said. "I have my finger in a number of pies, so to speak. Therapists aren't very well paid. And this particular therapist happens to owe some money. Not to American Express . . . to some people who are very impatient."

"I . . . see. Is this the only one you have?"

"No. I have them all," I told him. "There's eleven all told."

He cleared his throat. Swallowed hard. Then: "If I wanted these . . . letters, it would be to spare the possibility of . . . oh, I don't know . . . unnecessary embarrassment."

"If you have the money, there doesn't have to be *any* embarrassment," I said quietly. "Not for anybody."

"It's very easy to make copies—"

"They're no good," I lied. "Without the originals, they're meaningless. No professional document examiner would ever—"

"Document examiner?"

"Like they use in court," I said, watching his face. "The important thing about . . . some letters is the *date*," I said. "There's no date on any of the letters. And you can't tell the date from a photocopy. You can't test for the age of the paper; the ink won't—"

"I understand what you mean now," he interrupted.

"Do you want the letters?" I asked.

"I'm . . . concerned," he said. "A therapist shouldn't—"

"I agree with you, Brother Jacob. I make no apologies for my own position. Like I said, I'm a businessman. And the people I represent, they're business people. A therapist does have certain . . . obligations. Sometimes a person is obligated in more than one direction at the same time—I'm sure you understand. Let me see if I'm following your chain of thought," I said, gentling my voice. "You might be interested in buying back these letters so you can show them to Miss Dalton yourself. So you can prove this therapist to whom she entrusted her deepest secrets is actually not acting in her best interests. Is that about right?"

"Yes," he said. "That is right. Exactly right."

"Good. I won't waste your time in meaningless bargaining, Brother Jacob. This isn't a question of whatever 'value' the letters may have. After all, it's a question only of what the therapist owes my . . . employers."

"And that is?"

"Twenty thousand dollars."

"That's impossible!" he blurted out. "I don't have that kind of money."

"Well, we would have no way of knowing that, would we?" I asked reasonably. "Because you're the only market for these particular items . . . it's not as though we could put them out for bids."

"I understand. I mean . . . I know what you're saying. But I don't see how I could . . ."

"That's up to you," I said, holding out my hand for the letter.

"Is it possible to . . . compromise?"

"I'm afraid not," I said, still extending my hand. "I'm a salaried employee, Brother Jacob. I don't work on commission. If it were up to me, I'd do something about the price. I know why you're buying the letters, and I admire you for it. Not many people would spend a lot of money just to help someone else out. But there's really nothing I can do."

"What are you going to . . . ?"

"Nothing," I said. "Nothing at all. We'll explain to the therapist that there's no value in the letters. The money will have to come from someplace else. My employers thought it was worth a plane ticket to see if there was another possibility, that's all. I hope you don't feel I wasted your time."

"No. Not at all," he said, still holding the letter.

"Brother Jacob . . . ," I said, looking directly into his eyes.

He cleared his throat again. "Is there a way I could . . . pay it gradually?"

"Of course," I said. "You could pay for each individual letter. But if you wanted them all delivered at once, certain . . . security would be required."

"Security?"

"My employers are very serious people," I said. "These are not things you put in writing—it's a matter of honor, you understand? You give your word—you keep your word."

"Yes, of course. But if—?"

"There is no 'if,' Brother Jacob. Except for this one: *If* you want the letters, I am authorized to agree to a time-payment plan. Say five hundred dollars a month."

"I . . . believe I could do that."

"For fifty months."

I could see the gears turn in his head for a few seconds. Then: "Fifty! But you said twenty thousand. Fifty times five hundred would be . . . twenty-*five* thousand."

"That's the business my employers are in," I said, my voice going flat and hard, driving out the reasonable tone I'd been using. "Lending money. The therapist borrowed a bit less than the twenty, but it's gonna cost twenty to get square. You want to pay this off, you're borrowing twenty. It's gonna cost *you* some juice to get square too, okay?"

"I . . . how would I . . . ?"

"In cash," I told him, letting him hear the jailhouse and the graveyard in my voice. "Once a month. We can have somebody come by, pick it up. Or they could meet you, anyplace you say."

"How do I know . . . ?"

"Like I said, the letters aren't worth anything to us. You can have them all, up front. How's that?"

"That seems . . . fair."

"We operate on good faith, Brother Jacob. Like I said: We trust you with our money; we trust you to keep your word."

"All right."

"I appreciate it," I said. "You keep that one. I'll be back in a couple of weeks with the rest. I hand them over to you, you give me the first payment. After that, once a month, okay?"

"Yes."

"Thanks for your time," I said, getting to my feet.

He didn't offer to shake hands.

Wolfe was waiting in the parking lot, standing next to her old Audi, the Rottweiler by her side on a loose lead. As I approached, the baleful beast snapped to attention, glaring at me with his dark, homicidal eyes.

"This is her," I said, handing over a copy of everything I had on Jennifer Dalton.

"You talk to her yourself?" she asked.

"Yeah. And she rings righteous. At least for now."

"We'll take a look."

"Thanks. One more thing. Those addresses you gave me? The co-ops Kite owns. Can you get me a tenant list?"

"How deep you want to go?"

"Far as you can. How they pay the rent, canceled checks, leases, anything."

"Neighbors too?"

"Be careful you don't spook—"

"We know what we're doing," Wolfe cut in.

"I know," I said by way of apology.

A pair of elderly ladies strolled by arm in arm, steps slow but eyes alive. Pals, glad to be with each other.

"Look, Rosalyn," one said to the other, pointing at Bruiser, "isn't that one of those Wildenheimers?"

"Well, I think *so*," her friend said, raising her eyebrows at Wolfe.

"That's right," Wolfe told her, a merry smile on her face.

"Are they good watchdogs?" Rosalyn asked.

"Oh, *very* good," Wolfe assured her.

"That's good, dear. A young woman in this city *needs* protection these days. You can't be too careful."

The two old ladies moved on, yakking away. "A *Wildenheimer*?"
I said to Wolfe.

"That's a Jewish Rottweiler." Wolfe smiled at me. "Don't you
know anything?"

"**Y**ou know anything about the Gospel of Job's Song people?" I
asked the slim, hard-featured man. We were in a gay bar just
off Christopher Street, talking in the four o'clock dead zone between
the lunch crowd and the evening mating dance.

"The Psalmists? Sure. They're not *with* us exactly: homosexuals
aren't really welcome in their hierarchy, and none of us serve as
ministers. Not openly anyway. But when it comes to AIDS, they're
right there. I don't care for a lot of their doctrine—hell, I don't care
for *any* doctrine—but they stand tall against that 'God's punishment' obscenity."

"You ever have any dealings with them?"

"Not personally."

"Okay. Thanks for your time."

"Tell Victor I said hello," the man said.

"**I** don't like the hypnosis piece," I told Kite.

"Not to worry," he said smugly. "We're on all fours with *Borawick*."

"What's a Borawick?"

"A case, Mr. Burke. The proverbial 'federal case,' as it turns out.
The Second Circuit set the standard just last year. It's not a rigid for-
mula—they use the so-called 'totality of the circumstances' test. But
the factors the court must consider are *all* in our favor."

"Tell me."

"Very well. *Borawick* was the same set of facts: hypnotically refreshed memories of child sexual abuse recovered from an adult

who entered therapy for what she thought was an unrelated problem. That in itself is one factor: *why* the subject underwent therapy
in the first place. Then the court will consider the hypnotizability of
the subject, the qualifications of the hypnotist, the procedures uti-
lized, and any corroborating evidence."

"Which we have."

"Yes. In spades. But the most important issue is whether any
suggestions were implanted."

"How could any court tell that?"

He templed his fingers, gazed at me over the steeple. "The key is
whether there was a permanent record of the hypnosis itself."

"And . . . ?"

"Heather," Kite said, a tone of triumph in his voice.

Her heels clicked on the hardwood floor. I heard a cabinet being
opened, the sound of snapping plastic. I felt her come up behind
me. She gently placed a standard audiocassette in my lap and
stepped back.

"I presume you have an adequate machine available?" Kite
asked.

"Sure."

"What you have is a copy, Mr. Burke. I plan to introduce the entire history of Miss Dalton's sessions into evidence. And then I shall
step back and simply say what I have waited to say all my life as a
lawyer: *res ipsa loquitur.*"

He raised his eyebrows, but I didn't take the bait.

"It's Latin," he said. "It literally means 'the thing speaks for
itself.' And the tapes do. Eloquently, I assure you. And unlike
Borawick, in which the refreshed testimony was *not* allowed, *our*
hypnotist is not some amateur with a high school education and
no formal training who didn't keep adequate records. In *our*
case, Mr. Burke, if you will remember, the hypnotist was a *psychiatrist.* And a psychiatrist who not only kept written records
of his sessions; they were all preserved exactly as they occurred.
If ever one searched for the classic case to rebut the so-called
'False Memory syndrome,' one could not do better than what we
have."

Most investigators don't even know what the word means. You stop the cops from using informants, and the only crimes they'd ever solve would be those by deranged postal workers who came to work once too often. There're plenty of well-meaning amateurs, but they run around like headless chickens on crystal meth. Private eyes? They're mostly ex-cops with some contacts. Or find-out-if-your-husband-is-cheating-on-you keyhole peepers. Or hypertech guys who know all about code-grabbers and digital scramblers but don't get the concept of tire irons and duct tape.

I don't have a license, but the humans I learned from were the best teachers in the world. You want someone to find secrets, use a man who has plenty of his own.

When games have no rules, they're only games to the players who made them up. I never made up the games, but they made me a player when I was just a kid: ugly secrets, dark corridors, terror around every corner. I learned how to hide real good. And now it's real hard to hide from me.

Plus I was working my own city. Where I know how to find the best slip-and-slide men in the world. The Prof might have lost a step—maybe he wasn't up to bank vaults or high-security buildings anymore—but he could still go in and out of a regular apartment house like smoke through panty hose.

"Seven G," I told him, unfolding a floor plan. "It's a two-bedroom, top floor, rear. No doorman. I'll make sure she's not around when you go in."

"She bunks alone?"

"Guaranteed," I said, relying on Wolfe.

"And the other one?"

"That's a three-room. Third floor, right off the elevator. Furnished. Six and a quarter a month, utilities included. It's not a hotel, but nobody stays there that long. Mostly studios—she's got one of the bigger units."

"Same deal?"

"Same deal. You need the Mole to take down the basement?"

"That ain't the plan, man. I figure amateur locks, right? What you want, I'll be through in a half hour tops."

"Be a ghost, Prof."

"A *holy* ghost, Schoolboy."

"**Y**ou can't imagine what it feels like," the man said. "If you haven't been through it, you'll never understand."

"I can't *be* you," I said softly. "I know that. But maybe, if you'll help, I can get close."

"Mr. Kite saved my life," the man said, standing on the back porch of his upper Westchester house, looking out over a rushing gorge. He was in his sixties, thinning brown hair neatly combed to the side over a fine-boned face. His right hand was locked over his left wrist as tight as a handcuff. "He asked me to talk to you—that's good enough for me."

"How did it . . . happen?"

"'Happen.' That's a good word for it. Like a train wreck. I had no warning. My son had a wonderful life. We had the . . . resources to give him everything a boy could want. He was a soccer star, you know. When he was small. He lost interest when he started high school, but that's common, I guess. Once puberty hits . . .

"He had everything, as I said. His junior year in Europe. The whole Continent, Grand Tour. A new car when he was only sixteen. A Corvette. A black convertible—just what he wanted. We did everything together. As a family. Ski trips, Disneyland, ball games . . . the whole nine yards. He graduated fourth in his class. Phi Beta Kappa at my alma mater. Then he got a master's degree in English literature. And a wonderful teaching position." The man's voice trailed off, his eyes focusing somewhere out by the gorge. He never looked at me.

"Then he got married," the man said. "A wonderful girl from a fine family—we all loved her. I gave them the down payment on their house as a wedding present."

"You were very generous. . . ."

"Oh, I *had* it to give," he said. "I've done very well for myself. In business. And what good is money if you can't spend it on your loved ones? It was my pleasure. Always my pleasure."

"When did . . . ?"

"He got divorced. It was so . . . sudden. A very nice divorce, actually. No name calling, no public displays. She had money of her own anyway—there was no need to . . .

"And teaching . . . well, that doesn't pay very much. He never said why they broke up, but I found out later. He was gay."

"He told you?"

"No. He told his mother. That was before . . ."

"Before . . . ?"

"Before it all . . . happened. When he was still speaking to her. To us."

"How did you . . . ?"

"A telephone call. The most terrifying phone call a parent can ever receive. It was Tyler. Calling me from his therapist's office. He said it was time to 'confront' me. That's the exact word he used, 'confront.' God."

"What did he say?"

"He said I had *molested* him," the man said, so quietly I had to strain to pick up the words. "My own son. Saying that to me over the phone. He didn't want to be gay—that's where it all started."

"What do you mean?"

"That's why he went to that therapist. He was gay. Or at least he thought he was. Naturally, he was . . . disturbed about it. So he went for counseling. That's what he told me, that time on the phone. The therapist helped him 'unlock the memories. . . .'"

He was quiet for a few minutes, crying soundlessly, tears on his face. But his hands didn't move, still vised together.

"'Unlock the memories,' that's what he said. Of me . . . molesting him. When he was a little boy. I couldn't believe it. I couldn't believe what I was hearing. I thought it was some kind of sick . . . I don't know . . . joke, maybe. I was in shock."

"Is that all he said?"

"No. He said . . . a lot. He wanted to meet with me. Face-to-face, he said. I said I had always talked to him that way. Man-to-man. And you know what he said to me? He said: 'You're not a man.' I almost died. Right there on the phone, I almost died."

"Did you ever talk to him. I mean . . . that way?"

"No. Never. Mr. Kite told me not to do it. He said it was extortion. A common thing, he told me. He knew the therapist. Knew him by reputation anyway. He . . . this therapist . . . does this a lot. Convinces young people who come to him—who come to him for *help*, for God's sake—that they were . . . abused when they were children. Mr. Kite said there would be a demand for money. To be ready for it."

"And did it come?"

"Oh yes. Tyler didn't call it that exactly. He said it was 'reparations,' or some such garbage. He wanted money. And an apology. That apology, it was very important to him, he said."

"Did you pay him?"

"I did not," the man said. He drew a harsh intake of breath through his nose. "So he got some two-bit publicity seeker of a lawyer and he sued me. But *that* didn't work either."

"Because . . . ?"

"Mr. Kite got it thrown out of court. Thrown right out. Tyler didn't have any *evidence* or anything. Just what he said. And it wasn't really *him* saying it anyway, it was that damn therapist."

"So you never did speak to—"

"No, I have not. I haven't spoken to him, his mother hasn't spoken to him, and his sister hasn't either."

"His sister. Is she older or . . . ?"

"Two years older. A fantastic girl. Married, with three beautiful children. He called her too. He tried to turn her against me, but she wouldn't budge. Brittany knows something about loyalty. . . ."

"Maybe he thought she would be loyal to—"

"To him? Why? What kind of loyalty would that be? To a person who ruined an entire family."

"But if . . . ?"

"He *did* ruin our family," the man said. "Nothing is the same. Oh, his little scheme didn't succeed. He didn't get his 'apology' for something I never did. But my wife and I . . . it just shattered us. It changed everything we had. And Brittany, she has no relationship with him at all. He actually told her she could never leave her little boy alone with me. Can you imagine that? Can you *feel* what that must feel like? My own grandson . . .

"When you're an innocent man, an accusation like he made hurts worse than if it was the truth. A false allegation of child abuse is the ugliest thing one human being can do to another, I know that now. If it hadn't been for Mr. Kite, I might have done something very stupid."

"Such as . . . ?"

"You don't know what it feels like!" he said, his voice breaking. "You feel so lost, so alone. Tyler even tried to go to the police. To make a criminal complaint against me. But they wouldn't take it. . . ."

"How long ago was this?"

"He said it happened when he was—"

"No. I mean, how long ago did he make that call?"

"More than seven years ago," the man said. "And I still wake up in the night hearing that phone ring. My heart still jumps. For years I couldn't bear to be around any place there was a telephone, afraid it would ring. My business . . . I've lost everything."

"Did you ever want to get revenge?"

"Well, I did sue the therapist. But it was a very difficult standard. We had to prove it was malpractice. And with Tyler sticking to his story . . ."

"And that was the last time you ever heard from your son?"

"I got a letter," he said quietly. "The most hateful letter ever written, I think. I'd show it to you, but it's gone. I burned it. Mr. Kite was furious at me for that, but I couldn't sleep another night even knowing that filthy thing was in the world."

He stepped back from the railing, hands still locked. "It can happen to anyone," he said. "Nobody is ever safe from a lie."

"It's an industry," the young woman told me, sitting with her legs crossed in a semi-reclined ergonomic chair behind a chrome-trimmed bleached-wood desk. "Driven by a combination of ego and economics. The children may have been abused once, I don't deny that. But now they're being *exploited*. And the perpetrators are their own parents."

"How does it work?" I asked, watching her bright-blue eyes through the oversized glasses she wore perched on the end of a surgically small nose.

"It varies," she replied, "but not all that much. The ingredients are always the same. The child is molested—not by a family member, but not by a stranger either . . . someone in the 'circle of trust.' A drama teacher, a football coach, a religious counselor, a babysitter . . . whatever. Eventually, the child 'tells.' And it turns out that the abuse has been going on for a long time. The perpetrator is arrested. There's either a trial or a guilty plea, it doesn't much matter. The essential element is that the child goes *public*."

"Why is that so important?"

"Because the child then *stays* public, Mr. . . . ."

"Burke."

"Oh yes. I'm sorry. Forgive me. Mr. Kite sent you over on such short notice, and—"

"That's okay. By going public, you mean press conferences and all that?"

"No. That's a different manifestation. That's when the parents are operating off their own egos. When they don't see the economics."

"I'm not sure I—"

"The ego part is simple enough. The parents go on the talk shows. Or they talk to reporters. Maybe they're hoping for something like a book or movie deal, but that's not the real motivation. What they're really after is self-aggrandizement. Attention for themselves. Sympathy. A chance to be important. Of course, parents of molested children don't have the same impact as parents of murdered children. *They* get the most attention, those valiant symbols of bravery." Her voice was so heavy with sarcasm it dropped from her mouth like a safe off a high building.

"You don't think much of—"

"I certainly don't. They run around lobbying for their little laws—always named after the child, of course—as though having a murdered child makes them experts on criminal justice. It's all a media thing. It has no substance whatsoever."

"Okay, that's ego. You said something about economics . . . ?"

"Ah, yes. Some of these poor children, they become a road show all unto themselves. They travel with an entourage—their own makeup people, speechwriters, press secretaries. And of course, they have their own stage mothers too. It's disgusting. I have some videotapes for you—Mr. Kite said you'd return them . . . ?"

"Yeah, I will."

"Well, the tapes speak for themselves. Canned presentations, as carefully rehearsed as a play. The brave little child standing up to the horrible abuser. Guaranteed to make you reach for your wallet. They produce so-called 'self-help' films, write their 'own' books for children, act as 'consultants.' Like I said, there's a fortune to be made. And there's plenty of these kids making it."

"What's this have to do with false—"

"With false allegations? Very little. But it's another form of child abuse, that's for sure. Most false allegations come from exploitation. Children being encouraged to lie. *Rewarded* for lying, in fact. And this business of making the children relive the abuse over and over again just to keep media attention . . . well, that's another side of the same coin."

"**S**he was out of control," the Latina in the beige wool dress said to me. "I had to do a *Tarasoff* warning—the first one in all my years of clinical practice."

"What's a *Tarasoff* warning?" I asked her, watching her fuss with a pack of cigarettes on the top of her desk as though deciding if she was going to take a bitter pill.

"Mental Hygiene Law, section thirty-three thirteen," she said mechanically, pushing her thick black hair away from her face in an absentminded gesture that rattled one of her gold hoop earrings. "When a patient articulates a clear and present threat to another person, the therapist may break confidentiality and inform the potential target. She was obsessed with revenge."

"On the guy who abused her?"

"No," she said, a rueful smile on her face. "On the guy who left her. It was a stormy relationship. She was a very needy, very demanding young woman. And eventually, her demands strained the relationship to the breaking point. And all the pent-up hatred she felt for . . . her father got redirected to her boyfriend. He was in real danger."

"What sense does that . . . ?"

"Some patients suffer from a kind of moral dyslexia," she said, brushing her hair away from her face again. "They project the conduct of the abuser onto an innocent person. But what you need to understand is that only their *facts* are wrong. Their *emotions* are true. The abuse *did* happen. It's just that—"

"The wrong man paid for it?"

"He paid for everything," she said, finally lighting a cigarette.

"I'm doing a paper on it," the black man told me. His scrawny neck was so long it couldn't support his large head—his face listed at an odd angle. It was hard to hold his eyes.

"How long have you been—"

"Almost six years," he interrupted. "This whole ritual abuse thing has been metastasizing for longer than that, though. Despite the fact that there isn't one single documented case—not a single case authenticated by legitimate law enforcement investigation— the *number* of reported cases has been expanding exponentially."

"Because . . . ?"

"Because the *accounts* have been traveling through the survivor community," he said in a strong, vibrating voice, punching a thick-bodied black Montblanc fountain pen in my direction for emphasis. "We noticed a certain phenomenon a while back. Whenever survivors gather in groups, especially for allegedly therapeutic purposes, a 'Can you top this?' ethos emerges. One woman says she was an incest victim. The next says she was an incest victim too, but she had multiple perpetrators. The next says they took pornographic pictures. Before too long, they're up to ritualistic murder of babies and international plots."

"You're saying they make this up?"

"They are *induced* to the images," he responded, like he'd had a lot of practice answering that question. "And seduced by the power it gives them. They don't 'make it up'—they have the images implanted by others. They know they are in terrible pain. They seek reasons for the pain. They know they're hurting more than the last speaker, so they must have suffered more. Do you understand?"

"I understand what you're saying . . ."

"But you find it incredible? Good! A skeptical attitude is exactly what is needed in this area. The true believers have polluted scientific knowledge. So what we did, sir, is we *tested* our hypothesis. We used an 'artifact' method, deliberately introducing bogus material to see if it became absorbed."

"You sent a ringer into T-groups?" I asked him.

"That is precisely what we did," he said, a note of triumph in his deep voice. "We prepped and trained three talented actresses. They simply joined existing groups. Groups in which there had been *no* prior members who made complaints of ritualistic abuse. After a while, each actress introduced her own tale. And in *every* case, in *each* group, other members began to 'disclose' similar stories."

"Like group hysteria?"

"Exactly like group hysteria," he said. "And when my paper is published, the scientific community will understand that it has been practicing some group hysteria of its own!"

The man and woman looked two-of-a-kind: same height, same weight, same no-shape. Dressed alike in those brown mail order pants guaranteed to last a lifetime, both wearing white T-shirts with FREE THE BYRDS on the chest. Another woman, a younger one, in a dark blue shirtdress, stayed in the background, busying herself with affixing labels to a stack of newsletters piled up on a long folding table.

"We have a mailing list of almost four hundred," the man said. "But our circle of support is much, much wider."

"Do you know them personally?" I asked.

"We have *come* to know them," the woman said. "We didn't at first—just what we read in the papers. And from the TV. It was Laureen's case first," she told me, pointing at the young woman working on the labels.

"How do you get your cases?" I asked, ballpoint pen poised over my reporter's pad.

"There are certain things you look for," the man said. I had to look to make sure it was him—his voice was the same as the woman's.

"What things?"

"Media overkill, that's the first sign. Biased reporting. The Byrds were good citizens in every way. Home owners, taxpayers, churchgoers . . . you name it. That is *exactly* the type of person the media targets, you know. I mean, it's not much of a story if some known degenerate is accused, is it? The feeding frenzy really started a number of years ago. In Jordan, Minnesota. That was the original case for the movement. And after that, it became an epidemic. The media isn't interested in people on welfare committing abuse. The media wants white, middle-class victims for its witch hunt. Look at McMartin, or Marilyn Kelly Michaels. If you work in a day care center, why, you're at risk; it's as simple as that. The list is amazing, just amazing."

"And what they have in common is . . . ?"

"That they are all *innocent*," the woman said. "But their cases are tried in the newspapers, and the public finds them guilty without any evidence."

"And that's what happened to the Byrds?"

"Exactly!" the man said. "But it's not going to stop there. Appeals are pending. We have a complete fact-sheet on the case. Laureen . . . ," he called over his shoulder. But the young woman was already walking toward me, a stack of paper in her hand.

"You look the same," she said. I knew it wasn't a compliment.

"You too," I told her, ignoring how the brunette wig didn't sit just right. And the crow's-feet around her eyes.

"Aren't you sweet! But I only work out-call now," she told me, stepping back so I could come inside the studio apartment.

"Just tell me how the trick went," I told her. "Like I said on the phone."

"How'd you know about him?" she asked, eyes narrowing. "It was only that one time."

"You pay money, you get information," I said.

A pathological liar lies—that's what they do. But a professional liar treats truth no different from a lie—you use whatever works. So I told her I'd paid cash for what got me to her door—that kind of thing would make sense to her. No point explaining about the credit card receipts. If people weren't greedy, they'd never get caught. Businessmen have been charging whores to their businesses since forever, billing it as limo service, restaurant tabs . . . sometimes just "entertainment." If they just paid cash, nobody would ever know— but then they'd have to spend their own money. If you know what you're doing, you can follow the paper trail right into the shadows of their lives. I didn't know where Wolfe got hold of Kite's American Express receipts, but this was the only one that hadn't dead-ended.

"And you're gonna pay *me*?" she asked, absently rubbing at her coke-ruined nose. Only it wasn't a question.

"You know me, Penny," I said. "I work the same way you do. You're too high class to be grabbing front money, right?"

She sat on the unmade double bed, shifted her too-thin body inside the black silk robe. "I thought he was a trick too, okay? But all he wanted was to talk."

"Sex talk?"

"No. And he didn't want to wear my panties either, okay? Or have me spank him. He wanted to ask me about *another* trick."

"And you told him you didn't talk about your clients, right?" I asked her, putting it together finally. If Kite had offered her cash over the phone, she would have spooked. So he came in person, like he was a customer.

"Right. But you could see he wasn't a cop. I mean, I never saw *nobody* ever looked like him. Like he had all the blood drained out or something. And he already knew all about the trick. Just not what we . . . did, okay?"

"Okay. So you told him . . . ?"

"Yeah," she said, sandpaper in her voice. "I told him, okay? No big deal. It was nice just to . . . talk, for once. It wasn't like he was paying me to rat the trick out or anything. I mean, he wasn't the heat, right? He was doing . . . research, like. That's what he said. He was consulting me," she said, her voice loving the sound of the word in her mouth.

"And that was it?"

"That was it, Burke. No big deal. You want to pay me now?"

"Sure," I said, reaching in my pocket. "By the way, did you know that trick was a judge?"

"Oh yes!" She laughed, nasty-edged. "One thing you can always get from tricks, honey—they can't *wait* to tell you how motherfucking important they are."

I had other things to do besides Kite's job. I'm a professional—I work even when I'm flush, not living from score to score like some rookie. Like most criminals, I learned my trade in prison. On the yard, listening to the Prof preach the gospel:

"Every take ices the cake, Schoolboy. But you never finish working, see? It ain't a bunch of jobs, it's all *one* job. That's your *work*, got
it? So when the time comes you got to cut into the cake, the cash is
there, waiting. You don't got to do something stupid. You ain't in a
hurry. Keep that cake rich all the time, so when you got to slice, it
stays real nice."

All the scores don't pan out, especially when you work the
corners the way I do. And the *federales* have been crimping some
of those corners lately. Used to be I could always count on a
steady stream of firearms sales to halfass Nazis preparing for
the revolution, but their latest psycho fantasy is biological war-
fare—dump a load of botulism toxin in the water supply of
"Nigger Dee-troit" or "Jew York," wait patiently up in the hills
in their ramshackle little hate-houses to mow down the fleeing
survivors.

The feds even monitor the White Night shortwave radio traffic
now, and the FBI has a whole pack of undercovers working the sur-
vivalist beat. The feds cruise the Internet too, but that's still safe for
me—I make kiddie porn deals but I never deliver, satisfying myself
with the up-front cash. I guess I get some of Uncle's buy-money
mingled in there once in a while, but they'll never come close
enough to make a bust. Besides, it's the product they want—a lousy
fraud arrest doesn't race their motors.

I trade with the feds too, but I never took a CI jacket—Confidential Informants never stay all that confidential. I take it out in favors
instead. The way that works is so simple I'm surprised they haven't
caught on: I sell guns to some Nazi wannabe, then I drop a dime on
him and the feds get a good solid bust. They don't pay me for the
info, but I get a couple more cards in the Get Out of Jail Free deck
each time.

G-men are pretty neutral characters. They don't go native
like some of the NYPD undercovers do. Hoover's dress code
went out the window about the time he went into the ground, but
you can still spot the Gee at a hundred yards. Even across cyber-
space.

That's the latest frontier, the freshest stalking ground for predators. But the Internet's no different from any other piece of technology. It's neutral, like a scalpel. In the hands of a surgeon, it cuts out cancer. In the hands of a freak, it cuts out hearts.

The Net is paradise for lurkers: nameless, no-scent psychopaths. That's the way camouflage works—by blurring the outlines. Most people look to the edges for definition—when it's not there, they don't see anything at all. But camouflage doesn't help when the other guy's willing to defoliate the whole jungle.

There's a few heavy players working the fringe now. They climb on the Net, usually one of those "kids only" boards, and they get right into the pen pal thing. It never takes long. One of the freaks engages them, chats a bit, makes some promises, and sets up a meet. The freaks especially love airport hotels—in-and-out's their game anyway. They check into the room, and in a little bit, a kid shows up. Whatever they thought they were cybering with—a little Latino boy, a freckle-faced white girl—doesn't matter. But before they can get down to what they do, the door pops open and there's a real big, real angry man there. Turns out—it *always* turns out—that the kid is *his* kid. Somebody's gonna get hurt. Real bad. But if the freak spills out enough oil, *fast*, maybe he can douse the fire before he gets burned himself. All it costs is money. It's the old badger game, updated cyber-style. And the freaks never run to the Law.

I don't go in for that stuff myself. I don't like to operate out of my territory. But I know there's crews working in half a dozen cities. Probably more by now. Freaks lock onto the Net and start salivating. They never figure that in this world, there's creatures that prey on predators.

The world's nothing but crime. I don't do every kind, but I do more than enough. I've been playing this way for such a long time that I'm doomed to it now, dancing between the acid raindrops, waiting for that manicured hand to drop on my shoulder and read me my rights. That happens, I'm ready for it. Even with my record, I'm not risking a long time inside. Not with the way I work things now. I may sell guns, but I don't carry them.

And I keep swearing I'll never use one again.

The one place I couldn't risk the Prof invading was Kite's aerie. The way I had figured it at first, Heather was living there. The floor plan of the building backed me up on it—there was enough room for a large family in the penthouse. Wolfe had her living in that two-bedroom apartment over in the West Seventies, but I thought that was probably just a place to store her clothes and keep up appearances. Then I found out Kite owned the building she lived in. Not right out in the open—he had a corporation nested inside a holding company, and shares of that company were controlled by a real estate investment trust that also held a mini-mall in Tucson and an office building in Dallas—but he was Heather's landlord, all right.

"Bitch is a clean-freak," the Prof told me. "Joint's a fucking hospital. Got one of them filter machines, looks like a wastebasket it's so big. No carpet, nothing but tile and wood."

"Look like she lives there?"

"Yeah, I guess. Food in the fridge, stuff in the cabinets over the sink. Hamper got clothes in it, so . . . But she ain't no chef, I tell you that. All she had was them packaged meals. And a microwave."

"The food just her stuff, you think?"

"Oh yeah, bro. Ain't been no *man* in that place ever, except maybe to fix the sink or something. 'Sides that, she got a motherfucking shrine in her bedroom."

"Religious stuff?"

"Only if your boy Kite is God, Schoolboy. Got pictures of him everywhere. On the dresser, on the wall. Big bulletin board too. Bitch's got every article ever mentioned his name, it looks like. Got a trophy drawer too."

"His stuff?"

"Got to be. Only thing that ain't clean in the entire joint. One drawer, sealed, like. Got a handkerchief, pair of white silk boxer shorts—I know women be wearing that stuff now, but that Heather broad couldn't get her damn *leg* in the pair I saw. Man's shirt. An old watch. Pair of cuff links. All wrapped in tissue paper. Souvenirs, like."

"Cash? Jewelry?"

"Nothing worth taking. Cheap costume stuff. Except for the chains."

"Necklaces?"

"No, bro. Chains. You know, those little ankle bracelets. Broad's gotta have a couple of dozen of them, all different kinds. Gold, silver . . . platinum, one looked like. All different patterns too. She got them on little hooks in her closet. Like she puts on a different one every day."

"Prof, were the chains in pairs?"

"All single-o, bro. All the same exact size too—bitch has got some ankle on her! And for cash, she didn't have more than a couple yards loose, unless she had a real good hiding place. And it didn't smell that way . . . she's got that joint set up like nobody's *ever* gonna visit, understand?"

"Yeah. She have a computer?"

"Not even a typewriter. No diary, no notebook. Not even a pad to write on. She got a *big* TV set, though, got *three* VCRs stacked on top. Whole bookshelf full of tapes too, got a name and date on every one. Seems like she tapes all them daytime things, maybe watches when she gets home."

"What about books?"

"I went through 'em good, when I was looking for a cash stash. Decoration—they was new, like she never cracked them. Except for the porno . . ."

"Porno?" I asked. The Prof is a stone prude—what he thinks is pornography wouldn't raise an eyebrow in a church waiting room.

"Yeah. You know, paperbacks. Always got a broad and a guy on the cover. In them old-time costumes. Like pirates and shit."

So Heather read romances. And put Kite on the cover in her mind . . . ? "Nothing to interest the cops, huh?" I asked him.

"A *smart* cop, maybe. She got toys, bro. Brass knucks, steel snap-out baton, set of punch knives. This broad gets close enough to you, she could do some real damage."

"This is all I could put together on such short notice," Hauser told me in his gravelly voice. "The *Post*'s not on NEXIS that far back—I had to go to the morgue."

"Thanks. How're the boys?"

"They're perfect," he said.

"No kids are perfect," I told him.

"What do you know?" he sneered, throwing the electric-blue Ford Explorer in gear and lurching into traffic without looking.

Heather was telling the truth. About the lies. The clips Hauser pulled for me had it all, just like she said.

Except for the suicide note the professor sent her.

"This one was the flip side of the fat broad, Schoolboy," the Prof said a few days later, telling me about his toss of Jennifer Dalton's apartment. "Place is a pigsty. Stinks out loud. Got dirty clothes on the floor, roaches. Wouldn't surprise me she had a couple of little cheese-eaters hanging around too. Only decent-looking thing in the place was the answering machine—looked brand-new. Uses the living room for everything: eats there, probably sleeps on the couch too. The bedroom didn't have nothing but the bed. Not even a phone back there."

"What's she read?"

"Total trash, man. You know, space aliens spotted in a parking lot in Miami, getting it on with a bull gator. *TV Guide*. Confession magazines."

"No romance novels for that one, huh?"

"No romance *period*, brother. Joint *smelled* bad, I tell you."

"You come away with anything?"

"Got you this," the little man said, handing me a pair of keys.

"**S**he was a nice girl. I never said otherwise. And I still wouldn't today," the man in the blue blazer said, sitting behind one of the little gray metal desks they give salesmen in high-volume car dealerships. The gleam from the showroom washed into his cubicle, merging with the overhead fluorescent lighting to give his fleshy, well-scrubbed face a rosy glow under his short-cropped haircut. "It was just one of those things that didn't work out," he said in a brisk salesman's voice.

"Nothing . . . happened? Like a sudden event?"

"Nooo . . . ," he said slowly, drawing the word out. "It was just that we were sort of . . . thrust together. You know. Same church, same social events. Our families knew one another slightly. We didn't really have that much in common, but . . ."

"How long did you go together?"

"We dated for about a year. Maybe a little less. Then we got engaged. But we were just going through the motions—there was no spark, if you know what I mean."

"But you did plan to get married . . . ?"

"Plan? I'm not sure we had any real plan. Maybe that was the problem. We hadn't really thought things through. After a while, I just . . ."

"Met somebody else?"

"Not really. I mean, not a special person or anything. I didn't meet Melissa, my wife, until after me and Jennifer had broken up for a few months."

"Is Melissa also in the church?"

"Of course," he said, looking at me as though I had asked if it was daylight outside. "I am part of the church, and the church is part of me. I wanted children, and—"

"Did Jennifer want children?" I interrupted.

"I guess so. I mean, we never really discussed it. Like I said, we never really *talked* about very much."

"Did you like her? As a person, I mean."

"Jennifer is . . . rigid, I guess you'd call it. I mean, she's very nice. In every way, really. But she's not what you'd call a fun-loving person. Me, I'm more lively. I have to be *doing* something, you know what I mean? I'm very active in the church. And I'm a great sportsman too. Especially football."

"You follow the Giants?"

"The Jets," he said solemnly. "They are truly Job's team. And they will prevail. We must have faith. I have no use for fair-weather fans. The Jets were once mighty, but they have been suffering under a long period of adversity. I believe they are being tested. But we're going to get a lottery pick this year for sure—the *top* pick, as a matter of fact. And with the free agent draft plus—"

"Yeah," I said, cutting off the flow. "Would you say Jennifer was a religious person? When you knew her?"

"Religious? I guess so. I mean, she obeyed the tenets. She wasn't . . . passionate about our religion, but . . ."

"What about her character in general?"

"I'm not sure what you mean, her character."

"Was she an honest person?"

"Jennifer? She was one of the most honest people I ever met. She never lied, not about anything. It was one of the things I really liked about her. You know, the business I'm in, everybody has an image of it. The sleazy used car salesman. Like the crooked lawyer, right? Well, let me tell you something. In our church, lying is a great sin. One of the reasons I'm so successful is that church members would always prefer to deal with one of their own. But not because of what you might think. It's not clannishness—it's because Psalmists don't lie. If you buy a car from Roger Stewart, you're going to hear the truth about that car, new or used. And the word gets out. They tell their friends. I hope to have my own dealership someday. And when I do, it'll be because people know my word is as good as gold.

"That's the way we are. Any Psalmist who doesn't hold truth to be sacred would be shunned. Everybody knows that. Jennifer? She was a simple person. I don't mean stupid, just . . . straightforward. Nothing slick about her. Jennifer was a person who always told the truth."

"Ah, she was always in a fucking daze," the waitress told me, shaking her head hard enough to rattle her mop of carrot-color curls. "Couldn't get an order straight, dropped trays. I don't know why Mack hired her, I swear."

"Mack, he's the boss?"

"Boss? For here, I guess so. He's just the goddamned cook, that's all. But he gets to pick the girls, so I guess that makes him something. At least he thinks he is, anyway."

"How long did she work here?"

"Coupla months, maybe. I'm not sure. You gonna order something to drink with that burger?"

"Yeah. Give me a beer."

"What's 'a beer'? You want draft, bottle, what?"

"Whatever you got."

"You ain't particular, huh?"

"Not about beer."

"Ah, I heard about you private eyes," she said, twitching her hips a little, smiling to let me know she was just playing.

"How come she left?" I asked her when she came back with the beer.

"Left? She got canned, honey. Dumped out on her skinny ass. The customers here, they ain't too choosy, you know what I mean? But they don't go for screw-ups all the time. I mean, maybe they would if *I* was doing it"—she grinned—"but I know how to talk to customers. Men, especially—that's about all we get in here. Jenny, she didn't know squat. Girl probably didn't make five bucks a night in tips, even on a full shift."

"You do much better than that yourself?"

"Me? Honey, any night I don't go home with an extra fifty, I figure I'm losing it, you know what I mean? A joint like this, the guys like you to clown around a bit with them, you know what I mean? Jenny, she walked around like she had a sharp stick up her ass. Customer says something to her, she don't even come back at him. Me, I know how to handle myself. I know how to keep them in line, and I know how to play them too. That's part of the business. . . ."

"Ever had any other trouble with her? Before she split?"

"Like what?"

"I don't know. Swiping tips from other tables, dipping in the register . . ."

"Jenny? She was one of those Christian freaks, you know what I mean? One time, she was about ten minutes late. Anyone else, they woulda just told Mack the bus was late or something. You know what she says? She says she didn't get up on time, that's all. Mack told her he'd have to dock her pay. Just kidding around. You know, get a rise outta her. She says, that's okay—that's only fair. A real space cadet, like I told you."

"Thanks for your time," I said.

"You gonna drink that beer?"

"No."

"So why'd you order it, then?" flashing me another come-on smile.

"So I could leave you a bigger tip," I said, tossing an extra twenty onto the greasy Formica tabletop.

"**S**he always paid the rent on time," the stolid-looking middle-aged woman in the dull blue housedress told me, the chain on the door to her apartment still latched. "Every Saturday."

"She paid in cash?"

"You a bill collector?"

"Private investigator," I told her.

"What'd she do?"

"She didn't do anything. I'm just checking background. She might be in for an inheritance."

"Like in a will?"

"That's right. But we want to make sure she's the actual party."

"Huh?"

"Well, it's a common name, Jennifer Dalton. There could be more than one."

"Well, she's real thin. Scrawny, like. Never took care of herself. Real pasty-faced, like she never went out."

"Did she?"

"What?"

"Go out?"

"I mind my own business," the woman lied. "All I care about, they don't have nobody over in their rooms, that's all."

"Did she ever get mail?"

"Utilities included in the rent," the woman said. "And she didn't have no phone in her room."

"But . . . ?" I asked, letting her see the fan of ten-dollar bills in my right hand.

"She got two, maybe three letters all the time she was here."

"Personal letters?"

"How would I know that?"

"Were they window envelopes? Like you get from a company? Did they have stamps on them or a postage meter? Were the envelopes colored or white? Regular size or—?"

"Okay, I see what you mean now. They was little envelopes. And they wasn't typed. You know, handwriting. With stamps."

"Who were they from?"

"That wasn't on the—"

I stood there waiting, holding the money.

"There wasn't no name besides hers," she said. "All I could see, they come from New York."

"I could get in trouble for this," the black man with the shaved head said. "Real trouble, man." His arms bulged from the short sleeves of his white cotton orderly's shirt. A dull white patch of skin ran across his lower cheek. Knife scar.

"They're just photocopies, right?" I told him. "No big deal."

"Fuck if it ain't, man. They catch me doing it, I'm gone. Histor-*ee*, Jack. Just like that."

"Yeah. Well, it's already done, true? You got them right there in your hand."

"That's right," he said, neck muscles rigid. "And they ain't going in *your* hand unless I see some green."

"Five yards, like I said. I'm holding the coin—let me see the goods."

He spread the paper out across the scarred wood table in the barbecue joint, glancing over his shoulder as he did. I didn't touch the paper, just scanned it quickly with my eyes. The name and social security number matched what I had. Date of birth too. Okay.

"Let's do it," I said, reaching into my pocket.

"Hold up, man," he said, covering the paper with a large, thick hand. The nails were long, yellowish and horny, starting to hook. "Like I told you . . . this is hot stuff. Seems like there oughta be something more in it for me."

"There isn't," I said flatly.

"A couple more yards won't hurt you," he said sullenly.

"It's not in the budget."

"Yeah, well, fuck a whole bunch of that 'budget' shit. Man, that's all I hear at the hospital: 'Budget.' I got me a budget too."

"We had a deal," I reminded him.

"Yeah, well, deals get changed."

I held his eyes for a few seconds, the brown iris running into the yellowish white. The last time he'd been to prison, he probably got some strange ideas about white men—if I went a dime over what I'd agreed, he'd be thinking "fish," and that wouldn't do. "Maybe some other time," I said, ice-polite, getting up.

"Wait up, man! Don't be so cold."

"Those papers are no good to you," I said quietly, still standing. "They aren't worth a dime. Fact is, I don't take them off your hands, you got to burn them. I got five hundred dollars in my pocket. I'm gonna trade or fade, pal. Pick one."

He held out his hand for the money, muttering something under his breath.

I got what I paid for. The hospital had wanted to hold her after the emergency admission, but the "AMA" note at the bottom of the chart told the story. She had signed herself out Against Medical Advice. She hadn't opened up to the social worker who'd interviewed her—not a single mention of the hair-pulling. And not a hint of Brother Jacob anywhere in the slim file of papers.

A psychiatric resident had written up the case after speaking to her, laying it out in the cold language shrinks use to label human beings.

DSM III-R DIAGNOSES (DISCHARGE)

AXIS I:	A)	POST-TRAUMATIC STRESS DISORDER, 309.89
	B)	R/O DYSTHYMIA
	C)	R/O MAJOR DEPRESSION, RECURRENT, UNSPECIFIED
AXIS II:	A)	HISTRIONIC PERSONALITY FEATURES
	B)	R/O BORDERLINE PERSONALITY DISORDER
AXIS III:	A)	SUICIDE ATTEMPT
	B)	ASTHMA
AXIS IV:	SEVERE (JOBLESS, BROKE UP WITH FIANCÉ)	
AXIS V:	GAF CURRENT = 55; PAST YEAR = 45–65	

Back in my office, I used my own copy of the DSM—the *Diagnostic and Statistical Manual of Mental Disorders*—to decode the shorthand. The suicide attempt was the "presenting problem." The clinical picture was mostly guesses: "R/O" means "rule out"—a possibility they wanted to consider once they got her into treatment.

But that never happened.

They put down getting fired and breaking up with her boyfriend as "psycho-social stressors," writing it like they happened at the same time. Probably the way she told it.

And GAF was "Global Assessment of Functioning." The score was her highest level in the last year. A 55 meant "severe symptoms; significant interference in functioning." Good guess.

The whole file was nothing but outline sketches. Except for one handwritten note: "Patient states she has attempted suicide at least twice before. Expressed regret only in her lack of success . . . 'I even failed at this.' No insight exhibited during interview."

If Jennifer Dalton knew why she tried to take herself off the count, she wasn't telling.

Not them. And not then.

"**D**oc, you remember that guy you told me about, Bruce Perry? The one working on the brain-trauma stuff?"

"Yeah," he said slowly, waiting for the punch line. "You got a good memory, hoss."

"I got a case. A legit case," I assured him quickly. "And I think he's the man for me to talk to. Can you set it up?"

"I'm listening," Doc said, his wrestler's upper body shifting behind the cluttered desk, eyes homing in the way they did years ago when we first started talking. When I was inside the Walls. Telling me there better be more.

"I've been doing a lot of that myself—listening," I told him. "A girl says something happened. A long time ago. It happened, but she didn't know it. Or didn't remember it anyway. Until now."

"Recovered memory?"

"That's what she says."

"And *you* say . . . ?"

"I don't know what to say. That's the job—for me to say."

He leaned back in his chair, eyes still on mine behind the wire-rimmed glasses he always wears. "We go back a long way, Burke. You've spent more time studying child abuse than any Ph.D. I know. Your gut's as good as anyone's. What do you need Perry for?"

"He's a science guy, right? Hard science, not the blah-de-blah stuff."

"Like I do?" Doc asked. Not challenging me, just getting at it, the way he always did.

"What you do . . . it's only as good as the guy doing it, right?"

"Sure. Same as building a house. Or fixing teeth. Or playing the piano."

"But there's a *truth* somewhere, Doc. A true truth. Like the way they test for gold—you drop the chemicals on the metal and you see the truth."

"You think Perry's stuff is like that?"

"Don't you?"

"I'm not sure yet, hoss. Could be. Tell you what—I'll give him a call and tell *him* the truth. About you too, understand? He wants to go for it, that's up to him."

"Thanks, Doc. I owe you."

"Yeah, right," he said, waving me out of his office.

The flight touched down at Houston International at two-thirty, on time even with the transfer from DFW—there were no nonstops out of New York, and you couldn't pay me to fly out of Newark. When I got to the hotel, there was a note waiting for me at the desk.

Hi! We're already here, me and Jennifer. It's all set up. Dr. Perry said to call him as soon as you're settled.

The handwriting was rounded, immature. Signed: "H."

"**T**he best predictors of current functioning are past experiences. The most critical part of any evaluation, then, is getting a thorough, accurate history," the man said, smiling sheepishly as though he knew how pompous the words sounded. He was tall, well put together, with a frank, open face and thick tousled hair. Looked like a recruiting poster for North Dakota. "Childhood experiences have a grossly disproportionate effect on adult functioning . . . and those experiences are almost exclusively provided by adults."

"But what if the patient is the only source of that history, Doctor?" I asked him, watching my language, wondering what he'd been told about me. I'd already guessed the dress code wrong: I had on a dove-gray silk suit and a conservative tie; he was wearing a blue chambray shirt with the sleeves rolled up and a pair of weathered jeans over scuffed cowboy boots.

"It doesn't matter. I would still look for a set of emotional or social characteristics in the family which would increase a child's vulnerability—those factors which make children feel isolated, inadequate, lonely, unattractive, incompetent . . . *different*," he said, leaning forward, engaging me, telling me to ignore the heavy language and listen to the core. "A harsh, demanding, cold parent . . . an overwhelmed, depressed parent . . . absence of supportive extended family . . . social isolation . . . a parent who was raised abusively who hasn't come to terms with it—"

"Most families weren't the Brady Bunch," I said, cutting him off. I know there's always a price to pay for information, but I hadn't come all that way to listen to what I'd learned before this guy had been born.

"Sure," he replied, nodding. "But those factors tend to be transgenerational. It's rare to find an adult who was neglected, humiliated, unloved—made to feel worthless for whatever reason—who can easily provide optimal nurturing. You can't give something you never received."

"Yeah, you can," I said, greeting his sermon with a flat prison-yard stare.

He was quiet for a minute. "You think I'm sugar-coating it?" he asked.

"I don't know *what* you're doing," I told him. "It sounds like you're telling me someone like Jennifer could be an easy target because—"

"Look," he said, cutting me off. "Not all stealth predators are successful. Many are rebuffed—"

"Stealth predators?"

"Those who don't use force. They operate from within what the child believes is a safety zone—they're always people the child has been told can be trusted—and they proceed in highly stylized ways. They would call it 'seduction.' We call it what it is: hunting."

"And some kids just blow them off?"

"A good many do just that, in one way or another. But if the child was reared in a highly competitive or consistently humiliating environment, if the child's primary caregiver was overwhelmed or emotionally distant, that child might be susceptible to what feels like . . . caring."

"So for the kid to be set up, he doesn't actually have to be abused?"

"Emotional abuse is as devastating as any other form, Mr. Burke," he said, his voice not open to argument. "And it leaves as indelible a physical scar on the developing brain as a brand would on the skin."

"So your mother telling you you're a piece of shit is the same as your father fucking you every night?"

"Children don't react to inputs the same way adults do," he said, turning aside my deliberately coarse language, waving his hand to tell me to wait until he was finished. "Let me put it this way: The nearer the target, the more damaging even the slightest blow can be. And when the target is the developing human heart . . ."

"You think that's what turned her into a puller?" I asked, trying to get him off the soapbox and on to the reason I came.

"The trichotillomania? Most likely. That's very primitive, self-soothing behavior. You remember your college psychology? The 'fight or flight' reaction?"

I nodded so he'd keep going. I guess Doc hadn't told him everything when he'd vouched for me. Me, I had what you'd call a lower education. But the tuition had been a lot more costly than college. Started much earlier too.

"Well, it's palpable ignorance to believe a *baby* has those options," Perry said, anger flashing across his handsome face. "When a baby is threatened, she can't fight and she can't flee. And when the threat actually induces *terror*, sometimes the only option is to run to a 'safe' place . . . to dissociate. Cut off the pain and threat from the outside world and stay inside. Deep inside. Dissociation is connected to a release of endorphins—you know, natural opiates—and the result is soothing, pleasurable. The inner retreat 'feels' good to the baby. It is, if you will, rewarding."

I thought about Fancy, a girl I knew a long time ago—Fancy telling me how the taste of the whip got all the endorphins racing through her brain. Made her feel *good.* But I didn't say anything, just shifted my body posture enough to let him know I was listening.

"And because the brain 'learns' from experience," Perry went on, "behaviors and emotions that result in 'reward' are repeated. Eventually, the child continues to seek that reward even if the original stimulus—the threat or the terror—isn't present. That's one of the keys to the survival of our species. Would it surprise you to know that those same biochemical 'rewards' can be released when a baby smiles at a woman holding her?"

"The mother gets an endorphin rush?"

"If you like," he said, ignoring my tone of voice. "The point is that the woman holding the baby is rewarded for the baby's smile . . . and seeks that smile the same way a terrorized child seeks safety. That's part of the reason why mothers protect their children. But that capability, it's only a genetic potential. If the caretaker herself was never fed or held, never nurtured or loved as an infant, those biochemical 'reward' systems in her brain don't develop to the maximum. So when *her* baby smiles, the 'reward' isn't as powerful. And she's not as impelled to seek it again."

So maybe my mother's mother hadn't . . . I threw that thought into the garbage can I keep in my mind for things like that, looked him in the face, and took him back to Jennifer Dalton: "What if this 'reward' gets thin after a while?" I asked him.

"Thin?"

"Like dope. After a while, what used to get you high doesn't even get you off the ground."

"Dose-related, right," he agreed. "Are you asking if—?"

"If pulling didn't give her enough, make her feel good enough, could she start cutting on herself?"

"That happens sometimes," he answered, temporizing. "It's not always so progressive—we don't see that all the time. It does happen, but . . ."

"But it's rare, right?"

"Trichotillomania is rare, sure. So is self-mutilation. Pain signals have the ability to turn on the brain's endorphins, like I said earlier. Children living in a constant state of terror may overdevelop those systems, like a bodybuilder overtaxing a muscle to make it grow. The more you use *any* part of the brain, the more it develops. So instead of feeling more 'pain' when they pull their hair or cut themselves, they actually feel more soothed. Their brain systems are organized differently from those of the rest of us."

That's *you,* not *us,* I thought, thinking how violence had soothed me so many times when I was younger. Not my pain; someone else's. Sometimes *anyone* else's . . .

"What we're looking for is . . . plausibility," he continued. "A set of circumstances that could account for high vulnerability. We look for evidence in the individual's ability to give their own history . . . and then we look for 'dissociative' gaps," he said, using two fingers tapping against each thumb to make quote marks around the word, "spaces where recollection of key experiences is fuzzy, incomplete— or even missing entirely."

"Liars would have spaces in their memory too," I reminded him.

"Not usually," he said. "In fact, skilled liars—malingerers, we would call them—often display a richness of detail that the average, honest person might not."

I filed that one away—a professional never stops learning.

"The brain stores traumatic experiences differently from others," Perry went on. "Because when the brain is in a state of alarm, it pays attention. So words are stored much less efficiently than the nonverbal signals that are important to survival—facial expressions, body movements, sounds, smells. We remember trauma at some level, but suppression is a factor in that equation too. Recall is scattered—the resulting narrative isn't always linear or precise. So we don't rely on it totally. We try to determine how an individual feels about specific traumatic events . . . and whether they can identify trauma-related cues. That's why we use self-report forms too."

"You mean what patients say about themselves?"

"Yes, and the usual standard psychological tests as well. We want to examine various aspects of the patient's personality—coping styles, IQ, the themes of the patient's inner world . . . hopes, fears, wishes. But in this case, we have hypnotically refreshed memory, and that raises some other issues."

"Like . . . ?"

"We use the Stanford Susceptibility Index—we want to know if the patient is easily hypnotized."

"You can tell that from the way they answer questions on a test?"

"No," he said. "Here, let me show you. Follow my finger with your eyes."

He moved it left, right, up, down, finally looping his finger all the way up, way past my vision. "Okay, now, without following my finger, roll your eyes up as far as they can go."

I did it.

"So?" I asked him.

"Generally, the more white exposed on the extreme eye-rolls, the more susceptible to hypnosis the patient is."

"How'd I do?"

"Fine," he said, something flitting quickly across his face. "We also need a sleep history," he said quickly. "If the patient has chronic difficulty falling asleep, or wakes up suddenly—especially about three hours after they fall asleep—we have some indication of dysregulation of the noradrenergic system."

I wanted to ask him if he had an English-speaking translator on the grounds, but I settled for: "Nora-what?"

"Norepinephrine is a chemical—like the other chemicals I talked about for the reward systems—only these noradrenergic systems are the main mediators of the fear response. And when someone is exposed to traumatic stress—especially in childhood, when those systems are first organizing—those systems become hyperreactive."

"Even when the kid's asleep?"

"If the whole *environment* is stressful, sure. The key is the heart—it's only one synapse away from the brain. Trauma increases the heart rate. If the environment is heavily laced with trauma, you get an over-reaction to even the most simple stressors . . . and that brings on a major change in functioning. You see it in all traumatized individuals: anxiety, impulsivity, depression, aggression . . . even dissociation."

"So you put them on an EKG machine and wait for . . . ?"

"Pretty close. Actually, the instrument we use looks like a wrist-watch; kids get used to it in seconds. When we—or they—bring up a traumatic topic, the heart rate increases. And when the internal anxiety gets high enough, the brain has to 'act,'" he said, making the quote-marks sign again, "and this can be a primary, *external* behavior—like agitation or aggression—or a primary *internal* response: freezing, going numb, dissociation. If the response to threat is external, the heart rate stays elevated. But if the response is dissociation, the heart rate plateaus . . . and ultimately decreases. We can actually track this, in association with specific cues. And with time-sequenced video, we get a very precise assessment of what topics and what cues and what stimuli are associated with a deeply in-grained memory . . . the memory of the state of fear present in the original trauma." He took a deep breath. "Is any of this making any sense to you?" he asked in an apologetic tone. Perry used language in exactly the opposite way lawyers did—he didn't want to hide be-hind it; he wanted you to *get* it. A fucking genius without being ar-rogant, explaining the meaning of life with that "aw, shucks" farmboy front—he must be a killer on the fund-raising circuit.

"A normal person gets scared, their heartbeat goes up," I told him. "Eventually, that calms them. If they've been abused, the heart rate just keeps climbing until they go somewhere else in their heads. To a safe place. *Then* the heartbeat slows down. Like the tail wag-ging the dog," I said softly. Thinking how I learned to do it for my-self: staring at a red dot on my mirror, going *into* that dot until I wasn't afraid anymore. I didn't get all his vocabulary, but if you translated it, every abused kid in the world would recognize it.

He nodded, not saying anything.

I stayed quiet too, listening for my own heartbeat.

The hotel was set up right inside the hospital complex. For families who wanted to stay around while a patient was hospitalized, Perry told me. That way they could be close at hand, feel more a part of the process. I figured I'd stay there too, took a two-room suite for the duration.

After I unpacked, I took a stroll until I found a pay phone. Then I called Mama.

"All quiet," she said. "You okay?"

"Sure," I told her. I gave her the number of the hotel room, just in case.

I went back, took a shower, and started reading over some of the material Perry had given me, wishing I'd brought my medical dictionary along. I began reading this stuff years ago, swiping books from Doc's library in the prison. Doc never admitted he knew what I was up to, but whenever he left a book lying around for too long, I knew he meant me to take it. Maybe if he'd known I was running a nice little business writing phony psych reports another inmate clerk substituted for the real ones that went to the parole board, he wouldn't have been so eager to further my education.

I always returned the books when I was done. Couple of things I learned in prison: nothing you stole was ever really safe in your cell, but once it went into your head, no goon-squad shakedown could take it back.

When I was locked down, I used to read all the time—that's where I got my vocabulary. But I don't do it as much anymore. Like the guys who stopped lifting iron soon as they hit the bricks. There's other ways to pass time once you're free.

I'd forgotten how much I'd loved it, reading and studying. I'll bet if I'd been raised by humans instead of a collection of freaks and the fucking State, I'd have been . . . a scientist, maybe. I don't know.

I know I wouldn't have been what I am now. You don't get born bad.

jumped when the phone rang next to the bed. None of the crew would call me here unless . . .

"What?"

"Burke? It's me. Heather. I'm in the hotel too. You got my note, right? They're keeping Jennifer overnight. To run some tests or something. Did you eat yet?"

I glanced at my watch. Jesus! It was almost nine o'clock—I'd been lost in Perry's stuff for hours.

"Ah, no. I was just gonna—"

"Can we have dinner together? We don't have to go anyplace, okay? Just room service and—"

"Where's Kite?" I asked her.

"He's back . . . home. Working on the case."

"Yeah, okay. Dinner. You want me to—?"

"My room's really small. Could I come up there?"

"Sure. Whenever you're ready."

"I'll be right up," she said.

dug out the room service menu. Sounded pretty good, reading down the list. But they always do, I guess. It wasn't five minutes before I heard a tentative knock at the door. Heather. In a bone-colored business suit and matching pumps and stockings. The only traces of color were her black-cherry hair and a black lace bra she wore instead of a blouse under her jacket. And her orange eyes under long dark lashes.

"You look very nice," I told her.

"You too," she said politely, as though my white sweatshirt and chinos was an evening ensemble.

She took a seat on the couch, knees touching decorously. I handed her the room service menu. She studied it carefully, tracing each item with a blunt white-lacquered fingernail. "You want a steak?" she finally asked.

"Sure."

"Salad?"

"Whatever."

"I'll take care of it," she said, getting to her feet. She walked over to the desk and sat down in the straight chair next to it. She picked up a ballpoint pen and one of those cheap little pads you find in hotels, crossed her legs like a steno getting ready to work. "How do you want your steak?" she asked, looking over at me, poised to write.

I gave her the whole order, right down to a pineapple juice with plenty of ice. She called it in, speaking slowly and carefully, like it was real important to her that they got it exactly right in the kitchen.

"It'll be about forty minutes," she said when she hung up the phone. "Is that okay?"

"Yeah, it's normal. Eight minutes to microwave it, half an hour to bring it here."

"It's pretty late to be eating dinner, huh?"

"It just feels later—we're an hour behind New York down here, remember?"

"Oh. Yeah, I forgot. What do you . . . think of it? I mean, so far?"

"No way to tell," I said. "Anyway, it's only a piece of the puzzle, right?"

"Right. I mean . . . I guess so. But . . . this was your idea, wasn't it?"

"You mean, not Kite's?"

"Yes. He never even *heard* of this place," she said.

"You sound surprised."

"Well, I was a little. It's so . . . complete here. I mean, they have *everything*. I thought it would be . . . famous, like."

"It might be, someday. But it's brand-new now. And I don't think they're much about publicity—I'm sure the last thing they need is more customers."

"It's mostly kids, huh? I mean, when I was waiting. With Jennifer. It seemed like the place was full of kids."

"Sure. That's why we're here with her, isn't it? Something that happened when she was a kid?"

"I know. It's just that . . . you know what I was thinking? That maybe there should be a special place. Just for grown-ups who had it . . . happen when they were kids. Not a kids' place. You understand what I mean?"

"They have places like that, Heather. Places full of grown-ups who got all fucked up when they were kids."

"What . . . places?"

"Prisons. Whorehouses. Psycho wards."

Her face fell. "I don't *mean* that. There are plenty of . . . kids who didn't turn out like that. No matter what happened to them."

"That's true. I'm not arguing with you. Being abused . . . it's no guarantee."

"It's no excuse either," she said, looking at me with those orange eyes.

A gentle knock at the door. Room service. Guy in a maroon uniform with black piping on the sleeves, OSCAR on an aluminum strip over his heart. He wheeled in a table of food, spent a few minutes showily setting it up: uncapping the dishes, laying out the silverware, working hard for the ten bucks I eventually put on top of the bill after I signed it.

"Thank you, sir. Just call Room Service when you want the table cleared away."

The food was okay. Nothing spectacular. But the steak was medium-well, the way I'd ordered it, the salad was crisp, with no brown on the lettuce, and they didn't stint on the ice. Heather tore into it with gusto, cleaning her plate and uncapping the goblet of vanilla ice cream like a gold miner unearthing a plump nugget.

"I shouldn't eat so much," she said, smiling.

"Why not?"

"Because I'm *fat*," she said.

"No you're not," I told her matter-of-factly.

Her face flushed. She dropped her eyes, saying nothing.

It was past eleven by the time Oscar had collected the food table. I sat back in the only easy chair the hotel put in the suite, lit a cigarette, and closed my eyes.

"You have a headache?" Heather asked softly. If the cigarette puzzled her, her voice didn't show it.

"No big deal," I told her, wondering how she could have known. "They never last."

"You want an aspirin or something?" she said, making a circuit of the room turning off the lights. The curtains were open and the room was flooded with moonlight, strong enough to see by.

"No, I'm fine."

She went into the bathroom, closed the door behind her. I smoked slowly, letting the dark quiet comfort my headache. Just as I finished the cigarette, the bathroom door opened and Heather stepped into the moonlight. The only white left on her was her body. The black bra topped a matching garter belt, the hooks dangling loose against her round thighs. She was barefoot.

"Still think I'm not fat?" she whispered across the room.

The moonlight penetrated the bedroom too. Heather's pale body gleamed in the reflection. On her knees, her hands clasped at the intersection of her thighs, she looked down at me lying on my back, hands behind my head, listening, eyes slitted so she was a soft blur.

"I don't know a lot about . . . this part," she said, biting her lower lip. She reached behind her and unclasped the black bra. Her breasts spilled out in a lush tumble. She cupped them, pulling them toward her mouth, licked the top of each one. "I used to do this all the time," she said. "By myself. When I was alone. I wanted to know what it felt like."

I didn't say anything, just made a sound to let her know I was paying attention, waiting for the rest of it, whatever it was.

She dropped her breasts—they bounced hard against her rib cage. Her eyes narrowed and she unhooked the garter belt, tossing it aside. Then she put her hands on the insides of her thighs, pulling them apart. She was as hairless as a baby, not even a trace of a razor's shadow in the moonlight. A white-tipped fingernail disappeared inside her, orange eyes steady on mine. "I used to taste this too. So I'd know . . ."

"Know what, Heather?"

"Why he did it," she whispered. "It seemed so strange to me." She pulled her hand away, put the tip of her finger into her mouth.

"Did you ever figure it out?" I asked her.

"No. It even . . . hurt a little bit. It doesn't hurt now, though."

"Did he want you to . . . shave everything too?" I asked gently. Getting close to it, but leaving her room to run if she wanted to.

"It's not shaved," she said, spreading her thighs even further. "It's gone forever. Electrolysis. I had it everywhere."

"Damn! That must have been painful. Why did—?"

"I told you before," she said. "I don't mind pain. I know how to take it."

"Do you—?"

"I don't want you to talk about it. I want you to look, okay? Just look. How old do you think I am? To look at me, I mean."

"Twenty-eight?"

"I'm not, you know. I'm . . . older than that."

"It doesn't matter."

"Yes it *does*. You know it does. To a man, I mean."

"Different men are—"

"Men are the same," she said in a harsh whisper. "All the same. Every one I ever met. Except . . . one."

"Look, girl, you don't have to—"

"I don't have to do anything, do I? I know. That's true, now. I don't have to do anything. You don't have to either. But it looks like you want to. Do you?"

"Yes."

"Would you . . . do it like I want? I only . . ."

"What?"

"Could you . . . stand up? And not say anything?"

I got to my feet, watching her face.

"Come around. Behind me. Please."

I walked around to the foot of the bed. Heather bent forward and pulled a pillowcase off the pillow. She carefully fitted it over her head, all the way down to her neck. Then she dropped her shoulders to the bed, her buttocks high and elevated. The way she'd been on the floor of Kite's apartment after I'd climbed off her and released my hold on her neck.

I felt the baby oil girding my cock as I entered her. She was tight, but I couldn't feel even a trace of stubble—her sacrifice had gone deep. I felt the talcum powder on her wide hips, followed her deep-set spine with my eyes from the cleft of her rump until it disappeared under the pillowcase, heard her stifled breathing, felt the spasms inside her as she let go.

I was right behind her, locked in hard. She slowly slid forward on her belly, disengaging from me. Then she turned on her side and slowly pulled the pillowcase off her head. I lay down next to her. She burrowed her head in my right shoulder, whispered, "That was good, wasn't it?" a halo of anxiety around the soft words.

"Perfect," I lied, patting her black-cherry hair.

She drifted in and out of sleep after that. Every time she'd come around, she'd start talking. She never kissed or cuddled, but she'd always reach for my hand before she said anything.

"You didn't say anything about the . . . pillowcase," she whispered.

"I . . ."

"I know what you think. I have low self-esteem, right? But that's a lie."

"I don't—"

"That's those stupid talk shows. I watch them all the time. Hundreds of them. Every night, when I get home. I tape them all. For him. For the research. The people in the audience, they're . . . cruel. Some poor woman is sitting on the stage. All alone, telling her story. And no matter what it is, no matter what horrible things happened to her, some nasty smug little person stands up, grabs the microphone, and tells her: 'You have low self-esteem!' Like that's supposed to be so fucking brilliant. Like it's supposed to *fix* everything. Low self-esteem . . . those people, they don't know anything about it."

I knew most of it by then. But I didn't push for the missing piece—I knew it would come.

"**H**ow did you know, Heather?" I asked her later, still lying next to her.

"Know what?"

"How to do it."

"I *don't*. Not really. I mean . . ."

"Not . . . what we just did. I don't mean that. When you made the . . . false allegation. About that professor? You said you knew what to tell the cops. About what he supposedly did. If you hadn't actually . . ."

"He loved me," she whispered. "A true love. When I was little, he loved me. If I hadn't . . . matured, he still would have, I know. Not my . . . boobs. That was all right. Little girls sometimes have them early. I did. When I was only ten, I already . . . But the . . . other stuff: hair and all . . . As soon as I did, he stopped. Just stopped. That's when he left."

"Your father?"

She found my hand in the moonlight, squeezed it into numbness while she cried for a long time.

The clock read almost three in the morning, before she got to the part I didn't know. "I would *never* have sex with him," she said. "He doesn't do that. He's not like other men. He's like a . . . god. It was hard, at first. I thought it was just *me* he didn't want. I did everything I could to . . . but he never paid any attention."

"Maybe he's gay," I said, voice neutral.

"He's *not*," she snapped. "He's just . . . higher, that's all. Higher than other men. I'm with him all the time. For years. I even told him if there was something . . . special he wanted, I would do it. Whatever it was. But that's not the way he is. He doesn't have those feelings. He's pure."

"But he likes it when you . . . dress up, right?"

"No! I mean, it doesn't matter. He sees the way men look at me. Women too, some of them. He knows I like that. He knows I'm . . . weak, I guess. People are weak—he always says that. It's the truth, what he says. But that doesn't make it bad."

"No."

"No, it doesn't. You thought him and me, we—"

"Sure. Why not?"

"It would be like having sex with a priest or something," she said. "I didn't use to see that, but I do now. I would never . . ."

I looked into her orange eyes, and I got it then.

"When do you do the brain stuff?" I asked Perry two mornings later. It was almost eleven, the time he said he'd have free for me.

"Well . . . actually, *all* of this has been 'brain stuff.' We reviewed every available record, her self-report forms for past recollections and current symptoms, the cognitive and projective test results . . . and Jennifer has had a series of nonstressed, unstructured clinical contacts during which we monitored her heart rate. We videotaped all those interviews and time-sequenced the tapes with the continuous heart rate data. So up to now, it's all been relatively unintrusive. She has been exposed to a variety of our team members. I don't do any of the initial work—I just kind of float around the perimeter so they grow accustomed to my presence. When I sit down to do the actual forensic interview, I want to be richly informed, but I don't want to be the gatherer of the information."

"Because . . . ?" I prompted him.

"The nonstructured interview is a critical component," he explained. "But before we use that technique, we need to know some evocative cues: what will set them off. When it comes to memories, some of the most reliable and powerful cues are olfactory—smells. These tend to be very deeply ingrained . . . so that if a particular smell is associated with a buried trauma, one whiff and the patient can be right back there. A classic example is the smell of bleach; for many children, it is reminiscent of the smell of semen. Or ask a Vietnam vet about the smell of flesh and napalm—it doesn't go away. We see this with kids in here all the time, even when they're way too young to speak."

I still remember smells. From that foul war in Biafra. Dead flesh, ripe-to-bursting from the relentless jungle sun. And the terror stench from those packed-earth tunnels they called bomb shelters. That was just a stink—I've smelled it since, and I stay in control.

But I remember the smell of chains too. The chains they put on me in that basement of the foster home. To hold me against that post while they . . .

Maybe that's why the first time the cops tried to put handcuffs on me I fought them so hard they had to knock me unconscious. I came to, blood fogging my eyes, trapped, hate and fear struggling for supremacy in my soul, wishing for a gun with all my tiny heart. I was nine then. I shoved the memory away, reached down and grabbed my center, calmed my voice. Asked him: "So you just . . . watch them to see if they react?"

If he'd noticed anything, it didn't show on his face. "No," he said. "As a matter of fact, external observation is bound to give you inaccurate results. One of our most remarkable findings is that the heart monitor is often inconsistent with affect. A child can be telling us about his home, nothing intense, just describing a regular day. His heart rate is predictable, varying according to his narrative. But then we introduce an innocuous word, like 'bedtime,' and although the narrative doesn't change, the needles bounce to the sky."

"Like a polygraph?"

"No," he said, a hint of sharpness in his voice. "There's no real connection. The child isn't being tested for truth. It's an internal probe—it has to be tightly focused to really work. At different points during the interviews—while we're monitoring heart rate and videotaping—we collect samples of stress-response hormones: melatonin and cortisol. We ask the kids to chew some Trident, and at different points they spit into a little tube. Then we measure these hormones—"

"Which is where the brain . . . ?" I asked, starting to struggle a little bit.

"Again, all these things give us different parts of the whole picture of how the individual's brain is organized. How it functions; how it is regulated. And after all this, we look more directly at brain processing by putting EEG leads on the child's head and have her read a series of vignettes from her life, which we put together when we gathered her history. One would be an account of a neutral event; another, say, a sad event. And then an event that should elicit a 'trauma' response," he said, making the quote-marks sign. "We can examine how different parts of the brain are activated and which parts shut down. . . ."

"So you don't actually ask them questions?"

"Not at this point. Not about the actual . . . allegations. Later, during the final forensic interview, which I conduct, I will. We want to match those responses, not only against her individual patterns of brain reactivity but against those of individuals who experienced similar events at similar times in their development."

"Okay," I said, thinking it through. "But what if someone did a lot of reading? You know, on child sexual abuse. They'd already know what people who'd been abused were supposed to feel, right?"

Perry's face tightened, but his voice went on smoothly, as though he hadn't caught what I was really asking him. "One of the most useful procedures we will use this next couple of days is during the sleep study. In some people, we can see changes in their brain activity when they're exposed to sounds or smells associated with the original trauma. 'Lying' under those conditions, clearly, is not possible."

"But how do you know—"

"Excuse me for interrupting, Mr. Burke. Look, the brain develops over time. It doesn't just come as this minibrain that grows into a big brain, like a pumpkin from a seed—it grows sequentially and almost all in the first three years of life. First the brain stem, then the midbrain, then the limbic system, and finally the cortex—that part that allows us to 'think.' When we look at the data from *all* these comprehensive evaluations, we can literally place in what part of the brain the dysfunction resides. This allows us to fix the time, to some degree, when the disrupting event—the trauma—took place.

"See, when adults are traumatized, they will have *event-specific* changes in brain functioning. But when a child is traumatized—while the brain is still in development, still organizing—the trauma acts like a fault line, impacting everything that grows around and over it. The neurobiology of the traumatized adult will be different from that of the traumatized child. In a child, the alterations will be more pervasive. And those vulnerabilities may not show up until later in life."

"Like a scar? A scar you can't see unless you know . . . ?"

"More like a substance that fluoresces under a special light or turns color when exposed to a specific reagent. Like the field test for cocaine . . . ?"

"Yeah, I get it," I told him, meaning it.

A young woman with the face of an Indian princess and braided black hair to match rapped against the jamb of the open door to Perry's office. She was wearing blue surgical scrubs, her face set in severe lines. When he looked up, the nurse said: "She got a court order. She's coming to visit him. This afternoon. At three o'clock. What should we . . . ?"

"Set up the Munchausen camera," he answered her. "You know, the fiber-optic one? Tell Ronnie to monitor. If she makes a move on the kid, you stop her, right then and there, understand?"

"Yes!" The woman flashed a smile, as if someone had just given her a present.

Perry turned back to me like he'd never left the track. "The key to understanding the brain is to understand its role in mediating every signal that the organism receives. The brain processes information, and some early-childhood damage *changes* the way the brain works. If you wave at a little baby," he said, waggling his hand to show me what he meant, "the baby coos and giggles, right? But for *some* babies, when they see an adult's hand raised, you get a startle reaction instead. That's not because the baby has *learned* a raised hand means a blow; it's because, to that baby, the brain translates that raised hand so it *becomes* a blow, you see? It's not *learning*; it's processing."

"And once that's locked in . . ."

"Yeah, that's right," he said sadly. "It takes an enormous amount of work, highly skilled work, over a long time, to even have a *chance* of modifying it. Trauma generalizes—that's its nature. So instead of the child being afraid of the man who hurt her, she becomes afraid of all men, understand? The brain takes the baby to a safe place in response to chronic pain and terror. After a while, the baby does whatever it takes to get to that place. Sometimes that means dissociation. Sometimes it means hair pulling."

"Or homicide?"

"Yes. The mystery of life isn't why a tortured child becomes a serial killer—it's why so many children *don't*. If we could only understand how the brain learns new accommodations . . . But we *do* know this: it's some form of interference later on."

"Interference?"

"Some other input. A friend, a counselor—hell, a puppy . . . The brain develops over time, and even if it's set in motion one way, it doesn't have to continue on that path. Child abuse connects to crime, no question. Abused children are more likely to be arrested than nonabused children. But the overwhelming majority of abused children never get in trouble with the law," Perry said, fury suppressed in his voice. "There's nothing 'inevitable' about it. Anyone who says that abused children are doomed to carry on that same behavior is a hopeless idiot."

"But until they learn new ways, you can see how they react to stuff, right? So the younger the kid, the easier to prove abuse?" I asked him, trying to move him away from the social philosophy to the reason I was there.

"To prove trauma, certainly," he said. "Then comes the investigative component. We have to rule out all other possible causes of the trauma as well. But when we have a history . . . or physical damage . . . or a sexually transmitted disease . . ."

"Or pictures?"

"Photographs?"

"Kiddie porn."

"Yes. But that's relatively rare. We have to rely on other evidence. And that means accumulating a large enough sample from the heart rate monitoring and evoked potential—sorry: the brain wave—studies. Then we apply multivariate computer analysis to crunch all the data—the tests, the interview, the history, everything. There's the ultimate forensic value of our work. We eliminate the impossible, then the improbable, and finally . . ."

"You nail it."

"Sure. Once you've proved the existence of the trauma, the question becomes, What *else* could cause this totality of data? When we cross-compare to other, documented cases, the task simplifies radically."

"So when they say kids make lousy witnesses, that they have different memories . . . ?"

"Kids may not be articulate, Mr. Burke. But they are great communicators. Their internals speak volumes—it's just a matter of gathering the data, developing the protocols, training the personnel. . . . It *can* be done. And we're doing it, right here."

"How much does all this cost?" I asked him.

"In real money?" he shot back.

"What does that mean?"

"The work we're doing on your . . . client, that's the gold standard. Best of everything. When you include the full week's stay, all the personnel involved, the tests themselves . . . it's costing your Mr. Kite around fifteen thousand dollars."

"Damn! So there's no chance of all kids—"

"All kids don't *need* this extensive a workup," he said. "And our children's program is about ninety percent subsidized. As we treat children, we also gather data for our research. Most of the kids don't have insurance anyway. In fact, you're our first true paying customer. Once this is standardized, once the computer programs are set up, the costs will drop precipitously."

"You can't set up field hospitals in every city," I said. Thinking of politicians closing AIDS wards to save money.

"No, and we don't have to. Once local personnel are trained to do the initial screening, our methods will be called upon only in the most difficult cases."

"So what you really need is . . . ?"

"That's right, Mr. Burke. Money. We need about fifteen to twenty million dollars to finish the research, publish it, defend it . . . and make it exportable. But we're *already* doing the work . . . and the money will come," he said, hope and faith tangling in his voice.

"**G**irl call," Mama said.

It was around ten o'clock at night, and I'd invested over an hour walking around trying to find a pay phone that looked safe. I wasn't in the mood for mystery. "What girl?" I asked her.

"Say Pepper. You call her, okay? Very important."

"Yeah, okay. Anything else?"

"No."

"I'll call you—"

"You want Max?" Mama interrupted.

"Not down here," I told her. "I'll be back soon."

"**I**s Pepper around?"

"That's me, chief." The Pied Piper girl's voice bounced over the long-distance line.

"I got a message to—"

"Delta flight six eighty-two to Atlanta tomorrow morning at six-twenty a.m. Can you be on it?"

"Maybe. Why should—?"

"When you arrive, stay in the Delta terminal. Meet flight six oh three from La Guardia, okay? You can catch a return at three in the afternoon."

"There isn't much time to—"

"You already have reservations, round trip, Mr. Haines," Pepper said, mocking the voice of a super-efficient secretary. "You had enough frequent flyer mileage on Delta for an upgrade too, so you'll be going first class. Will there be anything else?"

"No. Thanks a lot," I told her. Especially for the message that the Arnold Haines ID was all shot to hell.

I came out of the deplaning chute carrying the black aluminum attaché case. In a medium-blue two-button suit, clean-shaven, with my hair combed, I was an anonymous fish in the entrepreneur stream that clogs the hub airports every weekday.

My flight had been almost a half hour late. I was thinking of where to meet Wolfe, when I spotted her standing behind the barrier. Hard to miss in that sunburst-yellow silk dress with the long strand of black pearls the only decoration down the front. Her hair was in a French braid, the white wings prominent against her high forehead. She raised her hand and waved, a smile sparking across her lovely face.

For just a piece of a minute, I felt like a man coming home to his wife. Or what I thought that would feel like anyway. I shrugged it off, not grieving for what I'd never lost.

Wolfe gave me a kiss on the cheek, took my arm, and steered me away from the gate. If you were watching, you'd never guess it was business. She was a pro, all the way.

"It's probably better if we find somewhere to sit," she said. "You have breakfast?"

"Not really. Airplane food . . ."

"Me too," she said. "I know a good place. Come on."

We ordered Atlanta breakfast sandwiches—sausage wrapped in French toast. Wolfe poured maple syrup over her sausage like it was mustard on a hot dog, but I didn't have the heart for that. She had black coffee; I had apple juice.

"I heard something," she finally said. "I don't know if it's true. But I didn't want to wait to tell you. And I didn't want to use the phone."

"About the—"

"Yes. Brother Jacob is on the Internet. At least, Chiara *thinks* it's him—she's the one who works the computers for us. There's a room on the Web. The server's somewhere in Europe, near as we can tell. When you go in, it looks like it's all about bringing Asian women to America. For marriage. You know, stuff about immigration laws."

"So?"

"There's a whole line of chat about 'dowries.' It sounds like they're trafficking."

"He wants to buy a girl to bring here and marry?"

"No. Chiara says there's a subtext. Not straight-up encryption, but some kind of code. She's still working on it, but where she is now, she thinks he has some kind of merchandise he's offering."

"Not a one-time sale?"

"No. A regular line of it. Whatever it is."

"Can you . . . ?"

"I don't know," she said softly. "It's a delicate probe, going in like this. If I were still on the job . . ."

"I may know someone," I told her. "A cop."

"Do I know him?"

"Morales."

"Oh *yes*, I know him." She smiled. "The only difference between him and a dinosaur is he's not stupid."

"He likes you too," I said.

We killed an hour or so just walking around the airport, Wolfe's hand on my arm. I told her I had to make a phone call. Went and bought her a white rose at the florist shop. She gave me a kiss and boarded her flight, not looking back.

I had a couple of hours to kill before my flight. I got a shoeshine, prowled through a bookstore, just walked around. Then I worked the pay phones.

Every line I'd thrown out was reeling in the same kind of fish. Every tile dropped onto the mosaic was different, but I already knew what picture was going to appear when it was done. So when I met with Perry for the last time the next morning, I wanted it without the frills.

"Bottom line, Doctor: Is she telling the truth?"

"Well, she signed the release, so . . . First of all, let me start by saying that whatever you do, encourage your client—Jennifer—to get some help. I can give you some names of good therapists in her community. I discussed this with her, and she seemed somewhat resistant; she said she's already *in* therapy, but judging from the test results, I . . ."

"I'll talk to her about it," I said, guiding him back to what I needed to know.

"All right. Good. Anyway, she has a set of primary symptoms—anxiety, dissociation, dysphoria, profound sleep problems, increased startle response, recurring intrusive ideations about specific humiliating experiences, poor self-esteem—all consistent with any number of DSM-Four diagnostic labels. But the most important aspect of her symptoms is that they do appear to be cue-specific. And in this regard, she would meet diagnostic criteria for PTSD. And for a dissociative disorder as well—a whole host of apparently benign cues produce dramatic heart rate increases, which are followed by classic dissociative responses."

Poor little bitch, I thought. Hung out to dry, trained to dance so hard she kept it up even when the music stopped. But every time she heard that music again . . . "Sure," I said, "but is she—?"

"With regard to her hair-pulling," he rolled on, refusing to be derailed, "both in her reporting to me and in her projective testing, she had confusion about intimacy, sexuality, and pain. Hair pulling—we have some on tape—was associated with the same decrease in heart rate that a dissociative response was. In other words, she does it because it soothes her. For Jennifer, it's like taking a little hit of morphine every time. The confusion about what is soothing and what is arousing, of course, makes her vulnerable to sexual exploitation. I'm sure you've seen that before."

"I've seen it cut both ways," I told him.

"It can," he agreed. He leaned back in his chair, rotating his head slightly as if he was working out some kinks in his neck. Then he leaned forward, elbow on the desk, cupping his chin in his hand. "With regard to trauma . . . it's clear from both her history and the corroborating neurophysiological reactivity—and her symptom constellation—that she has been exposed to multiple trauma at different times in her childhood, certainly some coming prior to adolescence."

He took a deep breath, looking me full in the face. "I'm told that you have considerable investigative experience in this area, Mr. Burke. What's *your* gut instinct?"

"That it happened," I told him flat out. "That she's telling the truth. That she was a damaged little girl. That this Brother Jacob sniffed her out like a shark spotting a belly-up fish. And that he had sex with her when she was a kid."

"Me too," he said, holding out his hand to shake, telling me we were done talking.

I couldn't think of another rock to turn over. Truth is, I believed her the first time I heard her. It was only Kite who kept me going, following every spot of blood on the tracks. It wasn't the money. I know how to go through the motions without actually doing anything. And I know more about killing time than a Peeping Tom knows about backlighting.

Later, when I was thinking about it—when I was trying *not* to think about it—I snapped to what had been going on, why I had been working so hard. I was finding the truth. Truth doesn't mean much to a con man. It's all presentation, not substance. Kite showed me what he had, put it right on the table. When it started, all I wanted was to get him off my back. And take his money. That's what I told myself.

He was an evangelist, I knew that. I didn't realize I'd become the congregation until I was down too deep.

And by the time I came out the other side, there was nothing to do but go with what I *really* knew.

"Please don't do that," Kite said.

"Do what?"

"Stare so deeply into my eyes—it's not polite. I suffer from nystagmus, and your staring makes me uncomfortable."

"Sorry," I lied, sitting in that butterscotch armchair. "Anyway, it's the real deal. It checks out every way there is."

"You're sure?" he asked softly. "There's no mistake?"

"Unless there's some more evidence lying around, I got it all," I told him.

His eyes flared behind the pink glasses. "Do you believe there *might* be some?"

"Might *have* been," I said. "But this Brother Jacob character won't be stupid enough to hold on to it. I'm done digging—there's no pay dirt left."

"Is there anything else? Anything you haven't turned over?" he asked, one long finger tapping a thick stack of documents on the little round table to his right.

"Just this," I said, pulling a list of names and addresses out of my jacket pocket. "It's not the coffin, but with everything else, it's damn sure another nail."

I handed it over. He scanned the list, shaking his head. "I don't see what this—"

"Third page, fourth name from the top," I told him.

"'Russell J. Swithenbrecht.' A post office box in Erie, Pennsylvania. What does that have to do with—?"

"That's him," I said. "Brother Jacob. He keeps the box under that name. Drives over about once a month. Only takes about an hour and a half, two hours tops. Always the same way. Drives there on a Friday night, stays over, hits the box Saturday morning—the branch is only open until noon. Then he drives back to Buffalo in time for his regular sessions on Saturday afternoon. Been doing it for years."

"And that proves . . . ?"

"What you have in your hands is a printout of a subscription list," I said. "For a little magazine called *Unique Yearnings*."

Kite's eyebrows lifted into a question.

"Girl-lovers, they call themselves," I told him. "Little girls."

"We have found the truth," Kite said, looking up directly into my eyes.

I could feel Heather standing behind me—feel the heat coming off her.

I met Morales in Bryant Park, right behind the Public Library, a block from where the heart of Times Square would be if it had one.

"This guy I'm looking at for Kite. If you ever hear anything—"

"What you got so far?" the cop asked.

It took another six weeks to assemble the ingredients. Then Kite dropped the bomb. Jennifer Dalton sued Brother Jacob in New York County Supreme Court. For twenty-five million dollars. Her complaint alleged sexual abuse, statutory rape, sodomy, extortion, intentional infliction of emotional distress, assault, battery, pastoral malpractice, and half a dozen other charges. The Psalmists were not named in the lawsuit—it was all Brother Jacob.

I caught it on the news, a thirty-second clip from a press conference called to announce the litigation. "Yes, we understand that these events occurred some time ago," Kite was saying smoothly, looking implacable and immaculate in a dark-chocolate double-breasted suit. "And while it is too late for the criminal justice system to act, we believe it is time for New York to join other, more progressive jurisdictions in providing a civil remedy for a child driven into a psychiatric coma by the deliberate, predatory acts of a sexual abuser. We are prepared to prove that the perpetrator's conduct was *calculated* to assault and impair the victim's reality-testing. This was no accident. It has happened time and time again. It is happening as we speak, to children all over this country."

The newspapers ran with it heavy, Kite piling on fact after fact, every detail displayed for the public, holding nothing back. They even broke out one of Kite's quotes in a black-bordered box in the middle of the article: "The statute of limitations was designed to be a shield to protect the innocent from claims filed so late that the evidence had disappeared. But now it is being used as a sword, a sword to attack the weakest, most vulnerable members of our society. When it comes to child sexual abuse, the statute of limitations has no place in a civilized society. This case isn't about the law. This case is about the truth."

The lawyers for Brother Jacob kept saying they didn't want to try their case in the press. But Kite maintained his assault, wondering out loud who was paying for Brother Jacob's defense. Tabloid TV reporters surrounded the house in Buffalo, blanketing the neighborhood for the usual empty quotes. Brother Jacob moved to an undisclosed location. A spokesman for the Psalmists appeared on a talk radio show. When he said something about the suffering of Job, the board lit up with enraged callers demanding to know if Jennifer's suffering meant anything. When the Psalmist spokesman tried to explain the church's position, the radio host called him a dirtbag and kicked him off the show.

Kite's legal papers ran almost three hundred pages, counting exhibits. Photocopiers at the courthouse pumped around the clock. The document became a best-seller overnight, turning up at coffeehouses and society parties and college campuses. Some commentators wondered out loud if Brother Jacob could ever hope to get a fair trial. And their colleagues pounded back, wondering with even more vehemence if Jennifer Dalton would ever get justice.

Just as the fever broke, a new wave hit. Five more victims came forward. With their lawyers. Three different lawyers.

Two of the victims were in their thirties. One claimed to have reported the sexual abuse to the police twenty years before. Even said she was interviewed by someone from the DA's Office. But nothing happened.

The other three victims weren't women. They were girls. One fifteen, one sixteen, the other just turning eighteen.

"The statute of limitations won't protect him from *this*," Kite crowed on TV.

Michelle was watching with me when they made Brother Jacob take the Perp Walk for the assembled cameras. He kept his head down, a coat over his wrists to hide the handcuffs, but he turned his face up just before he bent forward to get into the back seat of the police cruiser.

"He's got the look," Michelle hissed. "You can smell it right through the TV set."

I knew what she meant. They didn't all look alike, that was their camouflage. But they all had the same look when captured—that icy predator's glare promising no cage will ever change them.

"**C**op call," Mama said.

"How'd you know it was a cop?" I asked her.

"He say. Say, 'Tell Burke it's his friend on the force.' Okay?"

"Yeah. He leave a number?"

"No number. Say he call back. Tonight. Late. You wait here, okay?"

"Sure," I said, looking at my watch. It wasn't even nine.

When Max rolled in, he signed he wanted to play cards, but . . .

I understood what he was telling me. His taste for gin was gone forever—he could never recapture the magic of that last time, and he knew it. But we still had a few hours, so I figured it was a good time to teach him to play casino. Mama didn't know how to play either, but by the time Morales finally called, she was already giving Max bogus advice. And I was about a hundred bucks ahead.

"Look for a bitch on the stroll over on Lex in the twenties." Morales' harsh voice came over the phone. "She's wearing a long white coat, got a pair of black hot pants under it, you can't miss her. Name's Roselita. She got the key to a locker at Port Authority. Tell her your name's Mr. Jones, slip her a yard, the key's yours. Use it tonight—it's only good for twenty-four hours."

"You sure she'll be there? If she scores a trick—"

"She'll be out there walking, don't worry about it. Bitch owes me a favor."

"What if her pimp—?"

"She ain't *got* no motherfucking pimp. That's the favor."

She was where Morales said she'd be, a tall, slender woman with a Gypsy's long black hair and white plastic dangle earrings, slowly strolling the block but not calling out to any of the pussy-cruising cars that slithered by. When I tapped the horn, she swivel-hipped over to the Plymouth and leaned inside the passenger window, pulling the long white coat apart to show me her slim, flashy legs and small, high breasts bouncing free under a flimsy red tank top, while shielding the display from everyone behind her—a real pro move. One look at her face and I could see she'd had plenty of time to learn; the harsh tracks of the Life showed right through the stage makeup. You didn't need the VACANCY sign in her eyes to know her body was for rent.

"Wha's yo' name, hombre?"

"They call me Mr. Jones," I said, holding the hundred-dollar bill splayed between the fingers of my right hand.

"Hokay," she said, not even the trace of a smile on her greasy red lips. She fished a locker key from the pocket of the white coat, and we traded.

Later that night, Max took my back as I opened the locker at Port Authority. Inside was a chunky package wrapped in enough layers of plastic filament tape to take a strong man with a box cutter half an hour to open it.

Back at my office, I unwrapped it carefully, taking my time, half watching some old movie about gangsters with Pansy.

Once I saw what it was, I could see I'd need another kind of key to unlock it. I used the cellular to tap the Mole.

That was it, then. There was a lot of media buzz about the cases, but it went the way it always does, especially when the first judge assigned refused to allow cameras in the court. Kite objected, saying the people had a right to know. The judge just shrugged that off—a veteran of twenty years on the bench, he knew the value of a lawyer's speech. And that it wasn't "the people" who got him his job.

Besides, a serial killer was tying up prostitutes in Times Square hotel rooms and then making sure they took a long time to die. Media triage. And none of Brother Jacob's victims were all that sexy-looking anyway.

Besides, the governor was busy explaining why the newly passed death penalty hadn't stopped a freak from sodomizing a little girl to death in a housing project stairwell, covering her tiny face with his hand to stop her from screaming, doing it so tightly that she stopped breathing.

Even vultures prefer fresh corpses.

Then one cold, rainy Monday, Jennifer Dalton brought Brother Jacob back from the dead. The cellular buzzed. I picked it up, not saying anything. "You near a TV set?" the Prof's voice asked.

"Yeah," I said, watching Pansy watch me.

"Turn it on, bro. You not gonna believe this."

He cut the connection. I flicked on the set, rotating the channel knob until I found her.

"I lied," she told the freeze-faced reporter from one of those garbage-picking TV newsmagazine shows. The reporter kept nodding unctuously as *Exclusive! Exclusive! Exclusive!* trailed across the bottom of the picture.

"I made it all up," she said, crying into her cupped hands. "At least, I *think* I did. But I don't *know*. And now I know that's wrong. I can't go on with it any longer."

She kept talking as the screen cut to silent shots of newspaper headlines of the lawsuit. As the camera panned away, I could see a woman seated next to her, patting Jennifer's forearm. The other woman was dressed in a conservative business suit. The screen caption identified her as "Doreen Z. Landover, Feminist Lawyer."

Jennifer told the reporter the same story she had told me. Except that this time, Brother Jacob hadn't done anything to her. Oh, she'd had a schoolgirl crush on him, but he'd never taken advantage of it. She told the reporter about her broken engagement, about how she got so depressed she didn't want to live. Said she was drinking heavily, drifting. When she went into counseling, the therapist kept pressing her, she said. "He kept asking me about sexual abuse. In my family. He said that *had* to be the reason for all my troubles. It would explain everything, that's what he said. But I knew . . . my family had never . . . and that's when I told him about Brother Jacob."

"Do you mean about the alleged sexual abuse?" the reporter asked, smarmy-voiced.

"No. Not at first. I just told him . . . what had really happened. But he kept *after* me. And I was so . . . sad and depressed. After a while, it seemed to all make sense to me. And now I've ruined a man's life. I'm so ashamed. . . ."

She broke down then. The camera stayed on her sobbing face while they split the screen and showed clips of Brother Jacob doing the Perp Walk. Her new lawyer explained how Jennifer had been programmed, how she'd come under the spell of a "sincere but misguided" therapist. No, they weren't going to sue for malpractice. Hadn't there been *enough* lawsuits?

The reporter did a three-minute rap about false allegations, his voice throbbing with self-importance. "Isn't it ironic," he concluded, "that in 1996, in these days of space travel and the Internet, the Salem witch hunts are still a fact of life. But this time, one of the so-called victims has found the courage to come forward and speak the truth. And just in time to stop society, to stop *all* of us, from burning a man at the stake. Jennifer Dalton, a tortured young woman, lost in a life of sadness, sought some answers. And, as we have seen, some of those answers raise much larger questions indeed."

I didn't move from the set for hours. They finally located Kite. He spoke at a podium so loaded with microphones that only the top of his head was visible. He sounded lost. Distraught. "I assure everyone, and especially Brother Jacob and his counsel, that I personally investigated this matter thoroughly before the lawsuit was brought. I assure you that it was brought in good faith and only after I was personally satisfied as to its validity. I am . . . shocked. I don't know another word for it. This makes me question . . . everything. Not just this case, but myself. And my profession. I apologize to Brother Jacob and his family, personally and professionally."

"Are you dropping the case?" one reporter shouted out.

"There is no case," Kite replied. "I'm sorry. . . . I have nothing more to say."

A phalanx of bodyguards muscled Kite through the crowd of thrusting microphones. I couldn't see Heather anywhere in the crowd.

Every talk show in town vultured in, but Jennifer Dalton wasn't talking. Rumors flew that the tabloid TV magazine had paid her a hundred thousand dollars for the exclusive interview.

"This has nothing whatever to do with our case," the lawyer for two of the young girls told a newspaper reporter. "We are still suing Brother Jacob." When they printed that news, hostile letters to the editor flew like raindrops in a hurricane.

Brother Jacob was released from jail on his own recognizance.

Doreen Z. Landover announced that her client was giving a deposition to Brother Jacob's counsel in the other lawsuits. She said Jennifer Dalton was sorry . . . and she was going to do everything in her power to make things right.

"She's out."

"Stay with her."

"White on rice," the Prof promised.

I used my key to let myself into Jennifer Dalton's apartment, moving as carefully as a minesweeper. I wasn't there to thieve—I wanted to leave something for her.

The bedroom was the same filthy mess the Prof had described. I popped the portable video player out of the duffel bag I had carried over my shoulder. I was looking for an electrical outlet when the cellular buzzed in my pocket.

"She doubled back. Almost there. Just going into the lobby. Step quick!"

I moved over to the window. It was barred from the inside. No fire escape. I heard a key turn in the front door, snatched the video player, and moved behind the bedroom door.

I heard her come in. She turned on the TV set, then the sound suddenly disappeared, like she hit the Mute. I heard the refrigerator open, the sound of some liquid being poured. The springs on the couch made a faint protest. The TV sound came on again, some talk show. She was flicking the remote, changing channels so fast it was a sound-blur, when a sharp series of raps sounded on the front door. She hit the Mute again. I heard her walking toward the door. Sound of the peephole cover being slid off. Harsh intake of breath.

Heard the door open. "What do you want?" Jennifer asked.

"I want to talk to you." Heather's voice, rage in it like a bubble ready to burst. Sound of a grunt, door closing.

"Sit down!" Heather said. "Right there."

Sound of someone hitting the chair. Springs sagging heavy— must be Heather on the couch.

"Why did you do it?" Heather asked, her voice thick. "How could you do that to him?"

"He was the one who did it to me," Jennifer whined. "It wasn't my fault."

"He never did . . . Wait—who do you mean?"

"The therapist. He was the one who—"

"*Kite*," Heather said. "How could you do it to *him*? He *believed* in you. You know he did. How could you let him sacrifice his whole career, his whole *life*, for you when you knew it was all a lie?"

The room went so quiet I could hear Heather's harsh breathing.

"It wasn't a lie, Heather," I said, stepping into the silent living room.

Jennifer gasped, hand flying to her mouth. Heather whirled to face me. "You!"

I tossed the videotape cartridge at Heather. She didn't make a move to grab it out of the air—it landed against her chest. She didn't flinch, eyes only on Jennifer.

"It's all there," I said quietly. "Isn't it, Jennifer? Brother Jacob must have edited hours and hours of tape to make this one production, huh?"

"I don't know . . . ," she said softly.

"*Had* to be," I told her. "There's *years* of you on this. Everything you said. Lifting your skirt for the ruler. Playing with yourself while he watched. Getting on your knees and—"

"Stop it!" Jennifer screamed. "It wasn't my fault. I didn't want—"

"No, it wasn't your fault," I said, moving close to her. "It was never your fault. It was all the truth, so why did you . . . ?"

"I wasn't going to get any money," she said, face tightening into rigid lines. "The statute of limitations. I was too late. This way I get paid. I have to think of myself, don't I? I can get fixed now. Anything I want. Plastic surgery, even. It's only fair."

"You're dead, bitch!" Heather snarled, coming off the couch, the brass knuckles already fitted over her right fist.

I was ready for it this time. I swept the knife-edge of my hand down against Heather's wrist, spinning so my back was to her as I fired an elbow into her gut.

She gasped and went down.

"Just stay there!" I snapped at her, my foot right next to her face. I turned to Jennifer, holding out my hands like a traffic cop to keep her in the chair. "This is gonna be all right," I told her. "Just relax— I'll have her out of here in a minute."

I dropped to one knee next to Heather, put my lips close to her ear. "You owe me," I whispered. "It's you and me now. It's not about that sorry bitch over there. Come on."

She staggered to her feet, holding my arm, leaning heavily against me, tears blotching her face. "He—"

"Shut up now," I said. "There's plenty of time for that." I pushed her gently back onto the couch, keeping hold of her until she was seated.

I stepped away quickly, grabbed my duffel bag out of the bedroom, slung it over my shoulder.

"You can keep that tape," I told Jennifer. "A little souvenir. I got copies. I'll give you three days. Seventy-two hours. That's enough for you to get paid. Then you better get in the wind."

She sat there with her mouth open, like I'd slugged her in the gut too. I held my hand out to Heather. She took it. I hauled her to her feet, thumbed the cellular into life, hit the memory button.

"Go," the Prof's voice came back.

"All clear?"

"Quiet as the crypt."

I held Heather's pudgy hand tight all the way down the back stairs.

It took two complete loops of the FDR before she stopped crying. I finally found a place to pull in near the heliport at Thirty-fourth. I held her against me in the darkness. Her whole body trembled with what she knew.

"I don't believe it," she said finally. "The truth . . ."

"The truth is just a toy they played with, Heather. It's up to you now. It's your call."

"What are you going to . . . ?"

"Me? Nothing."

She was quiet for a long time after that. Finally, she turned in her seat. "I have to know. I have the key. Will you come with me?"

"It's not mine," I said. "I'm done."

She shifted her body against me, pulling at my jacket until I looked in her face.

"I love you," she said. "You found the truth."

I didn't say anything.

"Please . . ."

The concierge wasn't at his desk, the lobby deserted at that hour. We stood close together in the small elevator. "Breathe through your nose," I told her. "Stay inside yourself. Calm. You wanted the truth, Heather. You know where it is."

She opened the grille. I followed her down the hall. He was in the fan-shaped chair, like he'd been waiting for us.

"It was the *truth!*" Heather blurted out. "We know the truth. She—"

"Shut up, you cow!" Kite hissed at her. "What's wrong with you? Have you forgotten our work?"

"Our . . . work? To find the truth . . ."

"No!" Kite said sharply. "We *know* the truth, don't we? False allegations, *that's* the truth. All the pernicious lies, all the exaggerations. The phony therapists. The witch hunt—remember, Heather? There was only one way to stop it. Only one way to put a stake right through the enemy's heart."

"But you knew. . . . All along, you . . ."

"This is a chess game," he said in his empty voice, eyes shielded behind the glasses. "An intellectual problem. The real weapon in this war is propaganda. And I have just delivered the masterstroke. It will take them *years* to recover. Public perception will never be the same. *I* did this. Nobody will ever get away with a false allegation again—everyone is on the alert now. Just as I promised you when we started together."

Heather sat down on the floor and bawled like a little girl. A little girl who had lost her compass.

"No hard feelings?" Kite said to me, talking over Heather's slumped body like she wasn't there. "We're both professionals, you and I. And I appreciate the work you did—I admire it. You are the finest investigator I've ever worked with. But this was never about investigation."

"And you got paid."

"Did I? You know nothing about it, Mr. Burke. No, *you* got paid. And paid well. For myself, the payment is my syndrome. The *syndrome,* Heather," he said, shifting to a gentle, kindly voice. "You remember all the time I have invested in it? How important it is? Well, my syndrome is now the truth."

Heather's face snapped up. Her makeup was streaked, black-cherry hair hanging limp. Her movements were stiff, almost robotic. She caught her upper lip with her lower jaw, bit down so hard a drop of blood blossomed.

Kite returned her stare calmly, waiting for the dice to stop rolling.

"Can I still . . . ?" she asked, finally.

"Of *course* you can." Kite smiled down at her like a father forgiving a child. "Things will be just as they were. With us, I mean. There's still so much work to do. Now why don't you go into the bathroom and pull yourself together. Then you can show Mr. Burke out."

She got to her feet silently. I kept my eyes on Kite, listening to the tap of her heels on the hardwood floor.

"You're not planning on doing anything stupid, are you, Mr. Burke? I can't imagine you believe your . . . testimony would be worth very much in a court of law. And I know some things—"

"I'm all finished," I cut him off. "Can I just ask you a question?"

"Certainly. In fact, I'll even answer it for you. I was, shall we say, *retained* by a certain group in anticipation of certain lawsuits being filed. But the plan, the strategy, the tactics . . . they were all my own. Uniquely my own. And I have committed no crime. As I said, I did a full-scale investigation. And I proceeded in good faith throughout. And I'm sure you understand that I have a rather complete record of our . . . dealings. So . . ."

Heather came back into the room, face freshly scrubbed. "Will you please show Mr. Burke out, Heather?" Kite said, the control-leash tight in his voice.

She did an about-face and started down the hall. I followed close behind. At the door, I pulled her to me, holding her against my chest. "For your love," I whispered, pressing the brass knuckles into her chubby little hand.

I gave the videotape to Wolfe. Just in case somebody at NYPD decided to treat their copy like they had the French Connection heroin.

Jennifer Dalton disappeared the next day. The cops said there was no evidence of foul play.

Kite was a different story. A maid discovered his body in the penthouse a few days later. He'd been beaten to death. His files had been looted, picked clean. "It could have been anyone—we've got a long list of suspects," the lead detective on the case told the newspapers. "But whoever did it was a pro—they knew what they were doing."

They got that part right anyway.

I don't know where Heather went to. But wherever she is, I know her eyes aren't orange anymore.

AFTERWORD

Every year, millions of children in the United States are victimized by severe abuse. This maltreatment takes many forms, but all have this in common: they rob children of some percentage of their potential, some vital human piece of themselves. And by such robbery, all America is looted. The problem has been documented to the point of nausea. The media dutifully report the body counts, but the one-sided war rages on. Domestic violence, sexual exploitation, rape, sociopathic plundering, homicide . . . we remain under siege even as our "protective" institutions rot from within.

We know the root cause of our societal ills and evil—the transgenerational maltreatment of children. We know today's victim can become tomorrow's predator. We know that while many heroic survivors refuse to imitate the oppressor, the chains remain unbroken as abused children turn the trauma inward and lose their souls to self-inflicted wounds—from drug and alcohol abuse to depression to suicide. Their lives are never what they could have—*should* have—been.

We know the enemy . . . but where is the counterattack? More social engineering? More pious whining? More networking? More conferences? More unfocused, blundering incompetence? There is a Rosetta stone to societal decay. Child abuse, simply, modifies development of the brain. It alters "processing," so that the abused child (of whatever age) assimilates and responds to stimuli in distinctly aberrant ways. Most of those ways are self-destructive. Some destroy others. All, eventually, destroy *us* . . . as a country, and even as a species.

The CIVITAS ChildTrauma Programs at Baylor College of

Medicine are attacking child maltreatment in three distinct ways: (1) providing clinical services to desperately underserved children; (2) training a cadre of dedicated and superbly skilled professionals; and (3) carrying out these services and this training in the context of ongoing research. Without an understanding of what happens *inside* maltreated children, we can never hope for meaningful change but must expect only a continuation of our pitiful policies of appeasement and amelioration.

CIVITAS provides a multidisciplinary and interinstitutional spirit that synthesizes the complex social, legal, cultural, psychological, and physical issues related to child maltreatment. When is it safe to return an abused child to his biological parents? What about "false allegations"? What constitutes a truly professional investigation? What turns one abused child into a healer . . . and another into a serial killer? Are monsters born, or made? CIVITAS is answering these questions and, more important, documenting the answers, *proving* them again and again, developing a body of scientific knowledge to replace the psychobabble and guesstimates that pass for "truth" today. A major goal of CIVITAS is to develop, pilot, and evaluate innovative models for clinical service, training, and research in a *replicable model* for use throughout America.

Some of this research is now available. More is being developed every day. How can you help? By altering the *pace* of this vital work. What CIVITAS needs is resources. Financial resources. Given sufficient resources, we can not only find the answers, we can implement them. Do it for humanitarian reasons. Do it for self-interest. But do it now. Please.

If you want more information about CIVITAS; if you want to make a contribution; or if you want both, write to:

Bruce D. Perry, M.D., Director
CIVITAS ChildTrauma Programs
Baylor College of Medicine
Department of Psychiatry
One Baylor Plaza
Houston, TX 77030-3498

E-mail: bperry@bcm.tmc.edu

CIVITAS is a tax-exempt, not-for-profit organization. Checks should be made payable to Baylor College of Medicine (Tax ID 74-1613878) and marked for the exclusive use of Dr. Bruce D. Perry for the CIVITAS ChildTrauma Programs.

BURKE is back in...

CHOICE of EVIL

The new novel by

ANDREW VACHSS

•

A rally in Central Park, a protest against gay bashing. A murderous drive-by. Five people down, two dead. One of them Burke's girlfriend, Crystal Beth.

First the gay bashers celebrate...then they start dropping. Claiming responsibility is the mysterious "Homo Erectus," whose identity is as hidden as his mission is clear.

To most citizens, Homo Erectus is a serial killer with a political agenda. But to some, he's a hero and, like the police, they desperately want to find him. Unlike the police, they want to help him disappear before the dragnet tightens. They hire Burke for the job. Which is when things get really ugly.

ISBN: 0-375-40647-6 • $23.00

JUN 2 7 2023